LOOK BEYOND TODAY

By Mary Franceschini

Published by Mary Franceschini

This book is a work of fiction. Names, characters, places
and incidences are the product of the author's imagination or are
used fictitiously. Any resemblance to actual events, locales or
persons, living or dead is coincidental.

Printed in the United States of America
First Edition: October 2018

10 9 8 7 6 5 4 3 2 1

Franceschini, Mary
Look Beyond Today

ISBN: 978-1-941713-89-1

Cover design by Sylvia Frost

Book design by Andrew Benzie
www.andrewbenziebooks.com

*I dedicate this book to my late fiancé, Larry.
Thank you for believing in me!*

Most of all, thank You, God.

CHAPTER ONE

Marina fanned the charcoal in the burners until the water in the pot began to bubble. With her arm, she wiped away the drop of perspiration that trickled down her cheek. The butter colored rays of the mid-July sun shone through the open window and traced a path to the granite fireplace. She pursed her lips at the bandana that secured her shoulder length, dark brown hair.

A small potted plant of Miseria, thick with small dark blue flowers, soaked up water in a small bowl in the sink below.

She smiled wryly. The plant was supposed to bring 'Misery' or 'poverty' according to legend, but misery had come long before the little plant had found its place in the kitchen.

War had come first, for whatever reason that wars were fought, and people were dragged down into its abyss. Life couldn't be any worse than in this year of 1943 with the raging war, rationed food, and meager crops.

Benito Mussolini's grand speeches from Vittorio Emmanuele's monument in Rome were of no consolation to Marina or to her people in her mountaintop village of three hundred and fifty souls. Beef was hard to find, reserved only for the soldiers. If one *could* find some, it came with a hefty price tag. Chicken was for special occasions. Of the ten rabbits they'd had, only two had survived a mysterious disease.

"I can hardly wait to taste this cheese that grandmother gave us." Albina broke into her thoughts.

"I can hardly wait to taste anything at this hour." Rubbing her growling stomach, Marina turned to a soft 'meow'. "You're hungry, too, little one?" Soaking a piece of stale bread in a little milk, she placed it in Giada's bowl. "This will have to do for now, alright?"

The tortoiseshell kitty stretched luxuriously, wasting no time to enjoy her meal.

When the water in the tarnished pot broke into a gentle boil, Marina stirred in cornmeal for the all-too-usual *polenta.*

"Shall I set the table?"

"Yes, please. Mama and the girls will be home soon. Making faggots of kindling wood is hard work and we need plenty of them."

"*Oh Signore,* it's hard to imagine winter now." Albina shuddered. "But I hope that it won't be as freezing as the last one."

Marina's lips curved into a smile. Albina dark curls danced on her slim shoulders as she bustled about, humming softly.

In spite of all the hardships, Marina saw her world at peace in a bigger world ravaged by war.

A white monogrammed and mended tablecloth and napkins, treasures from their mother's dowry, adorned the old chestnut table. From the plate rack, five plates, one of them chipped, found their places. In the center was a large wood disk onto which the *polenta* would be poured. Next to this Albina placed the plate of cheese.

"Ahi, Gianni," Albina moaned as she stood behind a chair, empty for too long.

"We mustn't give up hope for our brother," Marina said.

"Hope? His last letter was almost a year ago, before he left for the Russian front. He could be dead."

Marina shuddered. Albina was right. She would never forget the day she had read the headline in the newspaper. They were hard to come by, but fate had assured that she read this one. She closed her eyes briefly, remembering that newspaper article, so full of bravado in spite of its grim news.

At the Don River on the Russian front in November of last year, the Italian Eighth Army had retreated when the Soviets broke through its ranks. Although they were allies, the German army left the Italian soldiers to fend for themselves. They walked for days to reach hamlets at the German border, where they asked for food or shelter. Some died from hunger and the extreme cold. Those who survived removed the clothes and boots from their dead comrades to keep warm.

Marina never ceased to ask herself if Gianni was dead or alive. If, by God's grace, he was alive, where was he?

"Ciao, bimbe."

Her mother's voice broke into her reverie.

Alda, entered the kitchen followed by Lisa and Daniela who trudged in, looking as weary as their mother.

From her dusty black apron, pinecones spilled into the wicker basket at the side of the hearth. Weary, she sat down at the table and loosened the bandana that secured her chestnut colored hair, which was now flecked with grey.

"Mama, you're home early," Marina said. "Good. This is almost ready."

"Can't they make these of anything else but wood?" Lisa winced and kicked off her *zoccoli*. She walked barefoot to the sink and eyed the pot full of *polenta* on the cooker. "Not that again. Can't you put together something else?"

"So much for peace," Marina muttered. She smacked the coated spoon down on the stove, where it hissed.

"Why don't *you* put together something else? For one who worked all morning, you should be grateful for anything. Who knows what Gianni is eating… *if* he is."

"Well, it certainly isn't *that* almost every day."

"I'm sure he would welcome it," Daniela grumbled. "I'm hungry so stop complaining."

"Good answer," Albina said, "at least someone appreciates something."

"Girls, please."

At the tired but gentle reproach from Alda, Lisa apologized. "I suppose there wasn't any mail today either?"

"No." Marina said and carefully poured the steaming *polenta* onto the disk. She ladled water into the pot to loosen the crust inside.

The peal of the church bell ringing noon floated through the open window.

Marina joined her family at the table. As was the custom in many homes before a meal, they recited the *Angelus Domini,* the prayer that recalled the angel's message to the Virgin Mary.

*　　　　*　　　　*

After the last of the dishes were washed and the kitchen tidied, Alda picked up a hemp towel from her handiwork basket. She frowned at the unfinished, red, cross-stitched monogram. "This has to be finished if we can be done with those blessed faggots. Your wedding will be here sooner than we think and there are other things to attend to."

Marina shook her head as her eyes filled with tears. "Mama, with Gianni away at war and not knowing if he's... he's alive or not, I'm not thinking about the wedding." She looked wistfully at the towel that would bear her initials, MF. Marina Fiori.

"Don't say that. You know that he wouldn't want you

to forsake your happiness. You and Giorgio love each other. It's your special day."

Marina hugged herself. Giorgio. He was the bright spot in her life.

"You've grown up so fast." Alda murmured. "It seems only yesterday that you were a baby in my arms."

How much the cares and woes of the past two years had affected her mother. Gianni had left for the war two years ago, and their father had died from a heart attack last year. Marina sneaked a glance at her. Her face was still youthful but her warm brown eyes had long ago lost their sparkle.

"Mama, go upstairs and rest now."

"I think I'll do that."

Marina joined her sisters on their little balcony that opened off the dining room. The sun had sunk to the west, and a gentle breeze wafted through the spreading branches of the cherry tree. Along the iron railing in the dappled shade, red and pink geraniums spilled over the pots. Clusters of red roses peeked up from the rambling rose below.

"Marina, I'm sorry about earlier," Lisa said softly as the breeze played with her dark curls.

"It's alright. We're all out of sorts. Is there anything else wrong with anyone? Speak up."

"Well, I have something good to say," Daniela announced with a big smile. "The school teacher would like to have me help tutor a few of the children with their grammar."

"When did this happen?" Lisa asked.

"I saw her yesterday when I was going to the store. She asked me to think about it. I may accept."

"This could be the start of something for you," Marina smiled because her sister was good with children. "Did you tell Mama?"

"Not yet. I wanted your opinions first."

"I think you should…"

Whatever Albina wanted to say was interrupted by cheers and shouts. She exchanged a quizzical glance with her sisters.

"What's this?" Marina hastened into the house. In a flash, she burst back unto the balcony, eyes wide and arms outstretched. "Girls… the… the King has arrested Mussolini."

CHAPTER TWO

News of the arrest reverberated from one end of the village to another. In Mussolini's place, King Vittorio Emmanuele had appointed Marshal Pietro Badoglio, also known as the Duke of Addis Ababa. Many chortled at this title. He had received it because under Mussolini's orders, he had led the successful invasion of Abyssinia. Never mind that it had been terribly brutal.

Marina welcomed the chance to get away for a few hours, if only for chores. Above and below her, common blue flax, starry Campion, and pinks bloomed in profusion among the grapevines. Carrying a sickle and a gunnysack, she walked the uneven, winding mule path and tried to recall how Italy had reached this point.

Il Duce. In his quest to bring glory to Italy, he had brutally conquered Abyssinia with the help of Marshal Badoglio, who had led the invasion. Italy had been condemned by the whole world with the exception of Germany. In turn, when Adolf Hitler had invaded Poland and later Czechoslovakia just as brutally, Benito Mussolini had no choice but to keep quiet. As time passed, everything pointed to an alliance between them.

With the invasion of Poland, Europe found itself in a war, and two years afterwards, Italy and Germany had declared war on the United States.

Where the path curved, she stopped to contemplate the valley below. The sky was deep blue and the mountains dressed in summer green. The Fegana River sparkled like diamonds in the afternoon sunlight and, next to its bubbling waters, someone tended to what might be a vegetable patch. Her family, too, had a piece of land next to the river where they grew *canapa,* the hemp that would provide spun thread for towels and bed linen, and they would harvest it soon. From down in the fields the tinkle of sheep bells and a rich, soprano voice reached her.

Maybe all isn't lost if people can still sing. She picked up the popular tune and resumed her walk.

"*Ehi*, Marina."

"*Ciao,* Carla." Marina greeted her childhood friend who walked towards her with a green shopping bag in one hand and an armful of kindling wood with the other. With her dark eyes, raven black hair that almost reached her waist, and a figure to envy, Marina envied Carla just a bit as a lovely woman.

"Are you going to the vineyard?" Carla asked.

"What else is new?" Marina laughed.

"Our life is what it is, alright." Carla shrugged and then fixed her eyes on Marina's face. "I saw Giorgio coming up from his vineyard. You found a good man, Marina."

"Thank you." The faintly spiteful edge to Carla's tone caught her by surprise. Yes, Carla had looked after Giorgio, but he had never looked at her. "You will find someone too," Marina said firmly. "He's out there searching for you."

Carla lifted her shoulders and let them drop. "We'll see. I'd better hurry home. For the price I paid for a little beef, and I mean a *little,* I can't afford to let it spoil. I'll see you in church if not sooner. *Ciao.*"

Marina watched her graceful form disappear around the corner. With all that she had gone through, she marveled that Carla had turned out to be the young woman that she was. Her mother had died when she was about six. Her father, perhaps from grief, took to drinking. He never abused her, thankfully, and did love her, but the habit was too much for him to handle. He died shortly afterwards and she was raised by an aunt. Not wanting her to feel alone, Marina had welcomed her in childhood games together with Gianni and Giorgio. The four of them had formed a close friendship. Perhaps too close? She shook her head, forgiving Carla for her moment of envy. Giorgio was a very good man. She smiled. Carla was right.

Marina's heart skipped a beat at the sight of a dark haired, tanned, young man trudging up the path ahead of her with a sack slung across his broad shoulders.

"Giorgio!" She waved and hastened her pace.

"*Gesu,* that path is steep." Giorgio huffed and let the sack slide to the ground.

Marina wrapped her arms around his slender body, his perspiration dampening her cheek. He was just a few months older than her at twenty. They shared the same dreams of a better life, but most of all, of a world at peace.

"What have you been doing with yourself?" She murmured, running her fingers through his damp, wavy hair.

"A customer has ordered a bedroom set and I am trying to organize myself to begin working."

"A bedroom set? That's wonderful." Marina smiled, elated. Giorgio took pride in his craftsmanship, but even though his word carving was praised throughout the valley, large orders did not come in often. Few had money for extravagances such as new furniture.

"Two dressers, the night stands, and a wardrobe will be a lot of work but the money will be a boon for us."

"Is your mother happy with the prospect?"

"Mama? If I so much as over-sleep, she comes to the bed and pulls at my feet."

Marina broke into laughter because it was just like Amelia to do that.

She had to ask Giorgio the inevitable question about what would happen now with Mussolini's arrest. He kept abreast as much as possible on the war news thanks to a neighbor who owned a radio. Local news came by way of word of mouth or someone might distribute a flyer.

He leaned against the weathered wood railing. "The war will continue but there is talk that the Marshal is meeting secretly with the Allies in the Vatican."

"Germany may turn against us."

"Even so, the Allies are gaining ground. Last month they invaded Pantelleria and Lampedusa, at the heel of Italy. Now they've begun bombing the coastal cities. I pray that they free us."

Marina shivered. How many would lose their homes and perhaps their lives as the country was freed?

"I'll still be cutting grass for the rabbits no matter who wins this war," Marina said ruefully.

"When the Allies win, our lives have to change for the better." Giorgio turned his gaze to the distant hills. "I want to improve my woodworking skills. Papa passed his trade on to me. I… I just wish that he was here to see my work."

Marina's eyes filled. Seven years hadn't dulled the pain of his father's death, caused by complications from a surgery. If memories kept loved ones alive, then both their fathers would live forever.

Giorgio cleared his throat. "Our *despensa* is almost finished, and I can picture the good things in it."

"Such as?" In his warm, brown eyes, she saw the familiar, faraway look that she had come to love.

"Oh, a crusty loaf of bread fresh from the oven and some of your peach jam would be nice. A big jar of olives from my trees sounds good, too."

If the war continues and food is still rationed, that might be all we will have in the pantry, she thought as goose pimples rose on her skin and a shiver coursed through her body.

"Marina, *cosa c'e?*"

"I don't know. Maybe I'm worried about Gianni, our future, and… and I still think about Papa." She rested her forehead against his. "Will we live through all this?"

"We will," he said gently and firmly. "You know that I'm here for you, but you have to let go of your father. You're not doing your family, and especially yourself, any good by harboring guilt."

She picked up her sickle and gunnysack. "It's getting late, *amore mio*. I'd better go."

He cupped her face and kissed her soundly.

"Giorgio!" She finally pulled away, her cheeks hot.

She *had* to go.

*   *   *

A little later, weary, her back aching, Marina sat on a large rock in the shade of a peach tree, whose rosy fruit peeked through the leaves. Peach jam. Dear Giorgio. He was contented with so little.

In the solitude of the vineyard, broken only by the chirping of the sparrows and a meadowlark's song, Marina relived the recent events of her life.

Gianni, her older brother, had left for the war, comforted that he had their father to care for the rest of them. She was working as a live in maid for a well to do family in the city of Lucca at the time.

When her father died, they were left reeling. She had taken the weight of his death on her shoulders and left her well-paid position in Lucca to come home. The weight of added responsibility she could handle. It was remorse that was hard to let go of. She could never rid herself of the notion that her father's death was her fault. Maybe if she had bitten her tongue, maybe… maybe. She shook her head and let her breath out slowly.

As much as she loved her sisters, she had to admit that Lisa, eighteen, Daniela, sixteen, and Albina, fourteen made for smooth sailing or for stormy seas, depending on the day. Getting up wearily, she began the climb up the path, asking herself whom she could blame for a war that turned people's lives upside down?

The questions were many and the answers few. Her only recourse was to turn to her mother and Giorgio for strength, but most of all, to the God of her faith.

*   *   *

Once at home, she rolled her eyes at the sight of the open kitchen door where a pot of red geranium was covered with blooms. She dropped the sickle and the gunnysack and stepped into the kitchen. It was buzzing with flies.

She grabbed a towel to shoo them away but became aware of animated voices behind the semi-closed dining room door. She detested eavesdropping, but something didn't feel right. She listened closely and heard Daniela and Albina. Although their voices were low, she understood every word.

"Where was this?" Daniela asked.

"In the keyhole. Wh… what are we going to do?" Albina whimpered.

"Marina mustn't know."

"What shouldn't I know?" Marina pushed the door open.

Daniela whirled around and crumpled the note in her hand.

"Nothing. It's mischief," Albina said.

"Give me the note."

"It's alright, Marina." Daniela tucked the hand holding the note behind her. "You know how… how people are."

"I said, give it to me!"

Daniela reluctantly obeyed.

"Whoever wrote this forgot what they learned in school," Marina said. Her eyes widened as she read the sloppily written note and gripped the back of a chair.

Watch Giorgio. He's betraying you.

It was rubbish, but she felt as if someone had punched her in the stomach. "You know nothing about this, and Mama and Giorgio mustn't know either, alright?"

"Tear it up." Albina reached for it.

"No." She smoothed the crumpled page and then folded it. "If I find out who wrote it, this is evidence." She put it in her apron pocket, went outside, and took the sickle and gunnysack to the basement. "Absurd," she said aloud at the idea that Giorgio was betraying her. Yet, again, she shivered for no reason.

CHAPTER THREE

That evening, a meadowlark's last song of the day contrasted with the grim news that had come out of Rome. Many had cheered *Il Duce's* arrest, but in the chaos that had erupted afterwards, the Marshal had had hundreds of people shot.

Marina sat outside with her family but couldn't focus on her embroidery. She had dismissed the note regarding Giorgio's so-called betrayal. What did worry her was his enthusiasm for the Allies. Mussolini had let himself be convinced by Hitler that they should join forces to fight them. As a result, Hitler sent his troops to Italy with whatever arms were necessary. Now, Italy found itself divided in two, with the Germans in the north and the Anglo-American forces in the south. There were those in the village who felt the arrest of *Il Duce* was an injustice and approved his going to war with the United States. By accident, she had found out that Giorgio had had a strong discussion with a villager, a Fascist. Giorgio had said that he welcomed the day that both Nazi Germany and Fascism would fall.

"Marina, are you feeling alright?" Alda asked.

A moment went by before she answered. "Yes, Mama, I'm just... just depressed with what has happened in Rome."

"Who knows what the coming days will bring," Lisa said.

"The world that we knew no longer exists." Albina's tone was wistful.

Marina thought of the newly arrived refugees in the village. Desperate to flee the bombings, they had come from Rome and from as far south as Calabria, willing to do any work just to put food on the table. Her heart ached for the little ones who had been uprooted by events that they didn't understand. If nothing else, at least here in the village they could sleep peacefully.

Daniela turned the corner from the street, her face beaming. "I get to help with the children when school starts."

"This will require lots of patience." Alda smiled.

Daniela bent down and kissed her mother. "I've had a good example in you."

"The village feast is coming up in two weeks," Albina said.

"How can we even think of a feast when we have Gianni away at war and... and Papa..." Marina couldn't continue.

"We have to hope and pray for better days, no matter how hard it may seem." Alda blinked back tears.

"We'd better do a lot of praying then." Lisa exclaimed.

Although they attended church the morning of the feast, Marina and her family didn't attend the dance in the evening.

*　　　　*　　　　*

As July gave way to August, Marina wished to be able to see into the future. The early morning sun had barely risen over the mountains when Marina helped Alda with the *bucato*. They brought the bed linen and towels down into a corner in the garden and placed them in the *conca,* a large terra-cotta container with a drain at the bottom. Over this, they placed a large porous cloth made of hemp or cotton, and on this they placed ashes from the fireplace or the outdoor oven.

Marina, with Daniela's help, carefully poured a cauldron of boiling water mixed with lye over the ashes.

Daniela wrinkled her nose at the *ranno* that slowly seeped through the ashes and the cloth. "I wish that we could have soap for the laundry. It would smell nicer than this." Daniela pursed her lips.

"I wish that we could have more soap for bathing. I'd smell nicer, too. It's all I can do to keep fresh with this heat." Marina protested.

They repeated the process until the water from the drain came out clear.

"I'm going to make more faggots of kindling wood." Alda waited until the last of the boiling water had been poured. "We might as well do as much as we can with the warm weather. "Be good while I'm away." She crossed the garden to the basement.

"Aren't we always good?" Daniela asked mischievously. Marina rolled her eyes.

They placed the clean laundry in large baskets and, with Albina's help, they carried them to the public wash area.

They crossed the *piazza* and entered the path below the homes that led to the area. The walk from their home to the public washtub wasn't that long, but carrying a basket of laundered linen on their heads had them out of breath by the time they reached it. Here, they rinsed the laundry in the natural spring that poured out of a pipe into the large tub.

When the laundry had been rinsed clean, they made the return trip with their heavy baskets. "We're in for a storm." Daniela panted as she stopped in the cobblestone road and looked up at the darkening sky. "I hope we make it home before it starts to rain. What a change from early this morning." August days were very warm, but the dark and foreboding clouds up above promised welcome rain.

"Let's stop for a moment up at Giorgio's house to rest," Marina said. She noticed that Amelia had a sheet out on the balcony railing. "Amelia is away this afternoon. I'd better put it in and see if Giorgio's home. Both of you go ahead." She crouched down and maneuvered her basket onto a wood bench at the basement door.

"We'd better wait a moment before we spread the

laundry on the hedges." Albina warned.

Thunder rolled and a fine drizzle, borne on the brisk wind, carried the fragrance of wet grasses. A few chickens, feathers ruffled, cackled and pecked at blades of grass on the cobblestone street. Alongside a hedge that bordered the street, a grey cat stalked stealthily, then pounced on a mouse.

Marina gathered up the heavy, still damp, hemp sheet from the railing. Her arms full, she managed to turn the key in the door.

"Giorgio?" she called out as she stepped inside the small dining room. No one answered.

She spread the sheet on the chairs at the table and turned to leave but paused at the sound of rapid footsteps coming down the stairs.

"Marina," Giorgio said in surprise, fumbling to button his shirt.

"I thought I would bring this inside." To her dismay, she felt warmth rise to her cheeks.

"Thank you. I just got back from the vineyard. I hope that Mama can find a place to wait this out." He cringed at a loud *bang* as the wind slammed an upstairs window closed. "I'd better close those, or I'll end up making new ones!" He turned to the staircase.

"I'll help you."

Giorgio took the steps by two, and she hurried after him.

The heavens opened in a deafening torrent of rain and

loud thunderclaps shook the house. The cross-current of stormy wind through the house slammed another window shut. Marina leaned out to gather a few items hanging from a line outside the window. The wind-driven rain sprayed her face and arms.

When she had closed the windows, she took a towel from the washstand to dry herself, but Giorgio took it from her and gently patted her face.

Touched, a surge of emotion overwhelmed her. *How like him to perform an unexpected gesture of love.*

He bent his head and she welcomed his kiss, happy to nestle in his embrace.

"You're not leaving now are you?" he murmured against her cheek. "Stay here a little while."

Her chilly body warmed in his arms and his heart beat strong and fast against her hands. The pounding rain had turned into a gentle patter. Time seemed to stand still, and she felt torn between her deepest feelings and her conscience. The temptation to forget everything in his arms was strong. She prayed for strength.

When he bent his head to kiss her again, she found her voice and her courage before his lips found hers.

"Giorgio," she whispered, "I... I better go."

"Why? Why can't we have a moment for us? Mama won't be coming home now."

"That... that moment," she inhaled deeply, "I know, will lead us to something more. We... we can't. And you know it."

"Who would know?"

"*We* would. We have a life ahead of us, please God. You understand, don't you? Please say that you do." Her heart ached at the longing and love in his eyes.

"I don't." He let her go. "All I know is work, a game of cards with friends in the evening. When I do visit you, we're never alone. Am I asking so much?"

Marina felt hurt and annoyed at his reaction. "I never realized that my family was playing watchdog over us. You don't seem to mind when Mama reserves a treat for you when you visit!" she shot back.

"I never said they are watchdogs."

"Short of it." She bit her lower lips, still vexed. "Listen, the war is hard on all of us. I can understand your frustration, but think of *my* frustration if I should find myself... oh, never mind." His expression showed no understanding. "Excuse me?" She asked as she tried to pass between him and the bed.

"You really want to go?" he asked, sullen.

"Yes."

She quickly descended the stairs. When she opened the front door, she came face to face with Amelia. She nearly gasped.

"Marina! *Ciao.*" Amelia greeted her warmly.

Marina felt sorry for her. Although she had an umbrella, Amelia's hair was damp and her dress wet. "I... I brought in the sheet for you." She stepped quickly aside to let Amelia in. "I'm going now." She turned to look at

Giorgio, who had gone pale.

"Thank you, Marina. It was good of you," Amelia said.

Marina descended the steps and leaned against the basement door. She dared not think what would have happened if she had given in to Giorgio.

*   *   *

Marina tossed and turned all night in bed. She felt frustrated because yes, she had wanted to stay just as much as Giorgio had wanted her to stay, and yet she believed that she had done the right thing. At dawn, she got up quietly so as not to awaken her mother with whom she slept, and crossed into the bedroom where Albina and Daniela were still asleep. Lisa was already down in the kitchen, ready to leave for her first day at work in the statuette factory in the valley.

"You look awful." Lisa frowned at her as she sipped her milk and *caffe' d'orzo*.

"I didn't sleep well."

"You're not making *polenta* again today, are you?"

Marina rolled her eyes. "Lisa, why don't you cook your own meals from now on so you'll be happy?"

"I'm going, thank heaven." Lisa got up, washed her cup, and turned to Marina. "I don't know what's wrong with you. You've been cranky since yesterday. Whatever it is, I hope it will work out. *Ciao*." She grabbed her little cloth sack with the food that she would eat later on and left.

Marina stood staring at the door feeling guilty. Lisa was right. Yesterday evening, she had answered her mother a little tartly and had snapped at Albina. This was her first crisis with Giorgio, and she didn't like it—especially when she took it out on those around her. The first thing she did was to apologize again to her mother and Albina. Later, she would apologize to Lisa. The morning went by with the usual tasks. After *pranzo,* she decided against going to the vineyard, as the rabbits had enough fodder. Instead, she would visit her *Nonna* Nelsa, her maternal grandmother, who lived outside of the village, halfway down the mountain.

Puddles of rain glistened in the warm rays of the sun. As she walked along, a young couple tended to their terraced vineyard above her. Clusters of grapes, some already showing their rich, dark blue, peeked through the leaves, and their cat scampered through the grass.

Although Giorgio was piqued at her, prudence had been the wiser choice. She would never forget the look on his face when he saw his mother.

She sniffed the air and turned into the direction of a haze in the woods. Even with the rain, the *carbonari* were diligently keeping an eye on the conical mountain of slowly burning wood, which would become charcoal.

Having walked the familiar, winding path all her life, she quickly reached the little stone house. Smoke curled from the chimney, hens and several chicks pecked and cackled among the snowball bushes alongside the path. In front of the door was a porch-like area. Here, her grandmother's black and white cat, Pulce, basked in the dappled sunshine beneath a wisteria.

"Bimba mia." Nelsa quickly rose from her small chair in front of the fireplace. A big black cauldron filled almost to the brim with milk, hung over briskly burning flames.

Marina exchanged a warm hug with her. "It's been a long time since I've been down here."

"Too long, child. How is everyone at home?" Nelsa pulled back a chair from the table for her.

"We're doing alright. We're thrilled that Daniela will be tutoring children when school starts again. Let me stir for a while. You rest a little."

Marina could appreciate the love and work that went into making the *ricotta* that they enjoyed. It didn't take long for beads of perspiration to form on her forehead as she sat in front of the fire. "I think we have something," she said as clear whey began to show in streaks in the rapidly thickening milk.

With a sieve, Nelsa slowly drew up the curd and placed it in a mold, gently pressing it down as the whey spilled out.

"That's done," she said, washing her hands. "I'll make us some *caffe' d'orzo*." Nelsa quickly disappeared into the little dining room and returned with a small plate of *biscotti* that she had baked the day before. "Here, have one." She presented the plate to Marina. "What news is there in the village?"

"Apart from the war, there's not much. The refugee children seem to be settling into their new life."

Nelsa joined her hands and raised her eyes heavenward. "When will all this end? How is Giorgio? Is he behaving himself?"

"Yes... he... is," Marina faltered. "He's busy with his work." She bit into the homemade wheat cookie and prayed that her *nonna* hadn't noticed her hesitation.

"How are your wedding plans going?"

"It's not easy to plan with Gianni at war."

Nelsa studied her a moment. "Marina, what's wrong? You're not you."

Marina took another bite out of the *biscotto,* struggling with telling her about what had happened between her and Giorgio. She hadn't even told her mother so as not to give her another concern.

"Marina?"

Marina raised her eyes. "Giorgio and I had-" she choked on her words. After a moment she poured out everything along with her tears.

To her surprise, Nelsa laughed.

"Marina, you're dealing with a man. You did right in being prudent and, yes, he was stubborn, but that's part of life when you love someone. Deep down, Giorgio would never have forced you to do something against your will. Give him time. He'll come to reason."

"What if... if I wasn't prudent?"

"I trust you to be so, but remember that I'm here for

you, no matter what."

"Mama and the girls don't know anything," Marina said.

"Have you ever known me to gossip?"

"No." Marina shook her head, her lips curving into a smile. She sipped the refreshing beverage, made from barley, that her *nonna* served in two, dainty demitasse cups. This amused her because here was her maternal grandmother, with her bandana a little askew on her head and who had just made *ricotta*, serving a simple drink in her best cups. She was a no nonsense woman. If there was anything that she should know, she wanted it straight from her family. Widowed for several years, she had never buried herself in her sorrow, but instead had put her life to trying to help others.

They chatted for a little longer and then Marina followed her grandmother down to her small flower and vegetable garden below the house. The lemon verbena gave off its lemony fragrance when Marina rubbed a leaf between her fingers. Pear shaped red tomatoes hung on their vines. An old barrel gathered rain water for the furrows of celery and basil. The terraced vineyard bore rows of carefully tended vines, two apple trees, a peach tree, and two fig trees. One was the so called "gold" fig, because, when opened, the flesh was gold colored and sweet as honey.

As she pulled out weeds here and there, Marina was convinced that if the world was as peaceful as this garden, it would be Eden all over again.

Immersed in the beauty that surrounded her, she realized with a start that the sun had disappeared behind the chestnut trees. There was no way that her *nonna* would allow her to go home without a small basket of nature's bounty and a bouquet of pink roses.

"Thank you," Marina whispered as she bade her grandmother goodbye.

"Remember, he'll come around, alright? If you're upset, he's even more so. Trust me." She waved as Marina began her trek up the gently winding path, refreshed in spirit.

*   *   *

Now, more than ever, Marina turned to her faith. She didn't pour out her frustration to her family, but it was agony waiting to see what would happen. A week had already gone by and neither she nor Giorgio had made any attempt to see each other. Hurt at his stubbornness and what she felt was his selfishness, too, she wasn't ready to apologize for holding her own. He should have respected and understood her wishes.

Sunday Mass had just ended, but rather than go home, she decided to remain in church a little longer.

Alda leaned down to her. "Marina, remember that we have Nonna invited for *pranzo* and I've invited Giorgio and Amelia too."

Marina's rosary fell onto the seat of the pew in front of her. Giorgio and Amelia were invited to eat with them. Her mind wrestled with the idea. She heard a soft footfall and turned to see Giorgio approaching her.

"May I join you?" His lips curved in a tentative smile.

She was struck by the shadows under his eyes, the taut lines of his face. Clearly, the week had been hard not only for her, but for him, too. Her stubbornness melted and she moved over to make room for him.

"Marina, I'm… I'm sorry about the other day." He sat down. "You were right. I was being selfish… not thinking of the consequences."

"You were so hurt and… and then I was hurt because you wouldn't…"

"I wouldn't understand." He took her hand. "I would die rather than force you to do something against your will. Sometimes it's just that—oh, I don't know." He ran his fingers through his hair.

She caressed his cheek with her finger. "It's alright, *amore mio*, it's alright."

He squeezed her hand. "I love you."

"I love you, too."

"I really do like your mother's *biscotti*, you know." He smiled crookedly.

Marina stifled a giggle. They turned at the sound of a low voice at the open door behind them, but no one was there. She shrugged.

"Let's go," Giorgio said, and took her hand. "I think

that this is going to be a lovely day."

*   *   *

"This is a feast," Giorgio commented later, as he sipped the last of his wine and sat back, contented.

"Yes," Alda said softly, "it is a feast." From her pocket, she took out a worn envelope and placed it on the table.

Marina exchanged a quick glance with her sisters and gasped. "*Oh Signore,* it's from Gianni!" She jumped up from the table as she recognized the beloved name in the corner.

"*Eviva!*" Giorgio's rousing cheer released everyone's emotions.

"*Sia lodato Dio!*" Nelsa and Amelia thanked God almost in unison.

Lisa and Daniela sat speechless.

"Mama, when… when did this arrive?" Albina asked.

"Yesterday. I… met the mail lady as she was coming to the door." Alda brushed away a tear. "It was hard to keep it a secret until today."

Although it wasn't the latest news, as mail traveled slowly, they read that Gianni had been spared the Russian front. He had become ill with pneumonia and was sent to a local hospital. It was from there that he wrote the letter full of concern and love for everyone. He trusted his sisters to take care of their mother and looked forward to the day when the Allies would win back Italy for its people. He remembered his childhood friend, and threatened to beat Giorgio at *briscola,* a popular card game.

Giorgio cleared his throat and toasted him with a little wine. "I'm looking forward to it, Gianni."

"Mama, we have to celebrate in some way. What… what can we do?" Marina asked.

"The time of mourning for your father is over. On Sunday, we celebrate the village feast, and go to the dance on Sunday evening." Alda let out a deep sigh. "It hasn't been easy for anyone lately, and God knows it's not going to get any easier."

"Mama, will you come, too?" Albina asked.

"No. I'll stay home, but I ask that you keep an eye on each other and be proper. I'm entrusting you to Giorgio's care."

"You better live up to that, my good man," Amelia said and gave her son a look of warning.

Giorgio's eyes twinkled and he grinned from ear to ear.

CHAPTER FOUR

Marina's happiness knew no limit during the following days. She and Giorgio were together and Gianni had written.

On Saturday evening, the candlelight procession wound throughout the village with the statue of the beloved saint, the patron of youth, on its platform, carried by the men. On Sunday morning, Mass was celebrated. The church was full and there was much excitement over the activities for young and old later in the afternoon down in the *piazza.* Later that evening, Marina and her sisters walked down to that same piazza for the dance.

Young couples, children, and the elderly slowly filled the large hall. A villager, adept with his accordion, sat on a chair on the slightly raised platform and played well-known tunes. Daniela and Albina joined a group of young people, while Marina and Lisa sat on the one of the wood benches alongside the walls, dressed in their best finery.

Couples strode to the center of the hall to dance a well-known waltz. Marina didn't miss Lisa's searching gaze as it traveled around the hall, nor how her face lit up when Doctor Marco Graziani walked up to her.

Doctor Graziani held out his hand. "Lisa, will you dance with me?"

"Doctor Graziani. I… why… yes."

Tentatively, they tried the first steps and soon picked up the rhythm.

Marina smiled at how well matched they were. Lisa's growing interest in the young doctor hadn't gone unnoticed by any of them. At first they thought it to be her infatuation alone but Doctor Graziani, in a discreet way, had let her know that he wasn't indifferent to her.

"*Ciao,* Marina."

"Carla, you look pretty." Marina turned to her friend, whose eyes sparkled just like the pin on her bodice, a cherished reminder of her mother.

"Where's Giorgio?" Carla asked.

"Somewhere around serving refreshments, I think. I just arrived and haven't seen him yet."

"He wouldn't dare *not* see you!"

Marina stared at her, not knowing what to make of the remark. In that moment, Giorgio walked up to her and made an exaggerated bow.

"May I have this dance?"

"I thought you'd never ask." Marina took his hand. "Carla, excuse me." She turned to her, but Carla had disappeared.

It was almost midnight when Giorgio walked Marina home. Daniela, Albina, and Lisa walked ahead of them in the company of Doctor Graziani.

"Am I mistaken," Giorgio whispered to her, "or do we have a romance in bud?"

"Ah, so you noticed, too. I rather like the idea of having a doctor as a prospective brother-in-law."

"This reminds me of when we first met," Giorgio said softly.

"Yes, it does."

When they reached home, her sisters went directly upstairs. Marina closed the kitchen window and twirled around and around into the dining room. The unexpected memory of Carla's snide remark interrupted the music in her head.

For no reason, she felt cold.

Later, in bed, Marina stirred. In her sleepy state, she heard what sounded like pounding on the door below. She sat up, not knowing whether it was a dream or for real. Again she heard the pounding along with a man's desperate voice. She jumped out of bed and raced through her sisters' bedroom. Downstairs, she opened the door to Doctor Graziani.

"Marina," he gasped, "something bad has happened!"

"Wh… what? Is it Giorgio...Amelia?" Marina asked, her heart pounding.

The doctor placed his hands on her shoulders. "Giorgio has been… assaulted."

She grabbed a shawl left behind on a chair and raced ahead of the doctor down the street as tears streamed down her face. *Why, Lord, why?*

*   *   *

His injuries were not life-threatening, but they were bad. Marina's family, in the meantime, roused by the commotion, had arrived almost immediately after she did at Giorgio's home. Marina remained with him after Doctor Graziani left, holding his unresponsive hand, trying to keep back her tears.

"*Bimba*, go home now and try to rest," Amelia whispered when the first rays of dawn were visible in the east.

"No." Marina shook her head. She turned to her mother and sisters, who hovered behind her. "You understand, don't you?"

"Of course we do," Lisa said and placed a hand on Marina's shoulder.

"I want to be here with him." She brushed back a lock of hair, still matted with blood, from Giorgio's forehead. His cheeks were swollen and bruised, his right wrist broken in an attempt to protect his head. "I knew this was going to happen," she whispered.

Giorgio moaned, opened his right eye a little, his left one swollen shut. "You... you warned me... more than once," he whispered.

"Don't talk."

"We're going now," Alda said. "I'll be back later, alright?"

"Thank you, Mama."

Lisa hugged her tightly. "Don't let go, Marina."

As she watched Amelia hover over her son, tears streaming down her face, Marina vowed that from now on, as far as she was concerned, everyone was both friend and enemy. Her faith told her to forgive, just as the Lord had forgiven. Maybe one day she would, but not now.

Immersed in her thoughts, she didn't hear Dr. Graziani come up the stairs until he stood next to her. He placed his fingers at Giorgio's wrist.

"Your pulse is strong but fast. God, how I wish I knew who did this to you." He sat down on the edge of the bed. "Go home, Marina. I'll stay for a while."

"I'm not leaving, but I want Amelia to have something to eat." She caressed Giorgio's forehead. "I'm going downstairs a moment, alright?" She motioned to the doctor to follow her. At the bottom of the stairs, she turned to him. "Will he be alright?"

"He'll recover, but it will take time. More than the wounds, it's his spirit that I'm worried about." Doctor Graziani rested his head in his hands on the table. "I don't mind being wakened for a birth but this... this, no. Amelia was so distraught when she came to me that I didn't understand what had happened or how." He shook his head.

"Amelia told me that after... after he walked us home, he stopped to check on his work in the basement. Two men, faces covered, rushed in and began to beat him. He cried out, but Amelia didn't hear him. After a while, she went down to tell him to come to bed and found him. They… could have… could have killed him." Marina covered her mouth with her hand.

"No, it was a warning. They left a note on the door."

"A note? Wh… what did it say?"

The doctor bit his lower lip. "Next time, you're dead."

Marina covered her face, and fought the urge to break down. *"Don't let go,"* Lisa had told her. No, this wasn't the time to let go. She needed every ounce of strength to get through this ordeal.

After the doctor left, she was able to convince Amelia to have something to eat and to go and rest.

Marina gently bathed Giorgio's face, which felt hot to the touch. Although the sun was up, she felt exhausted and lay down next to him. She finally fell asleep with her head against his shoulder, her right arm lying across his body.

Exhausted from tension, Marina awoke before noon. Her head was still against Giorgio's shoulder, but he had managed to turn a little towards her. His left arm lay across her body and his hand covered hers.

*   *   *

The following day, Giorgio managed to sit up in bed, propped up against the pillows. Marina sat next to him, spoon feeding him the savory broth that Amelia had prepared the day before.

"This is good, Marina. Thank you." Giorgio gratefully

chewed a small piece of bread soaked in the broth.

"Later I'll give you a little cheese and a peach. You have to regain your strength after what has happened."

Giorgio sat back against the pillow. "The way I feel now, I wonder if I'll return to being the man that I was."

Marina forced herself to smile encouragingly. "You'll be even better, *amore mio*."

*　　　　　*　　　　　*

August came to a close with the news that the Allies had landed in Southern Italy. Giorgio was ecstatic. The swelling on his face had gradually disappeared, although he was still black and blue. Except for his wrist, his wounds were slowly healing, but it was the inner wound that worried Marina. He startled easily and at times was withdrawn. She was able to reduce her visits to him. But today, Amelia was out all day helping a neighbor in her vineyard and had asked if she would spend the day with him. Giorgio had gone for a little walk.

Marina wiped her floury hands on her apron when she saw him come in. "How did it go?"

"I walked a little and then sat in the sunshine. I wanted to try and do a little work but didn't have the courage to open the basement door." He shook his head glumly. "I can't do that forever."

"Take it one step at a time," she said, hugging him.

Giorgio kissed her lightly on the lips. "I love you. What

would I have done without you?”

"Well, now, let me think…" She smiled mischievously.

"Your love and encouragement have done more for me than any medicine." He caressed her face. "Do… do you remember the last time we were alone together here in the house?"

Marina nodded. There was no way that she would forget that day. "I-I have carried that moment with me," she whispered.

"So have I."

The thought that she could have lost him was more than she could bear. She met his gaze and was convinced that they had read each other's minds. He let her go and walked towards the dining room, his hand outstretched to her. She placed her hand in his.

Unlike that day, there was no storm but pure silence instead. Later, she rested in Giorgio's arms, her head against his bare chest. Come what might, at least this moment had been theirs.

*   *   *

A week later, what everyone expected came true.

Marina didn't go to Giorgio's, as she was baking bread. Her mother sat outside shelling beans. She kneaded the dough and stopped to listen to voices outside the open kitchen door. One voice was Giorgio's, clearly excited.

Giorgio burst upon her in the kitchen. "It's happened!"

Marina stood transfixed. "What's happened?"

"The… the Marshal has surrendered Italy to the Allies."

Marina exchanged a look with Alda, who had entered the kitchen, concerned.

"Now what's going to happen?" Marina asked. She raised a silent prayer to the Virgin Mary, whose feast day it was, September 8.

The next day brought more shocking news. The Marshal had given orders to the soldiers to cease hostilities. Those who obeyed were disarmed by the Germans, and those who refused were shot. Many soldiers were taken prisoner. The Commander of the Allied Forces had told the Marshal to train his five divisions of soldiers in Rome to fend off the Germans that held Italy from Naples all the way to the north. Instead, fearing for his life, the Marshal fled south with the King to Brindisi. Rome was left to its fate with his soldiers leaderless. The Roman populace, desperate to save themselves from Germany, fought in desperation but not without a heavy toll of lives lost.

The betrayal shocked all of Italy even if the majority of the people were jubilant at the fall of Fascism. The Fascists were seething. Reluctant to let go of their hold, their troops were still seen in the city streets. The Germans were seething, too. They would now treat Italy like any other occupied country.

Marina smacked a dishtowel on the sink. "They left us to the Germans and now we're an occupied country. What treachery!"

"We have to learn to survive, Marina." Alda cast a wary glance at her infuriated daughter. "The Germans may arrive here, too, and if they do, we will carry on our everyday life and not attract any attention. I just pray that Gianni, if he is alive, doesn't do anything rash, such as joining the movements that are arising."

Many Italians had no love for either the Fascists or the Germans, but there was the fear of deportation to Germany and the concentration camps there. A new movement called *La Resistenza* "resisted" both. This was also comprised of *Partigiani* or Partisans, mostly Italian soldiers who had made their way home but were afraid of deportation or of being recruited by the Fascist Army. Marina thought it a melting pot. Anti-Fascists, those too young or too old to fight, and even those who had never been drafted, joined the Partisans. One cause united all of them—helping the Allies to win.

Daniela and Albina entered from outside. Daniela threw her arms in the air, frustrated. "Can we never have a moment's peace? *Nonna* has fallen and hurt herself!"

Alda was instantly alert. "When did it happen? Who told you?"

"Thank heaven for her new neighbor across the way," Daniela said. "He went to visit her and found her sitting on the porch in pain with a sprained ankle. She had stumbled on a crack in the porch and fell down. He helped her to a chair and came up as fast as he could to tell us."

"I have to go down and see how bad she is." Alda

rushed upstairs.

After she left, Marina tried to figure out a plan. "Nonna can't stay down there much longer, and we can't always be down there to keep an eye on her. We have to find her a place here, but where?"

"I don't think there are any," Daniela said. "The refugees have filled the few homes that were empty. She'll have to stay with us."

Marina bit her lower lip. The only room they had was Gianni's. It would have to be her grandmother's for as long as was necessary. If Gianni came home, please God, they would have to figure out other arrangements. For the time being, they had no choice.

"I'm going, girls," Alda said. She carried a large cloth bag with some essentials.

"Mama, I'm coming down with you," Daniela said firmly.

"You don't have to. I'll be alright."

"I want to see *Nonna*," Daniela pleaded. "I'll stay a little bit and then come home."

"Alright. Let's go."

Marina stood with Albina at the door watching them leave. "Well, can anything else go wrong?" her sister asked. Marina rolled her eyes.

*　　　　*　　　　*

The gentle patter of rain on the roof the next morning

slowly roused Marina from a fitful night's sleep. Her emotions were as unpredictable as the weather had been all week. Added to the worry of the German occupation and her concern over her *nonna,* was the thought that she might be expecting a baby. Neither she nor Giorgio regretted that moment together and he was ready to assume his responsibility if she was with child. Her concern was how her mother and sisters would react. Lisa was bonding with Doctor Graziani and she didn't want to be a bad example to her.

Now that her mother was with *Nonna,* Marina felt a little lonely in bed. She got up and opened the inside shutters. She tiptoed into the next room. Daniela and Albina slept, but Lisa was already up. For a moment, she stood looking at them as they slept peacefully. She sighed deeply and sent downstairs into the kitchen. After lighting the fire, she prepared *orzo* and warmed some milk. The first rays of the sun had broken through the clouds and wisps of fog nestled into the ridges and chasms of the hills. If, in the weeks before, the fire had added to the summer heat, now its warmth felt good.

"I'm off to work." Lisa yawned. "After the weekend, Monday morning is so hard. I wish I could visit *Nonna.*"

"I hope that we can have her with us as soon as possible." Marina poured a little milk into her cup and dipped a piece of bread into it.

Daniela entered the kitchen with Albina and looked around dourly. "It's odd not having Mama here."

"We'll be fine," Lisa said, smiling. "Mama said to keep busy with our everyday lives. If… if the Germans should come here, too…"

"Lord, help us. The last thing I want is to have anything to do with them." Marina shuddered.

"Remember that we're talking about the soldiers, not the everyday person who is trying to survive." Daniela warned.

"I'm leaving." Lisa rose and gathered her little cloth bag with her food for later.

"I'm tutoring my first student this morning." Daniela sat down with a smile on her face and sipped her milk with *orzo*. "If it stays sunny, this afternoon we can do the bedrooms. We won't be keeping the windows open for much longer. I can undo the beds."

"Why don't we go searching for mushrooms tomorrow? People are finding them," Albina suggested. "We have the grapes next week."

"That's a good idea," Marina said. "We might find some for *Nonna,* too."

"I'd better go to the vineyard this morning, so this afternoon I can do the bedrooms with Daniela." Albina drank her milk thoughtfully.

Albina left a little later. Marina stood a moment longer at the door, watching her sister walk briskly towards the vineyards. She couldn't help smiling. Her sisters were intent on keeping life as normal as possible. Somehow, they would all survive this moment. She turned back to the kitchen and began to tidy up. After a little while, she heard a knock on the door. It opened and Giorgio stepped inside.

"Amore mio," Marina dried her hands and kissed him.

"I saw Daniela and she told me about Nelsa. Is there anything that I can do to help?"

"We're doing alright." Marina wrapped her arms around him. "How are you feeling?"

Giorgio looked away, biting his lower lip. "I… I feel fine. Marina, it was wonderful to… to-"

Marina felt warmth rise to her cheeks as she recalled that afternoon. "I know. It *was* wonderful. But now, I have to wait and see…"

Giorgio cupped her face. "I'm the baby's father and you're my wife. Remember that."

Marina happily nestled into his arms. She never doubted Giorgio's integrity but to hear him declare his devotion, made her feel that she could face whatever the world presented her.

*   *   *

Later that afternoon, up in the bedrooms, Albina wiped dust from the walls and swatted a spider. "How I'd like to swat the Germans."

"How will we survive?" Daniela asked.

"If the Allies can continue their advance, they won't last long. I hope to heaven that it's soon."

"Be careful how you talk, especially in public," Daniela warned.

"It's the truth."

"Can you trust anyone in this moment? You don't know what can happen. Marina always said that Giorgio is cheering for the Allies. Look what happened to him."

Albina paused, holding the broom. "Do you think he was assaulted because of that?"

"I wouldn't be surprised. He isn't the only one who's been assaulted. There was someone else a few years ago, only he wasn't so lucky to live. He was an anti-Fascist. No one ever found out who did it."

"That's scary. Giorgio could... could have died," Albina said softly.

"But he didn't. Enough of this talk." Daniela waved her hand. "Let's finish the rooms."

Satisfied that both rooms were dusted and swept, Daniela mopped the terra cotta floors before the beds were made. She carried the bucket downstairs to the little balcony and tossed the dirty water over the railing. A piercing scream from down below froze her on the spot.

Albina had just come downstairs and cringed at the scream. "Who... what-?" She stepped quickly onto the balcony.

"I'm... I'm afraid to look and find out. I... I tossed the water without looking..." Daniela whimpered and pointed to the railing. She winced at the irate words that floated up to her.

Albina stepped to the railing, looked down, and turned to Daniela. "Not when it's Marina you don't."

The kitchen door opened and Marina stepped inside. Her wet hair clung to her shoulders, her cardigan and skirt were soaked from the slosh of cold, dirty water.

"Oh, Marina, I'm so sorry." Daniela approached her with apprehension.

"Not as sorry as I am." Marina grimaced and walked to the stove where a kettle of hot water was always handy.

Albina stoked the fire while Daniela rushed upstairs to bring her a large ceramic washbowl, a ewer, and two towels.

"We're going upstairs so you can freshen up, alright?" Albina said soothingly.

"Thank you." Marina wrinkled her nose at her dirty cardigan while shivering at the same time.

Albina and Daniela retreated upstairs thinking that the less said to Marina, the better. They exchanged a glance, ran into their mother's room, quickly closed the door behind them, and burst into laughter.

*   *   *

The next afternoon, Marina and Albina left to go searching for mushrooms.

As they walked down the street, the sight of the refugee children in the company of their new friends on their way to school took Marina back to her school days. She would give anything to be able to sit down with a book in her hand, but that luxury was for winter.

They crossed the *piazza* and continued under the *portici,* arcades that supported the balcony of a large home up above. Lovely geraniums spilled over their pots, which were lined along its railing. Marina had seen the inside of the house a few times and a twinge of envy came over her at the memory of the spacious rooms and delicate stenciling on the walls.

When they reached the chestnut grove, gold and russet leaves heralded autumn. Spider webs shimmered like strings of diamonds in the low-lying brush. Marina sniffed deeply of the air that smelled of damp earth and mushrooms. "Albina, look," she whispered, as if afraid to break a magical spell.

A patch of *porcini* lay just ahead of them, their light brown umbrella caps peeking through the damp, varied-colored leaves on the ground. Albina knelt and carefully picked a chubby mushroom. "Aren't they lovely?"

They gathered as many as possible, careful not to damage the little ones that would provide another crop. Marina lifted the basket to her head.

"I'll carry it for you."

"No, I'd better carry it. You may stumble and the basket will fall."

Albina shrugged her shoulders and followed behind her.

They exited the grove onto the path that would take them back. All went well but when they were in sight of the village, Marina stumbled. The expertly balanced basket tipped, slipped, and the precious find flew out.

Albina covered her mouth, hard put to keep from laughing.

Chagrined, Marina stood speechless but at the sound of voices she quickly dropped to her knees to pick up broken stems and caps, some of which had rolled off into oblivion.

Albina knelt down to help her. When their eyes met, they burst out laughing.

"So much for *you* stumbling," Marina gasped. "Here, carry the thing."

A moment went by before Albina composed herself enough to carry the basket.

When they reached the *piazza*, they found groups of people gathered together, talking animatedly. There was no mistaking the news. Marina and Albina exchanged glances.

"Mussolini e' liberato!"

CHAPTER FIVE

The news of Mussolini's liberation proved as shocking as the news of his arrest. A German lieutenant had flown a glider to where Mussolini was held, rescued him, and then flown him to Hitler's Headquarters in Germany. From here, he was flown to Northern Italy, to Salo', where he was proclaimed Head of the new Italian Socialist Republic. He would continue with the Fascist ideals even if, according to him, the Italian people had disappointed him.

Marina made little of *Il Duce's* woes. If he was disappointed, so were many others, especially the mothers of those young sons who had lost their lives in his quest to bring glory to Italy. Besides, she had her own concerns about her possible pregnancy and chores that needed to be done before the weather turned cold.

The familiar, winding path to her vineyard immersed her in the beauty of the season. Clusters of Muscat grapes in red and white and the almost black *Aleatico*, grown to make a dessert wine, peeked through the red and gold leaves of the vines. Although the air bore a slight chill, the sun shone warm and bright on her. She longed to capture its rays to brighten the coming days.

"Marina, *ehi!*"

Carla broke into a run to catch up with her. In her hand she held a bouquet of zinnias.

"What lovely flowers."

"I'm going to pay a visit to Mama's gravesite."

Marina's heart ached because she couldn't imagine losing her mother at the age Carla had. "I haven't seen you since the dance."

"I haven't been well."

"I'm sorry. What happened?"

"Nothing to worry about," Carla shrugged. "How are you?"

"I'm fine."

"How is Giorgio feeling? How terrible it was, what happened to him."

"He's doing nicely now and working again, but it was a bad moment."

"Are you still planning to marry? Sometimes, when persons have been through an ordeal, they prefer to put things off."

She sounded hopeful, but that snide edge was still there. Marina didn't answer right away. "Why shouldn't we marry? More than ever I want to be with him and maybe sooner than we'd planned."

Carla's face colored slightly and her expression turned hard. "I... I have to go," she said abruptly and brushed past her.

Marina resumed her walk and watched Carla reach the junction where she disappeared around the corner. Something didn't feel right but she hastened to her task because tomorrow was to be dedicated to her *nonna.*

*   *   *

Marina, her sisters, Alda, and Giorgio were gathered on the porch at her grandmother's little home.

Nelsa had come to the conclusion that she was not getting any younger, and it was hard to keep up with everything. "I have lived a lifetime here." Her eyes rested for the last time on the garden and the vineyard below the house. "This was your birthplace," she said brokenly to Alda.

"I know, Mama, but it's the best for you. Everything isn't lost. We will soon pick the grapes and the fruit. After all the hard work that you put into tending them, it would be a sin to let them go to waste."

"Nonna," Marina said, "Giorgio is going to dig up the dahlias and the small red bourbon rose and move them for you. We'll pick the vegetables and the basil."

"I'll have to kill the chickens." Nelsa bit her lower lip. Ridiculous as it seemed, she had named all six of them.

"Now why would you want to kill them? Alda's chickens can use some company. Just think what a happy henhouse it will be, and, of course, the happiest will be the rooster," Giorgio said with a twinkle in his eyes.

Nelsa arched her eyebrows and then dissolved into laughter.

"One more reason to love you," Marina said softly and kissed Giorgio on the cheek.

The winding path was narrow. Giorgio had secured some of Nelsa's belongings on Pallino, his donkey, who clipped clopped up the path to where it joined the wider road. Everyone followed behind, balancing baskets with linens and towels on their heads. Nelsa's neighbor, who had helped her when she had sprained her ankle, had offered his cart to help with the move, and waited at the junction. A comfortable cushion was provided for Nelsa to sit on. In her arms, she held Pulce, her cat, secured in a box with holes cut in it to provide plenty of air.

Marina sat down in the cart along with her mother and sisters. She raised herself up on her knees among the baskets of linen, pots and pans. "You'll be fine," she reassured Nelsa and placed her cheek against her grandmother's satiny one. The remainder of the trip was devoted to talk of the new prospects that Nelsa had in front of her.

The first haul completed, Nelsa freed Pulce, to let her get acquainted with her new garden. Giada warily circled around the newcomer, who slowly advanced and touched noses with her.

"Well that's a good beginning," Nelsa said with a note of relief.

It was late afternoon by the time Marina got Nelsa

settled in Gianni's room. She picked a bouquet from the red rambling rose bush as a finishing touch for the dresser. Tomorrow there would be another trip. Life today was good.

*   *   *

"Marina! Marina!"

Daniela's frantic voice from the dining room below tore through Marina the next day. She had just returned from another trip to bring Nelsa's things over, and was freshening up. "Oh, dear Lord, what happened?" She cried as she raced down the stairs.

In the kitchen, Nelsa, Albina and Daniela attended Alda, who sat pale on a chair.

"What's wrong? What hap…" Marina gasped at the bloodied bandana wrapped around her mother's right hand. "What did you do?"

"I don't know. I… I was clearing out an area of weeds in the garden, and I tripped and fell on the sickle. The blade *would* have had to be facing up."

Marina gently unfolded the bandana and exposed a half- moon gash in the palm.

Her grandmother clucked her tongue. "You're lucky that only your hand got the worst of it. Wash it out and get to Doctor Graziani right away." Nelsa ladled water into a bowl and searched for a clean towel.

"I'm not dying." Alda winced as she tried to move her fingers. "It just hurts."

"It's your fault," Albina flared at Daniela.

"*My* fault?"

"Why weren't you with Mama? Why did you wander off?"

"I didn't *wander* off. I had to…"

Nelsa brought her hand to her forehead, her eyes raised to heaven.

"*Basta!* That's enough. Come, Mama." Marina gently took her mother's arm as Albina and Daniela shot dark looks at each other. "Can we hope to find you in one piece when we return?" Marina fumed at her sisters.

The doctor's home that also served as his practice was at the uppermost part of the street that wound past their home.

"Don't be irritated with your sisters, Marina. I don't know why, but they've been biting at each other all morning."

"I'm surprised at Albina. She's always sweet and calm. I suppose she's at that age when you're no longer a child, and you're trying to get used to being a woman."

At the corner, they climbed the two steps to a little terrace where Doctor Graziani lived. The door opened to the small entry hall that served as a waiting area. Those present willingly let Marina and Alda go in ahead of them when he called his next patient.

"*Signora* Alda." He took her arm and led her inside. "What happened?"

Marco Graziani was in his late twenties. He had taken

over his uncle's practice after his retirement last year. His parents lived in the valley, but he hoped to have them established in the village at some point. Tall and slender, his deep blue eyes and fair complexion contrasted with his wavy, black hair.

His touch was gentle as he cleansed the caked blood from the wound. "The sickle wasn't rusty and that's good, but it requires sutures." He carefully washed his hands and placed a clean white towel under Alda's hand. "If the pain is too much, *signora* Alda, tell me, and I'll stop a moment."

Marina felt her body grow tense as she placed her hands on her mother's shoulders and averted her gaze.

Doctor Graziani worked slowly and kept Alda engaged in conversation throughout the procedure. "Are you alright?" He asked when he snipped the last suture.

"I am now," Alda managed a smile.

He dressed her hand. "You'll be fine," he reassured her. "Come again tomorrow morning and I'll change the dressing."

"Doctor Graziani, tell me what I owe you," Alda said.

"There's no need to worry about that. What matters is that your hand heals."

"Doctor, I… I am so appreciative of all you have done for Giorgio." Marina knew that it took more than medications to help him heal.

"I'm happy that he has mended." His expression turned hard. "I would give anything to know who attacked him."

"I don't think we ever will. On a lighter note, Lisa enjoyed dancing with you so much." Marina said warmly.

"I'm afraid that I stumbled more than anything else." He smiled. "Lisa was very kind to put up with me."

"I think she was happy to stumble with you." The words came out before Marina could stop them. It was abominable for her to have said that, but the look on Doctor Graziani's face showed that he didn't mind at all.

"Thank you." Doctor Graziani's face lit up like a lamp.

As far as Marina was concerned, the sooner they were out of the office, the better. Only when they were out of earshot of his windows did Marina speak. "Now I've done it. If Lisa finds out what I've said, she'll never forgive me."

"God has a way of working things out, Marina." Alda smiled. "Let's leave it up to Him."

CHAPTER SIX

With getting Nelsa settled in and taking her mother to change the dressing, Marina marveled at how fast the week flew by and suddenly it was Saturday. Lisa was home and the laundry had to be done. Today it was towels. When they were ready to be rinsed out, they carried the wide baskets on their heads and headed out to the public washtub.

The air was chilly, the water cold. Marina felt grateful that they were rinsing out just towels and not the hemp sheets that, when wet, took a herculean strength to carry. She worked quietly, the only sound being the twittering of the sparrows. Intent on rinsing, Marina didn't notice Lisa contemplating her.

"You're unusually quiet. Are you feeling alright?" Lisa asked.

Marina smiled up at her. "Yes, I'm… fine."

The hesitancy in her voice didn't escape Lisa, who laid down a towel. "No, you're not. Out with it. I know you too well."

The last thing Marina wanted was to tell Lisa what she feared was happening with her body. "I'm fine, really."

"Ma-ri-na!"

Marina couldn't control the tears that sprung into her eyes. She grabbed the edge of the tub and took a deep breath. "I'm afraid to tell you," she said softly.

"Something *is* wrong." Lisa stepped over to her and placed an arm around her shoulder. "What is it?"

"That day when I stayed with Giorgio while he was mending from the assault and Amelia had to be away all day, he had gone for a little walk. When he returned, he told me how... how much my seeing him through those terrible days meant to him." Marina raised her head to Lisa's concerned gaze. "We'd had a moment alone before, and we avoided... avoided..." Marina hesitated.

"I know what you're saying," Lisa said.

"This time, it was stronger than us. I... I could have been strong, but the thought of everything that he had gone through and... and what could have happened was too much for me. We... we went upstairs..."

Lisa brought her hands to her face. *"Oh, Signore,* you didn't-"

Marina nodded. "Yes... we did and I think I'm pregnant." She blinked hard. "I'm sorry, but I don't regret it."

"There's nothing to be sorry about. We're human beings. Does Giorgio know that you may be pregnant?"

"Giorgio said immediately that if... if I was expecting, he loved me, and would take up his responsibility. It's just... how am I going to tell Mama and the girls?"

"Mama may be a little harder, but as for the girls, you

tell them that things happen sometimes because we're human."

"I should see a midwife to find out." Marina shook her head. "But I don't know where to find one."

"Maybe Marco, I… I mean Doctor Graziani can help. I want to go with you to your appointment."

Marina smiled at her. She hadn't missed her slip of the tongue. "You don't have to do that."

"I want to. Please. In the meantime, you do what you can do. I'm your sister and I'm here for you. You know that, don't you?"

Marina hugged Lisa tightly, grateful to have bared her soul to her.

*   *   *

"Oh!"

Marina turned around at the exclamation as a plate shattered on the floor. Her mother stared chagrined at the broken pieces.

"I'm totally useless," Alda moaned.

"Mama, it's alright." Marina knelt down to pick up the pieces. "Be grateful that your hand is healing."

Alda handed her a broom. "I am grateful, but it's frustrating at the same time to be like this. I'm not able to help much with any tasks and the *vendemmia* is almost upon us."

"It will be fine." Marina reassured her. "We're fortunate that we're not alone in the tasks."

Chores had to be done even with the war, and those families whose sons or fathers were away at the front found themselves helpless. Every Sunday at Mass, Don Antonio, the resident priest, would mention the names of families in need of help.

*　　　　*　　　　*

The *vendemmia* had arrived and the son of one of the families was another childhood friend of Marina and Giorgio. He was at war, and had left behind his wife, Anna, who was due with their second child. Sadly, their respective families had become estranged over a trivial disagreement. Marina and Giorgio both volunteered up to help Anna.

"How heartless they are. Stefano may die in the war. Will they continue like this forever?" Marina bristled.

"Carissima," Giorgio said as they walked home from church, "not everyone sees things the same way that we are fortunate enough to see them. Tomorrow is going to be a busy day, but worth it."

*　　　　*　　　　*

"The whole village seems to be out today," Marina commented as Pallino clip-clopped down the path. The gentle creature carried on either side two *bigongie*, small, oval barrels, one inside the other, in which the grapes would be placed.

Marina carried a basket with bread and cheese, a little fruit, and a flasket of wine for a mid-morning snack.

"Let me know immediately what happens tomorrow, alright?" Giorgio asked.

"Don't worry, you'll know. This waiting is just as bad if not worse than if I knew for sure."

He squeezed her hand. "We'll get through this moment."

They reached the vineyard where a small orchard of apple, fig, and apricot trees stood between the vines.

"This is beautiful." Giorgio's eyes took in the lush vines.

"You helped make it beautiful. Anna couldn't have managed this vineyard without you."

Giorgio breathed deeply and headed for the farthest end of the row.

They both worked side by side and when two *bigongi* were filled, he made his first trip with Pallino.

"You take it easy now and rest, Marina."

On a large rock in the shade of an apple tree, Marina took off her bandana and ran her fingers through her hair, which was damp with perspiration. The gentle breeze caressed her face and rustled the grasses around her. Bees hummed around the clusters of grapes.

Vines of white Muscat, Aleatico, and ruby colored Rossetto grapes made up the greatest part of the vineyard. Immersed in the peace of the morning, which was broken only by a meadowlark's song, Marina found it hard to believe that there could be such peace amid turmoil at the same time.

Germany had set up The Gothic Line of Defense that crossed a section of the valley farther down to the west. In the town of Diecimo, they had taken over the railroad station. From that point, the Gothic Line continued all the way to the Adriatic coast to the east.

Life had strange twists and turns. Shortly after she had let on to Doctor Graziani that Lisa had enjoyed dancing with him, he had met Lisa returning from work by chance. In a round-about way, he touched the subject of the dance and magic happened. Love was in bud. This sweet happening had made it easier for Lisa to talk to Doctor Graziani, now Marco, about finding a midwife in Lucca. Lisa promised Marina that she would find an excuse to go with her to the appointment.

Rousing from her musing, she realized with a start, that Giorgio hadn't returned. Worried, she placed the basket of food in the shade with the intent of going to see what had happened to him. She hastened to the path just as he was leading Pallino down the slope.

His expression was a mixture of excitement and emotion.

"What happened? I was coming up to find you."

He ran his fingers through his hair. "We… we have a boy!" His words tumbled out.

"Eh?" For a moment Marina didn't grasp what he

meant. "Oh, Anna! Stefano… a baby boy!"

"I arrived just as Marco was coming out of the house."

"Is she alright? The baby?"

"They're fine and… and… she named him…" Giorgio's eyes filled and he was unable to continue.

"Stefano?" Marina offered.

He shook his head. "Giorgio," he whispered.

Marina was elated that Anna had named her baby after him. A new life and a new hope had been born that morning.

Afterwards, they ate quietly in the shade of the apple tree. It seemed as if they were immersed in their own thoughts. Curiosity finally got the better of Marina. "What are you thinking, *amore mio?*"

"I don't know if I should tell you."

"What do you mean?"

"How a life can be born from the love of two people. If that isn't a miracle, I don't know what is."

"It is a miracle," Marina whispered and touched her belly lightly.

The last of the grapes were finally picked, and when they arrived at Anna's home, Marina entered the kitchen to inquire about her and the baby. Her little two-year-old girl, Maddalena, sat at the table playing with a doll. Fortunately, Anna's sister, who had always remained steadfast to her, was there and sent Marina upstairs to visit.

"Come in, come in," Anna called. She was holding her little boy and a bubble of milk glistened between his tiny lips. "Come and see our son."

Marina stood a little away from the bed as her clothes were dusty and a little stained. Even from there, she saw how much the baby resembled his father.

"I can't thank you and Giorgio enough for all your help. The best I could do was to give him Giorgio's name."

"You made his day."

That night, when Marina undressed, her more thin than slim body reflected back to her in the oval mirror on the dresser. No sign of a baby yet. Giorgio loved her in the full sense of the word, but tomorrow she would know for sure if her suspicions were true or not.

*   *   *

Arm in arm with Lisa, Marina's mind was a whirlwind as they sat down on a stone bench. The midwife had confirmed the pregnancy. A strong wind scattered leaves along the street.

"How can I tell Mama? What am I going to tell Daniela and Albina?' Marina covered her face with her hands. "I should be an example to them, and I'm not."

"Oh, stop it," Lisa said. "Just tell them what I told you. Things happen. There is no reason nor is this the time to put yourself down. If anything, you need to take care of yourself for your sake as well as the baby's. Somehow we'll manage. The wonderful thing is that Giorgio holds you in the palm of his hand."

Marina contemplated her sister, whose dark eyes flashed with determination. The young woman who had complained about always eating *polenta* was her stout ally.

"Thank you," she whispered. Buoyed by Lisa's words, she smiled to herself. "I wonder if the baby will be a boy or a girl."

"To be truthful, I hope it's a boy. It would be a welcome change."

Marina smiled through her tears. They talked a little longer and then headed for the bus that would take them home. Her first concern when she arrived would be to tell Giorgio.

*   *   *

Although she loved her dearly, Marina was grateful that Amelia was out on an errand. Giorgio greeted her with an anxious yet relieved expression on his face.

"Tell me everything." He had her sit down on a gunnysack full of sawdust and knelt in front of her with her hands in his.

"We... we're going to have a baby."

Giorgio leaned back against the wall. "I'm going to be a father," he said with wonder in his voice. "You've been with me through the good and the bad. As far as I'm concerned, you're already my wife. We'll have a small wedding as soon as possible and tonight we'll talk to our mothers and be done with it."

"There will be gossip," Marina warned.

"Who cares?" His smile was wide and happy. "I'm marrying the woman I love."

In her family's dining room that evening, Marina sat with her hands clasped as she broke the news to them all, including Amelia. The silence was worse than any outburst and seemed to last forever.

It was her mother who spoke first. "I don't have to tell you that I'm disappointed." Alda closed her eyes a moment to absorb the news.

"I know we made a mistake," Giorgio said and took Marina's hand, "but I love Marina. She and the baby are *my* responsibility."

Marina felt a surge of pride at this newfound maturity in Giorgio. He didn't quail before the new chapter in his life that had unfolded earlier than he had expected.

"Amelia?" Alda turned to her.

"You know I will stand by your side." She smiled.

"I knew you'd say that. Just like twenty-five years ago."

Marina frowned. "Mama, what do you mean?"

Alda raised her eyes heavenward and took a deep breath. "I… I have a confession to make about your father and I when we were like you, young and in love." She paused and then continued. "Your father always dreamed of studying medicine. He wanted to help people. But one day, our love was stronger than our will and I… I found myself expecting a baby."

Marina leaned back in the chair. *Twenty-five years ago... Gianni! Her mother had once filled her shoes.* She turned to Nelsa as she remembered their conversation when she was upset with Giorgio. "What... what happened when you found out, *Nonna?"*

"Your grandfather and I were not happy, but more than because of your mother, it was because of that witch of your father's mother, your *grandmother,"* Nelsa said through clenched teeth.

Marina never heard her *nonna* spit out a word as she did now. She wondered why her mother and father rarely spoke of her. More than being concerned about her baby, now she was worried for the revelations she might soon hear regarding her parents.

"Your grandmother never approved of our loving each other because she thought I wasn't good enough for your father." Alda's voice turned bitter. "His family had more land, was a little better off than many of us, but that didn't keep him from loving me."

"How cruel and heartless of her," Lisa exclaimed. "Mama, don't talk any more about it if it's too painful for you."

Alda shook her head. "It's better for all of you that you know what happened. She... accused me of ruining your father's life. I told your father that he was free not to marry me, that I would understand but... but he wouldn't hear of it. He loved me and there was no dissuading him. Your father and Paolo, Giorgio's father, were close friends.

Your parents, Giorgio, opened their door to him because he could no longer stand living with his mother. He couldn't stand the way she was treating me. We married in spite of her opposition and, oh, how she made us pay for it!"

Giorgio sat quietly, intent on every word but at this revelation, he turned to his mother whose eyes were wet with unshed tears. "Mama, you never talked about this. Why?"

"There would have been too much to explain," Amelia said softly.

Marina saw the pieces begin to fit together. Through the years, her parents had tried to bring her paternal grandmother to know her grandchildren but to no avail.

"Your father and I had a simple wedding, but she didn't attend. When Gianni was born, I received flowers, pretty baby items. Do... do you know what she sent to me?" Alda's voice broke. "A... a letter telling me that if... if my baby ever found himself one day in a war... that he should be the first one to receive a bullet!"

"Mama, no." A sob escaped Daniela as Lisa and Albina sat stunned, their faces ashen.

Giorgio cursed, which was something that he never did, but Marina understood. She knew how deeply he cared for his childhood friend. They had all grown up together; she, Gianni, Giorgio, Stefano, Carla. She remembered how he had cried with her the day that Gianni left.

"I can't begin to imagine what you and Papa went through and then when—Papa died because of me-she—

she hated us all the more." Marina felt drained.

"No!" Alda cried out. "Stop torturing yourself. You had a strong discussion with him because she never acknowledged any of you and he knew you were right. He… he tried to calm you because there would have been too much to explain. When he put you on the bus for Lucca the next morning, he met her on his way back home. Why on earth he told her that you worked in Lucca, I don't know. She reprimanded him for allowing you to be out in the world because "who knows what she will become," she told him.

"Where did this woman come from?" Giorgio asked.

"From hell, as far as I'm concerned," Nelsa said firmly.

Alda gave Nelsa a sideways glance and continued. "Your father defended you. When he came home, I… sensed something was wrong, and he told me everything. A moment later… he collapsed here in the kitchen."

A moment of silence followed before Alda continued. "It's terrible of me to say this, but in a way, she died just the way that she lived. May God forgive me!"

Marina knew that to be true. Her grandmother had died shortly after her father. Her mother had found her along a path, dead, with a faggot of wood at her side and a viper slithering around her body. She, who wanted nothing to do with her family, had come to a sorry end.

Marina frowned, feeling angry now. "Mama, all this time, you let me go on feeling guilty that Papa's death was my fault. Why, why didn't you tell me the truth right away? Why didn't you just come out and tell me all of what happened to you and Papa?"

"Because I was ashamed to admit what I did. Was it easy for you to come and talk to me tonight? Was it? Well, it wasn't easy for me to talk to you either," Alda cried out.

Marina had never seen her mother like this before. She heard her sisters' muffled sobs. She hardly breathed as her mother continued to vent her hurt.

"I'm trying to raise you and your sisters to be responsible women and your mother wasn't responsible. It was wrong of me, and you have every right to be upset, but don't accuse me of keeping secrets from you. All... all I can say is that I'm sorry. I'm so sorry, Marina. Forgive me. I love both of you."

Marina sat dumbfounded.

Giorgio turned to her. "Let it all go, Marina. This is a new beginning for all of you. Your mother is hurting, and she needs you. Let it go." Giorgio spoke in a low tone, his eyes misty.

Marina rose on shaky legs and slowly approached her mother. Giorgio was right. She had to let it all go. "Mama?"

Alda raised her head.

Marina gently drew her mother to her body. "It's alright, Mama. It's all over," she said, and let her pour out her pent up sorrow, her frustrations, and her fears for the son whom she had borne and whom she might never see again.

CHAPTER SEVEN

Now that her mother knew about the pregnancy, Marina felt a burden lift from her shoulders. She could face the coming days and months with a happier spirit. A few days afterwards, she and Giorgio met with Don Antonio.

Tall and thin, Don Antonio's hair had greyed considerably with the war and the responsibility of trying to guide his flock through it.

"Please sit down." He smiled warmly as he welcomed them into his office at the rectory. "How may I help you today?"

Marina exchanged a glance with Giorgio, who fidgeted.

"We… we have to marry earlier than we planned, Don Antonio," Marina said and lowered her gaze.

"I see." Don Antonio nodded in understanding. "Don't be afraid to tell me everything."

Marina drew courage from his gentle tone of voice. "I'm… I'm expecting a baby."

"And I love Marina," Giorgio added quickly, reaching for her hand. "I'm ready to assume my responsibility."

"Have you told your mothers?"

"Yes." Marina nodded.

"What you did wasn't right, and I know you realize that now." He contemplated them for a moment and then smiled. "I've seen both of you grow up, and I want you to feel comfortable coming to me with any concerns. Now," he rubbed his hands together, "let's get this wedding underway."

Marina and Giorgio exchanged a look of relief.

Hand in hand with Giorgio on their way home, Marina couldn't contain her joy. "We have so much to be grateful for. I can hardly wait to begin my life with you in our home. *Our* home, Giorgio! Isn't it wonderful?"

"Yes. My work is progressing. The *despensa* is finished and ready to be put to use."

"Well, we'll have to wait for the peach jam." Marina laughed. "But we can look forward to your olives."

Giorgio drew her to him and kissed her. "Life is good."

Marina saw smoke curling out of the chimney of her home. She wrinkled her nose at the dirty task that had to be done before winter arrived.

"Giorgio, do you feel up to helping us clean the chimney as you always have? You have to go on the roof and that worries me."

"I can't live in a shell. What kind of a man am I?" Giorgio shook his head vigorously. "Later today, I'll clip some hedges, and we can clean it tomorrow morning."

*   *   *

"Please be careful," Marina pleaded as Giorgio climbed the ladder to the second story with a thick rope coiled on his arm.

To protect the kitchen from soot, she hung an old sheet in front of the fireplace and secured it to the mantelpiece with pieces of firewood.

The hedge clippings were knotted in the middle of the rope and Giorgio dropped one end down to her. Between Marina in the kitchen and Giorgio on the roof, they sawed the rope up and down so that the clippings scraped the inside of the chimney clean.

Giorgio came back into the kitchen with an old broom and lifted a corner of the sheet to brush down the heavy chain used for hanging the cauldrons. Everything was fine until he started to sneeze. Anxious to get out, he raised his head a moment too soon and hit it hard on the underside of the mantel.

Marina winced. "Are you alright?" She placed her hand against his sooty cheek.

Giorgio muttered a word of frustration as he rubbed the top of his head.

To her dismay, Marina began to giggle. "You should see yourself. You look like a pirate."

Giorgio glared at her. "I look like a pirate, eh? Well, pirates plunder and kidnap and I'm kidnapping *you*."

"Giorgio, no!" Marina backed away with her arms straight in front of her but he grabbed her by the waist.

"I'm carrying you away to my private island!"

"Let me go!" Laughing and pleading, she struggled as he tried to lift her.

"Call me a pirate, will you?" He held her tightly.

The thought of hurting the baby froze her on the spot. "Giorgio! The baby!"

He let her go and led her to a chair. "Are… are you alright?"

Marina sat still a moment. "Yes, I'm fine."

"I have to remind myself that things have changed for us."

Marina rose to her feet and gently removed the bandana from his head. She touched his head where a nice lump had formed. "You're a *good* pirate," she murmured, "but if we don't get things in order, Mama will have us set sail."

"That looks better," Marina smiled later, looking around with satisfaction. They had cleaned up all the soot and a new fire crackled briskly in the fireplace.

"It's starting to sprinkle," Giorgio said. "I think I'll go home now unless there's something else for me to do?"

"No, you've done enough. If you're at the house tomorrow, I can start to bring down some linens."

He kissed her on the nose. "See you tomorrow, then."

*   *   *

Marina awoke to the early morning sun peeking over the mountains. Wisps of fog hung around the chasms and gorges and the air was fresh after the night's rain. Today would be a good day to take some linen to her home.

In the next room, Daniela and Albina were still sleeping soundly. She quietly descended the stairs and opened the shutters in the dining room and the kitchen. With a little kindling wood and a few pinecones, she soon had a nice fire going. She also placed a little charcoal in the stove to warm up some milk.

At the sound of a meow at the door, she opened it to Giada and Pulce who lost no time in going to sit in front of the hearth.

Lisa had already left for work but her cup sat, washed and dried, on the table.

"Buon giorno."

Marina turned to her grandmother whose grey curls framed her face. *"Buon giorno, Nonna.* Did you sleep well?"

"Oh, yes. How about you?"

"I always love the patter of the rain on the roof." Marina smiled as she bustled about in the kitchen.

"It's good to see you like this, child. You're happy." Nelsa kissed Marina on the nose.

"I have so much to be grateful for. I have Giorgio, who loves me, and an understanding family. How can I not be grateful?"

Marina poured the warm milk into cups and placed a few slices of bread, baked the day before, on a small plate. This morning they had the luxury of an egg each, thanks to her grandmother's chickens. She sat down next to Nelsa to enjoy breakfast with her.

Alda soon joined them, followed by Daniela and Albina.

"Mama, thank you for letting us share your experience," Marina said softly. "It must have been very difficult for you."

"It was." Alda nodded. "But somehow, now that I no longer carry that burden, I feel relieved. I had so much closed up in my heart. God works in mysterious ways. If it wasn't for your pregnancy, I would probably still carry everything inside of me."

"That's all in the past now. I want to focus on my baby and my life with Giorgio. God knows there's hardly anything else to focus on that's good, except for *Nonna* living with us and Lisa and Marco, who seem to be in love with each other."

"The war is getting closer to home, too close for comfort." Nelsa shuddered.

"Now that Italy has declared war on Germany, Giorgio says that the Allies are not about to allow the Germans to get the upper hand, but Germany is determined to do everything to hinder the advance of the Allies." Marina shook her head, wondering how much worse conditions could become in the valley.

"You and Giorgio will have to forsake your honeymoon now that the railroad service is interrupted," Alda said.

"Honeymoon? There is no way that we are going

anywhere. We'll find ways to celebrate at home." Marina sighed. "Even if I'm already expecting a baby."

"Why did I know you were going to say that? *Santo Cielo.* Don't let your mind be invaded by guilty feelings. You're not the first one, nor the last one. You have a life ahead of you," Nelsa admonished her.

Marina squeezed her grandmother's hand. "Thank you, *Nonna.* Winter will be here before we know it, and I know that Giorgio can hardly wait to enjoy *mondine* on cold, winter evenings."

"He may not eat any roasted chestnuts if we don't begin searching for them, and it's already October." Alda turned to Nelsa. "Mama, do you feel like going with me to the grove below the house to see what we can find? My hand has almost returned to normal."

Nelsa's eyes sparkled. "Giorgio has my mouth watering."

Alda brought her hand to her forehead. "I forgot that we also have to sow hemp. If Lisa should marry, I don't want her to lack for linen."

"I'll help," Nelsa said quickly.

Marina laughed. No, her *nonna* wasn't one to be idle.

*   *   *

The harvesting of the *castagne,* even if they were a staple, was a tedious, back breaking task and, sometimes, the nut had to be extricated from the bur. Marina had learned from experience that the best way to avoid pricked fingers was to use a sturdy twig. The chestnuts could be roasted, boiled, or sent to the mill to be ground into flour. If they were sent to the mill, they were prepared in a drying shed, a two story structure, sometimes located in the vicinity of the homes. The second story was accessed by a window and the floor was composed of slats where the harvested chestnuts were laid. On the ground floor below, a fire would burn slowly for two weeks, drying the chestnuts. Afterwards, they were fed into a machine that removed the skins, and then they were sent to the mill.

The chestnut flour could be made into *polenta* that was sweeter to the taste than cornmeal. *Necci,* were like thin pancakes and were cooked between two metal plates over a fire. *Vinata,* was made by mixing red wine with the flour and cooking it. The *castagnaccio* was a flat cake made with flour, water, olive oil, and rosemary. Adding orange peels to the mixture turned it into a real luxury if someone was fortunate enough to have purchased oranges. Marina especially liked the *castagnaccio,* even if it was a little oily.

In early afternoon, Marina headed for her new home, balancing a basket of towels on her head.

From the *piazza* she walked up the road to the other side of the village and saw Carla walking towards her.

Marina felt at odds. Because of the last time they had met on the path, she didn't know what to expect from her. She shivered and with her free arm, tightened her thick wool shawl around her body. "Carla, how are you?" she greeted her.

Carla raked her from head to foot with a hard glance. "So you and Giorgio are getting married soon."

"Yes, we are. We've decided not to wait until spring."

"All you could talk about was a springtime wedding. I'm really surprised but then only *you* know why you're marrying earlier."

Marina didn't miss the "you". She was about to retort rudely but instead chose not to do so. "You're free to think what you want." She left her and continued up the street.

The village was crescent shaped and her home stood almost at the top of the other side of the village. To the left of the front door, the tendrils of a young jasmine planted in the ground reached the upstairs bedroom windows. Marina sniffed the heady fragrance of one of its last blossoms. She turned the key and stepped into the *soggiorno,* the living room that also served for dining on special occasions. Facing her was the staircase that led to the bedrooms upstairs. Under the staircase was sufficient space for the *despensa* that was hidden by a curtain in a flowery print. To her right was another door that opened onto a small square balcony with a little garden below. The *cantina* could be accessed from the garden as well as a larger room that served Giorgio for his workshop. She was happy that he had more space to work in and a larger window for fresh air. Grateful, she offered a prayer for Giorgio's father, who had bought the house with the idea that one day it might become useful.

She stepped inside the kitchen, warmed by the fire. "Giorgio?" she called cheerily in spite of her irritation with Carla.

Giorgio sensed that something was amiss the moment she entered the kitchen. "Are you alright?" He helped her to lower the basket.

She told him what Carla had said.

He frowned. "I don't understand it. Avoid her if possible."

"How are you doing? That's nice." Marina said looking at one of the two new windows that Giorgio had just finished. From here, they could see a wide sweep of the Fegana Valley below and all the way to the south.

"My wrist is a little stiff today. Maybe it's the cold."

"I have muscle." She jokingly held up an arm.

He laughed but then turned serious.

Her spirits sank. "What's wrong, Giorgio? Are you having second thoughts about everything?"

"No," Giorgio said emphatically. "I'm just afraid of not being able to provide well for you and our baby. I'm catching up with my work but money is slow in coming in."

She cupped his face. "Do you want me to marry you?"

"You know better than to ask that."

"Then don't you *dare* think I will lack for anything."

"If... if anything should happen to me, remember that I'll always love you."

"Why should anything happen to you? Haven't you been through enough?"

"German troops have already appeared in Riteglio. It's only a matter of time before they will be here, too."

Riteglio, a little more populous village, lay situated to the north, about a forty-minute walk away, with the Apennines looming above it.

"Let's look forward to our wedding next Saturday and then worry about everything else."

*   *   *

The late October Saturday morning was crisp and bright when Marina stepped into the street where her neighbors had gathered to see her. Instead of wearing the pretty dress she'd always dreamed about for her wedding, she wore a beige wool suit and brown pumps bought with the help of her savings. Her dark hair, covered with a beige veil, fell in soft curls to her shoulders. She carried a little bouquet of white chrysanthemums picked from the garden, artfully wrapped in a white doily made by Albina and tied with a white satin, ribbon.

When Marco arrived, she slipped her arm through his and kissed him on the cheek. He had offered to give her away since she didn't have anyone else to do so. "Thank you for being father and brother to me today."

"Thank you for Lisa," he whispered, casting a loving glance at her sister, who stood behind Marina.

That Marina could be this happy seemed almost like a dream. She was marrying Giorgio, and she had love and support from her family and Amelia. To complete her happiness, a letter had arrived from Gianni, which she would answer as soon as possible to tell him everything that had happened.

With all the family behind them, including Marco's parents, Bruno and Valentina, Marina walked up the winding cobblestone street to the church. She climbed the five steps that led up to its richly carved wood doors, and paused a moment to catch her breath.

She saw Anna, her childhood friend and Giorgio's, too. Anna's face clouded as she looked towards the bell tower at the corner of the church. Marina followed her gaze, and, whether it was her imagination or not, she thought that she saw Carla standing there. It was only an instant as Carla turned the corner abruptly. Anna's expression hovered between shock and disgust.

"Are you ready?" Marco asked with a wide smile.

Marina diverted her gaze to look up at him. "Yes… yes, I am," she said softly.

Some of the villagers who had gathered alongside the church entered behind the family.

Marina's heart skipped a beat when she saw Giorgio standing proudly at the altar steps, with a big smile on his face.

Kneeling next to him, she raised her eyes to the nave above her. How many young women before her had knelt here over the centuries since the year 900? Below it, the candles flickered on the main altar, which was adorned by a beautiful altar cloth with a wide crocheted border of roses.

Don Antonio approached them, ready to begin the ceremony. Marina breathed deeply. It was her turn now.

*   *   *

After the wedding Mass, family and close friends including Don Antonio, gathered around the dining table in the *soggiorno*. She couldn't think of a better way to initiate her home.

Cups of hot chocolate, almond biscotti, almond and rice tortes baked by her family and Amelia graced the table.

"My dear, may God forgive me, but today I feel like a glutton with this fare," Don Antonio said, as he savored his cup of chocolate.

"I promise not to tell anyone," Marina whispered.

Anna was able to come for the refreshments with little Giorgio, whose big brown eyes surveyed everyone and everything.

"I'm so glad that you came." Marina kissed the little boy on the forehead.

"I had to give him some refreshment beforehand." Anna laughed and then her voice became wistful. "I only wish that Stefano was here, too."

"He is in spirit." Marina placed her arm around Anna's

shoulder. Her presence meant a lot to her. She would have liked to know what had gone on at the church door, but this was her wedding day, and she wouldn't deal with that.

Anna stepped away to speak with Don Antonio.

"We'll have another wedding soon," Giorgio said, nodding towards Lisa and Marco as he enjoyed a slice of his mother's chocolate torte.

"They're glowing." Marina smiled. "Lisa confided that they want to marry in the coming year. I'm so happy for her. I love all of my sisters but Lisa has been such a support for me."

"*Carissima,* you're glowing, too."

"God has been good to us. I want to savor this moment."

The reception continued into late afternoon. When the last of the guests left, the family helped to tidy up the *soggiorno* and the kitchen. By the time they finished, it was dusk outside.

Later, in Giorgio's arms, Marina recalled the anonymous note regarding his betraying her. Here she was, feeling his heart beating rhythmically against her hand as he slept. Whoever had written the note must be sorely disappointed because it had been absurd then and was more than absurd now. God had blessed them beyond measure. She didn't delude herself that there would be no ups and downs, but tonight she was happy and placed a hand on her belly to let their baby share in her happiness.

CHAPTER EIGHT

Marina and Giorgio floated on a cloud the first few days after their wedding. Happy as they were, though, life had to return to normal. Giorgio left for the valley to purchase supplies necessary for his work and Marina's first priority of the morning was to buy some food. Meals were still frugal, but she had learned to work with the rations to make them tasty. *Polenta* was enriched now with gravy made with *porcini* mushrooms. Happy as she was to be expecting, just the thought of cooking or eating made her queasy.

She glanced outside the kitchen window and lowered her gaze to the patch of land directly below. The old shed had withstood many storms through the years. In the back of her mind, she remembered Giorgio saying something about the property and that his father had gained rights to it. Every now and then, Giorgio would cut down the tall weeds. Two forlorn rosebushes tugged at her heart. It remained to be seen if the land would be of any use to them. She shook herself. There was shopping to be done.

The walk to the store was uphill now, but along the way, she stopped to talk with people that she had rarely seen before. She purchased what she needed, and talking amiably with the shopkeeper, stepped outside with him. A very irritated villager, a woman, rushed towards him, holding a bundle in her hands.

"Buon giorno," the shopkeeper greeted her.

"Don't 'good morning,' me." The woman walked to the stone bench to the side and opened her paper bundle. "I may be poor, but not to the point of eating rice with slivers of marble in it!"

The shopkeeper stood shocked, taken aback by her outburst. "Marble? What are you talking about?"

The woman, on the verge of tears, pointed to the open bundle. "See for yourself and then tell me if I don't have a right to be mad! Having rationed food is bad enough, but at least give us good food."

The shopkeeper sifted through the white rice. He blanched. "I paid good money for this rice. I've always sold good food!"

Marina turned away as the shopkeeper darted about, venting his anger with a few colorful curses at being cheated, while the woman was at a loss as to what to put on the table for *pranzo*. Marina pursed her lips, frustrated at all the consequences that people had to face because of war.

She arrived at her family home, eager to visit them. She was turning the key in the door when she heard voices on her right. Two young soldiers and their commanding officer, whose expression was anything but amiable, were walking towards her. There was no mistaking their uniforms. Germans! Behind them was Giorgio, gesturing with all his might for her to go inside.

Hands shaking, she opened the door, darted through, and closed it behind her. She leaned against it, her teeth clenched. What did the Germans want with them? The door nudged against her back suddenly, and she jumped away with a scream. "Oh, Giorgio, you scared me." She brought her hand to her chest to calm her racing heart. "I thought you had left."

"I was on my way when I saw their jeep driving up. I didn't know what was going to happen, so I turned around."

The door burst open as Nelsa quickly entered, her face ashen, her armful of wood tumbling to the floor. "The… the Germans are here! What are we going to do?"

"What's happened?" Alda raced into the kitchen from upstairs.

"We're under occupation, Mama. They've arrived. Oh, dear God, help us." Marina clasped her hands. She thought of her sisters—Lisa was at work and Daniela at school. "Where is Albina?"

"She's… she's looking for Giada who's been missing for a couple of days," Nelsa said, easing herself on a chair.

"Giada is no longer young to be straying." Marina frowned. As much as she loved the kitty that was a part of their family, she was more concerned about Albina being out at this moment.

"Let's all stay calm," Giorgio said firmly. "Wringing our hands isn't going to do us any good."

Marina knew that he was right. There was no need to be afraid. *Yet.*

The initial shock of the troops eased somewhat, and the morning went by uneventfully.

"Don't go home. I'm happier if you're here while I go back down for supplies." Giorgio told Marina.

"I'll do that, but be careful, alright?" Marina followed him with her gaze until he was no longer in her sight. She turned to look at the young soldier placed as a sentinel just past their home where two roads formed a junction. His commanding officer spoke to him and continued down the road. She suspected that there were others assigned throughout the village.

To her relief, Giorgio returned in the early afternoon. "I wasn't comfortable staying away longer and bought what I needed for the moment. I can always go back in a few days." He noticed Albina's eyes, damp with tears. "You didn't find Giada, did you?"

Albina sniffled and shook her head.

"We'll go out afterwards. We'll find her," Marina said and caressed her cheek.

Later in the afternoon, when school ended, Daniela burst into the kitchen, out of breath. "They've come," she gasped.

"As if we don't know," Albina mumbled.

"That solider is hardly older than I am." Daniela shook

her head in disbelief.

"His officers don't care," Alda said.

"It's not right," Daniela protested.

"It's not right for Gianni, either." Marina flung a kitchen towel on the sink.

"Someone's at the door." Daniela looked from one to the other, uncertain of what to do.

"Open it slowly," Giorgio cautioned.

Daniela opened the door. She didn't see anyone but then lowered her gaze and screamed.

Giorgio jumped to his feet and seized her, thrusting her behind him.

Daniela brought her hands to her face, ran into the dining room and up the stairs.

"Wh… what happened?" Alda cried, as she and Nelsa ran after her.

Giorgio found nothing untoward outside until his gaze fell on a box at the side of the door. "No." He recoiled, his stomach turning.

"What is it?" Marina asked with Albina close behind her.

He pushed them away. "Get back!"

Inside the box was Giada, her head smashed.

*   *   *

It was almost dark when Giorgio gently lowered Giada, shrouded in a pillowcase, into a shallow grave under the cherry tree where she loved to nap. He then covered the site with two heavy rocks.

Marina stood motionless. Giorgio's efforts to shield her and Albina from seeing Giada had proved useless. She had managed to take a peek at the poor animal that had become a part of the family. She closed her eyes. Another ugly moment flashed in her mind. She saw Giorgio, battered and bruised. The only reason that he had survived was because of Amelia and even then, that threatening note had been nailed to his door.

Albina sniffled. She picked up Pulce and gently stroked her. "Please, don't *you* go wandering off."

"I don't believe that she wandered off. I don't believe it," Marina said through clenched teeth.

Giorgio straightened up and frowned. "Are you saying that someone killed her here?"

"I don't know. Maybe they… caught her in some way and… took her away and then killed her and brought her back. What's going to happen next? What? *You* could be lying in a grave. Now Giada is dead. What does this mean?"

"I'd love to know who did this." Daniela clenched her hands, her nails digging into her palms.

"We're dealing with people who will go to any lengths to get their message through." Giorgio's expression was grim.

"God in heaven, is it because you favor the Allies? If the Fascists are behind this, how I hope that the Allies give them and Hitler a good thrashing." Marina burst into tears.

"I knew this was going to happen," Giorgio shook his head. "You were brave the whole time through my ordeal, but deep down you harbor resentment towards whoever assaulted me." He held her by the shoulders. "Is it worth it for our baby?"

"They left a note on the door saying that next time you would be dead!" Marina cried out. "Don't tell me that the Fascists didn't have anything to do with that or with Giada. This was another message."

"I'm sorry, but I'm not going to renounce my support for the Allies to do them a favor."

Marina locked her eyes with his. This time he was stubborn for a good reason, and she couldn't do anything but believe in the freedom he longed for. "You know I'll always support you." Marina sighed resignedly. "And I'll keep praying for Italy's freedom."

It was almost dark when she walked home arm in arm with Giorgio. October had come to a sad close.

CHAPTER NINE

The second of November brought the commemoration of the dead. Before dawn, Marina and Giorgio took part in a candlelit procession from the church to the cemetery. After prayers were offered for the repose of the departed, the lighted candles were placed at the gravesites of loved ones.

Marina, with her family, lingered at her father's gravesite adorned with ferns and a vase full of russet and purple chrysanthemums.

Giorgio approached them. "Are you ready? It looks like it's going to rain."

"Yes," Marina nodded. "Let's go." Her hand in Giorgio's, she walked out the gate to the narrow cobblestone road. Although she was dressed as warmly as she had been for the wedding and was wearing a heavy shawl, she shivered.

"Are you alright?" Giorgio stopped.

"Yes, but I don't know why I feel cold."

Carla passed by them without a word.

"Now I know why." Marina looked at Giorgio, who didn't answer but looked as if he felt the same chill.

Marina left her family at the crossroad where the path from the cemetery joined the one that led to the *piazza* to the left and to the right between two retaining walls. Past the walls, one could access the vineyards to the left or continue straight to a few homes outside of the village as well as to continue walking down to the neighboring town in the valley that lay to the west.

Giorgio quickly lit the fire, thankful that they had arrived before it had begun to rain. A brisk wind had risen. "I don't know what the matter is with Carla." He frowned. "But her way of acting is bothersome."

Marina shrugged. "I don't remember doing or saying anything to have hurt her feelings."

"I don't either but, as your mother always says, the truth will come out someday."

"I have other concerns at this moment."

"What is it? Is there something that you're not telling me?" Giorgio turned to face her, worried.

"I'm fine except for the nausea, but I'm concerned over Daniela. I hope that she doesn't dwell on the sentinel posted at the house."

"What do you mean?"

"She feels sorry for him which, in a way, I do, too, but I hope that she keeps her head on her shoulders."

"She sees him as young and maybe scared. She'll be fine."

"I hope so," Marina said and then smiled, placing a hand on her belly. "I want our little one to feel happy. I wish I could know if we'll have a boy or a girl."

"I just want the baby to be healthy." Giorgio smiled.

"Spoken like a true father. You know, the bed is a little chilly. We should warm it with the *scaldino* before going to bed."

Before they let the fire die down, Marina scooped up embers and placed them in the small earthenware pot with a handle, covering them with a little bit of ashes. She went upstairs and folded back the bed covers, then hung the *scaldino* inside the igloo shaped, wood arch. Carefully, she then pulled the covers over the arch.

When she slipped into bed a little later, she stretched luxuriously in its warmth.

*   *   *

"I love Marco so much!" Lisa hugged herself the first day up after being in bed with a cold. "Was it like this for you and Giorgio when you fell in love?"

"Yes, and here we are, married."

"With the baby on the way. I can't imagine what you must be feeling."

"Well," Marina wrinkled her nose, "I could do without the nausea."

"Does it last for the whole time?"

"Signore Gesu', I hope not. Mama says it's the first three months or so." She remained for a while to catch up with her family's news. Her mother gave her a little basket

of chestnuts to take with her when she went home. The overcast sky promised snow.

At the corner of the house, she met the soldier's gaze. A hint of a smile appeared on his face. Marina felt a twinge of guilt. Daniela was right. He was hardly older than her, thrust into the fray to become a man and one with a rifle at that. She acknowledged him with a nod and continued on her way.

She saw Amelia outside on the balcony and waved to her.

"Marina, *ciao!*" Amelia called out, waving her hand. "Come and visit for a moment."

Marina stepped inside the dining room and couldn't help remembering the day that she had brought in the sheet for her.

"I haven't seen you lately. I was wondering if I scared you away." Amelia pulled two chairs away from the table on which a basket held fresh chestnuts.

"I'm sorry, but these days just fly, and we're still saddened over Giada."

"Don't speak of it. Whoever did that is full of hatred. What will they do to a human being, if they hurt a defenseless animal?"

"Remember Giorgio?"

A shadow clouded Amelia's face. "We still don't know who did it, which, I suppose, is just as well because if I ever find out, that rolling pin in the corner will come in handy."

Marina stifled a giggle. Her mother-in-law would think nothing of doing just that. "We have to let it go, Amelia. Giorgio wants me to focus on our baby."

"You're right, but sometimes it's hard to let it go."

After a quick visit, Marina left Amelia, just as flakes of snow began falling. She smiled up at the sky, feeling the flakes melt coldly on her face.

Giorgio would have his *mondine* tonight.

*   *   *

Marina gasped at the view from her bedroom window when she opened the shutters the next morning. The peach tree in her neighbor's garden was outlined in white and, underneath, a few late chrysanthemums bent their crown of flowers beneath the gentle weight they bore. Total silence reigned except for a rooster's song.

Giorgio was already up and probably lighting the fire. Marina descended the steps into the *soggiorno* and hastened into the kitchen, welcoming its warmth.

"This feels so good." She rubbed her hands together in front of the cheery flames.

"Did you look outside?"

"It's magical." Marina hugged him as tightly as her body would allow at almost three months. "I guess it's *mondine* for you again tonight."

"I feel like a pig because you don't eat as many."

"You're one pig that I like."

"Well, I guess that should make me happy."

Marina burst out laughing but was soon silenced with a tender kiss.

The sun broke through the clouds and promised a beautiful if very cold day.

"I'm going to shovel the snow away from the house down to the *cantina*." Giorgio rose from the usual, frugal breakfast. "Don't go outside, alright? I'll bring up wood when I've finished."

"Don't worry, I won't." Marina hummed as she began to tidy the kitchen. Today, she would sew the curtains for the kitchen windows with the new fabric that she had put aside for them a long time ago. She was eager to use the Singer sewing machine that her mother had given her as a wedding gift. It was the same one that she had used when she and her sisters were growing up.

The front door opened and she heard a woman's voice calling her.

"I'm coming." Wiping her hands on her apron, she went to the door but no one was there. She was about to close it when she heard a sharp report, like a rifle shot.

"Giorgio! Giorgio!" Fear gripped her heart when he didn't answer. The snow was cleared enough that she walked gingerly down towards the garden. He wasn't there. Thinking that he might be in the *cantina*, she called out again.

"Giorgio! Are you..." Her words disappeared in a scream as she tumbled down the three steps into the garden.

*   *   *

Marina stirred and blinked. She turned her head as confusing images flashed through her mind—Giorgio's desperation as he carried her into the *cantina*, blankets underneath her, her neighbor's frantic race to call Marco, the terrible feeling of warmth flowing from her body, and finally Marco's broken words to Giorgio—"I'm so sorry."

"Mama?"

Marina winced as she stretched her legs. Her body was bruised from the fall and her left wrist was swollen. By God's grace, she hadn't hit her head, although in this moment she wouldn't have cared if she did. At least she would be with her baby.

Alda sat on the bed, one hand holding hers, the other caressing her face.

"I… I lost the baby, didn't I?"

Alda nodded, blinking hard.

"Why? Oh, why," Marina broke into uncontrollable sobbing.

Alda placed her cheek against hers. "Maybe God needed another angel."

"Where's… where's Giorgio?" Marina gasped. "Something… something happened. There was a shot… I… I… fell… no, no… I felt something… on my back."

"Giorgio's downstairs with Marco and the girls." Alda turned to rapid footsteps coming up the stairs.

Daniela and Albina flew in and rushed to the bed.

"Please say this didn't happen. That... the baby is alright," Daniela exclaimed.

"The baby is gone. Gone forever," Marina whispered. "We... were so happy and... we were choosing names if it was a boy or a girl."

"Zitta, zitta..." Don't talk. What matters now is that you rest," Albina soothed her.

Giorgio appeared, his face taut and his eyes red from weeping.

Daniela and Albina stepped aside, each looking at the other, shocked.

Marina reached out to Giorgio. "I'm so sorry. I'm so sorry."

With a sob, Giorgio took her in his arms and caressed her hair.

"I... I felt something at my back," she said.

Giorgio frowned, looking at her intently. "What do you mean?"

"I don't know. I just felt something and then...I... fell."

Giorgio shook his head, his face darkening. "Don't talk anymore now, alright?" He laid her back on the pillow.

Marco trudged into the bedroom. Giorgio nodded for him to step towards the window a moment. He looked at Marina, who had closed her eyes.

"There's more to her falling than an accident." Giorgio spoke softly.

"What do you mean?"

"She says that… that she felt something at her back."

Marco paled. "Giorgio, everything is so confusing for her now in this moment." He inhaled deeply. "Sadly, what isn't confusing is that she lost the baby."

Giorgio sat down on a chair, feeling helpless.

Marco walked over to the bed, still shocked by what had happened. "Marina, I'll give you something to help you sleep, alright?"

"Give me enough to not wake up." Marina sobbed into the pillow.

*   *   *

Could life continue? Marina asked herself. A month after the miscarriage, she still struggled to come to terms with her loss. She spent most of her days in the bedroom, getting up now and then but always retreating to bed. The baby she had borne now rested in the cold earth, blessed by Don Antonio. With Marco's help, Giorgio had fashioned a little box so that their angel should have the dignity of a resting place.

Although not fully formed, the baby was a boy and so they named him Gianpaolo. He bore Gianni's name as well as Giorgio's father.

The morning was sunny. A sharp contrast to her heart.

"Marina?" Alda called her.

"Mama." She smiled at her mother, who seemed to have aged lately.

"Anna is here."

"Have her come up."

Anna entered quietly and rushed over to her. "Oh, Marina!" She placed her cheek against hers. "What can I say?"

"There's nothing to say, Anna. How are Maddalena and little Giorgio?"

"My sister is watching them for a moment. I nursed Giorgio, and he's napping now."

Marina felt a twinge of jealousy at the look of tenderness on Anna's face, but she quenched it. She had every reason to be happy with her little ones.

Anna's smile faded. "Marina, what happened?"

"I… I don't know." Marina leaned back against the pillow. "One moment I was calling Giorgio at the top of the steps and the next moment, I tumbled down the steps. I… I felt something at my back. As if hands had… pushed me. I can't understand it." Marina frowned at the look on Anna's face. "Is… is something wrong? You looked troubled."

Before Anna could answer her, Alda entered the room again. "Carla is here to see you."

Anna turned quickly to look at the door. She got up, her face ashen. "I'd… better go, Marina. I promise to come and visit you again."

"You don't have to leave." Marina held her hand tightly.

"I have to go. We'll talk more in another moment,

alright?" She turned to leave, just as Carla entered. Anna looked once again at Marina and cringed as she walked past Carla.

Marina found Anna's manner odd. It seemed that she recoiled from a snake.

Alda exchanged a quizzical glance with Marina. "I'll escort Anna to the door. I'll be downstairs if you need me."

Marina pushed herself up against the pillows.

Carla tip-toed over to the bed. Marina extended her hands and Carla reached for them, holding them tightly. "I'm so sorry. I don't know what to say."

"It's good of you to come," Marina said. "Sit down."

Still holding on to her hands, Carla sat down. "I know that I have been rude to you lately."

"I… I couldn't understand what I did…"

"You didn't do anything. You and Giorgio have always been close to me. I knew that you and Giorgio would marry. But at the same time, I felt like I was losing you. You would have your own life to live."

Marina sighed with relief at the revelation. "Carla, do you really think that Giorgio and I would forget our friends, especially those that we grew up with?"

Carla lowered her gaze. "Can you forgive me?"

"It's over. You've brought a little ray of sunshine into my life." She remembered the voice she had heard at the door. "Did you call me that morning?"

Carla fidgeted. "Yes. I was coming to visit you but…

but stopped because I saw someone looking around the house and down in the garden."

Marina shivered. "Was it a man, a woman?"

"A man. It was a man," she answered quickly. "I waited a moment until he was gone. Then I heard the shot. I… I was frightened and ran away."

"I heard the rifle shot. That's when I went to check on Giorgio and… and…"

"That's when you fell."

"I don't know what happened. I felt something at my back and fell forward."

"There was no one when I reached the door. Where was Giorgio?"

"He was in the *cantina* or in his workshop." Marina raised her arms and let them fall. "I wonder if someone was on the lookout to harm him again or worse."

Carla rose abruptly. "We've talked enough and you need to rest." She took her hands once more. "Be brave, Marina." She kissed her on the cheek and left.

Alda was on the balcony when she heard Carla come down. "You're leaving, Carla?"

"Yes, I'd better go. I hope that Marina gets stronger every day. I'll come back and see her for sure."

"Yes, please do."

Alda walked her to the door and was about to close it, but paused a moment, instead. When she closed the door, she frowned.

*   *   *

Marina twirled the spoon in her *minestrone*. In another time, she would have relished the hot vegetable soup, lovingly prepared by her mother for *pranzo*. Today, they were alone because Giorgio had to go to the valley to take measurements for a window.

"I want you to finish that. Not even a bird can live with what you're eating," Alda pleaded.

"I'm not hungry, Mama. I'm just not hungry."

Alda raised her eyes, and joined her hands. *"Signore, aiutami!"*

Marina leaned back against the chair, frustrated at her mother's invocation for God's help. As far as she was concerned, God was too far away now.

They turned at a knock on the front door.

Alda opened it to Don Antonio and drew him inside. "Don Antonio, *please* come in."

Marina quickly ran her fingers through her hair, hoping she looked decent.

"I'm... I'm going down into the garden, Marina, alright?"

Don Antonio paused a moment before he walked over to Marina and took her hands.

"Please sit down, Don Antonio. Thank you for coming."

"I'm so sorry."

"Not as sorry as I am."

"There is no answer for what has happened, but your little one is cradled in the arms of God."

"I would have preferred to do that." She looked away.

"You will, Marina. Give yourself time and you will hold a little one in your arms."

Marina knew that even if she did, it never would be like the first baby. "I don't know that I want any more."

"Do you really feel like that? Think about it."

"I wanted to die." Marina couldn't help lashing out, even at Don Antonio.

"Of course you did. How do you think Giorgio feels? Have you ever thought of *his* feelings?"

Marina sat up straight. "*I* bore our baby!"

Don Antonio sighed. "You bore the baby but remember that he had a pretty important role in this. Without him, you wouldn't have carried it in the first place. If you don't come out of your shell, you will send *him* into one."

"A… a wall seems to divide us. We're barely talking. What can I do?" She covered her face.

"In the name of heaven, talk to him." Don Antonio urged. "It's the only way that both of you are going to heal."

Marina felt her defenses shatter. "Will he… talk?"

"Why don't you try and find out?"

She wiped her face with her sleeve. *Poor Giorgio.* She had to bring their lives back to normal, to the happiness that they had once known. She straightened her shoulders and smiled.

"Thank you, Don Antonio. Thank you."

That night in bed, Don Antonio's words played over and over in her head. He was right. She had wallowed in her sorrow and ignored Giorgio's hurt. He lay with his back turned to her, but she sensed that he wasn't sleeping. She turned towards him and tentatively slipped her arm across his body, her head pressed against his shoulder. "Giorgio?" she called softly.

"Yes?"

Her heart skipped with joy that he wasn't sleeping. "Will… will you hold me? I… love you."

Giorgio turned over, his eyes damp with unshed tears. Marina drew his head to her shoulder. He shuddered and a sob escaped him.

CHAPTER TEN

Marina was up early with Giorgio the next morning. She was determined to appreciate the beauty of the new day ahead. As much as she loved her baby whom she had never seen, Giorgio was her concern now, and his happiness was her happiness. What exactly had happened in the moment before she fell, she still wasn't sure. She had to trust that the truth would come out one day.

"Ahi," Marina looked out the kitchen window at the frost-rimed valley below. "Look at that. Aren't we fortunate that the sun kisses us good morning?"

"Speaking of a kiss, I wouldn't mind another one." Giorgio walked up to her and kissed her gently on the lips. "I'm happy to see you like this."

"I'm sorry that I've been selfish, just thinking of myself."

Giorgio cupped her face. "What matters is that you are healing."

"What matters is that we are healing together." She hugged herself from the cold. "I think you'd better light the fire."

Warmth permeated the kitchen as Marina prepared the *caffe' d'orzo* and warmed up some milk on the burner. She looked out again at the broad sweep of the valley beneath her. She had been so out of touch with everything lately. "I'm almost afraid to ask this, but is there anything new in valley?"

Giorgio pursed his lips. "The Germans are piling up their ammunitions in the tunnels. The valley is in their grip now, but something is going to happen because I saw an Allied fighter plane flying overhead a few days ago."

"A fighter plane!" Marina's eyes widened.

"They're probably scouting to see what the Germans are up to."

"They'll be bombing…"

"Not here," Giorgio reassured her, "but the valley for sure. We have the curfew now and must be very careful that the shutters are closed tightly against the window panes when it gets dark. It's also dangerous to be outside. If the Allied planes should fly overhead to scout for German activity, any light they see could be a target for them."

"But in summertime the days are longer." Marina pursed her lips.

"There's a notice in the *piazza* that says that in winter, no one should be out after 6:00 p.m. In the summer, it's extended to 10:00 p.m."

A sizzle told Marina that the little saucepan of milk had spilled over. She quickly removed it from the heat and poured the milk into the prepared *orzo* in their cups. Thanks to her mother, they could enjoy bread, baked the day before, and some cheese. "Shall we eat?"

Marina realized how dear these moments were—eating and talking about their plans for the day. Giorgio would give the last finish to the bedroom set.

"I'm going to visit Mama. She doesn't need to come."

"You haven't been out for a month. I'll go tell her that you're up and about." Giorgio smiled. "But stay inside for today."

"Thank you," Marina said, feeling joy at the sparkle in his eyes.

To Marina's surprise, Alda arrived before noon with her *nonna* close behind her, carrying a rice torte.

"I had baked this for you, so here I am," Nelsa exclaimed.

"*Nonna,* you didn't have to do that."

"I can do whatever I please. Almost," she added in a conspiratorial whisper.

Alda began to slice the torte. "For me, it's a miracle to see you dressed and here in the kitchen."

"Thank Don Antonio for that. I think Giorgio's a little dazed." Marina smiled as she arranged plates on the table.

"I'll go and call him to join us," Nelsa said.

Marina sat down to savor the treat normally reserved for special occasions. Happy as she was, she was worried about Daniela. "Is Daniela alright?" Her happiness was clouded with worry about her.

"If you mean regarding the soldier, the age factor doesn't seem to bother her anymore," Alda assured her. "This morning she took a few pieces of firewood for the little stove in the classroom. She says it's freezing in there."

Nelsa was back in the kitchen with a quizzical look on her face. "Has Giorgio gone out?"

"No. He was working downstairs. Isn't he there?"

"No."

Marina frowned. He never went anywhere without telling her. The front door opened and to her relief, he walked into the kitchen, carrying a little bundle in his arms.

He greeted Alda and Nelsa. "Marina, close your eyes a moment," he said with a mischievous look on his face.

"Why?"

"Close your eyes," he repeated.

Alda and Nelsa exchanged baffled looks.

Marina did as she was asked. She felt a gentle kneading, and then purring. She opened her eyes and gasped at the furry kitten that stared up at her and meowed.

"Oh, Signore! Oh, how lovely she is." She gently picked up the tortoise shell kitten that couldn't have been more than a few weeks old.

"Actually, it's a 'he'." Giorgio rubbed his hands together, happy that she was happy.

"He's Giada all over!" Marina rose, holding the kitten to her shoulder and kissed Giorgio. "Thank you," she whispered. "Where did you find him?"

"He was born from the stray that was always around our house. Mama can't stand to see anyone or even an animal suffer hunger so she began to feed it. He was from a litter of six. Now, Mama is trying to find a home for all of them and mama kitty is as happy as can be to have a home."

That night, Giorgio fell asleep the moment he slipped into bed. The kitten was curled up in a box in the hall. Marina, for the first time in a long time, offered a prayer of thanksgiving to God. She also prayed that He would give her courage for tomorrow.

*   *   *

Giorgio's strong hand on her shoulder was just what Marina needed in this moment. She approached the gravesite, marked by a rustic cross, where their baby lay. She knelt down with Giorgio and touched the cold earth. "So warm… so warm inside my body and now our baby is in the cold, barren earth."

"Our baby's spirit is beyond this grave just as our fathers' are," Giorgio said softly.

Marina's eyes grew dim as she turned towards her father's resting place alongside the path with its grey, stone cross. She rose to her feet and walked to the grave. She knelt down and caressed the cross. On the other side of the path lay her paternal grandmother. Marina bit her lower lip. She had never been able to bring herself to offer a prayer for her, not even here. But, now, after losing Gianpaolo, she had let her conscience become more her guide. Hesitantly, she walked over, took a deep breath, and offered a prayer.

Giorgio walked over to her. "Hadn't we better go? It's getting colder."

Marina nodded. "Yes, let's go."

She walked hand in hand with Giorgio, comforted by the thought that as they always kept their fathers alive in their hearts, they would keep their baby alive, too. As they reached the crossroad, German soldiers marched past them.

Marina drew in her breath. "Where are they going?"

"They have their camp on the road that goes down to Nelsa's former home. I was able to see it when I went down for supplies."

Marina wrapped her shawl tightly around her body. The occupation was here to stay.

At home, she checked the calendar by the fireplace. Christmas was two weeks away.

*   *   *

Marina and Giorgio woke up to a bright, frosty Christmas morning. The fire burned brightly in the fireplace as well as in the new brick oven outdoors in the garden. Giorgio had ordered it built when they married, and now it was ready to use. New white curtains that she had sewn hung at the kitchen windows, a sign of renewal.

Her family and Amelia had provided two chickens, which Marina cut into pieces.

In the *soggiorno,* Chicco, their kitty, bounced, leaped, and chased after a ball of old yarn.

"This is our first Christmas in our home," Giorgio said. "You did invite Don Antonio, didn't you?"

"How could I forget him?" Marina said softly. "My family, your mother, Don Antonio, Marco and his parents, Valentina and Bruno, will be here. We'll have a full table." Marina's happiness slowly faded and she covered her face.

"*Amore mio,*" Giorgio put his arm around her. "No."

"I'm sorry. The bad moments still sneak up on me," Marina took a deep breath, "because not everyone is here."

"We must be grateful for those who *are*. Those who have gone beyond us are only a thought away. As for Gianni, I'm going to toast his safe return, and I still aim to beat him at *briscola.* "

"You're right," Marina said, dabbing at her eyes with her apron. "I had better get to work."

She arranged the chicken pieces in a roasting pan with olive oil, garlic, and rosemary, both picked from the garden at her family's home. She poured olive oil in another large roasting pan and placed their new crop of small, round potatoes in it and added more garlic and rosemary.

On a small side table, in a copper, low rimmed cake pan

was her almond torte which she would slice later on.

In the *soggiorno,* she contemplated the *credenza,* the hutch, where some of her *nonna's* best dishes and glassware, given as wedding gifts, shone through its flower stenciled glass doors. From a drawer, she took out her best tablecloth and spread it on the chestnut table. On this, she arranged the dishes and cutlery.

Nonna Nelsa had told Giorgio to cut down one of the small junipers at her former home. This stood upright in an old bucket full of heavy rocks hidden by moss. Little handmade ornaments from their childhood hung on its branches. The crèche and two shepherds, adoring the Baby, were placed on a small side table.

"Giorgio, would you go and check the oven, please?"

Giorgio sped out the door.

In the kitchen Marina checked the time on the clock. In a little while, her guests would arrive.

*   *   *

Buon Natale!" Lisa hugged her sister tightly, vying with Daniela and Albina to be the first to step inside the door. Behind them were Alda and Nelsa.

"Merry Christmas to you. I hardly see you anymore." Marina hugged her again.

"I know, but I'll make up for it today."

When Giorgio brought up the pan of potatoes, Marina tested them with a fork and was chagrined that they were slightly undercooked.

"No meal turns out totally perfect," Amelia said. "Besides, you have four men out there with good appetites, so don't worry."

Valentina turned the key in the door. "Here we are." She carried a tray of almond *biscotti.* Bruno entered with a flasket of wine.

Marina welcomed them. "Sit here in the *soggiorno* or in the kitchen. It's a moment yet before *pranzo* is ready."

When the bell tower rang noon, and the *Angelus* was recited, everyone sat at the table. Lisa and Marco's love for each other brought smiles and laughter all around. They also talked of the war and, as Giorgio promised, the meal ended with a toast to Gianni as they enjoyed the almond torte. Valentina and Bruno were delighted to have been able to share in the feast, and it proved to be the perfect way to get to know Lisa's family.

"This was beautiful." Don Antonio beamed as he kissed Marina on the cheek when he was ready to leave. "You're doing fine, Marina. Good girl."

"I'm trying my best," Marina said.

"Keep it up!"

Sitting in front of the fireplace later that evening, Marina and Giorgio talked about the day.

"I think that everyone had a good time." Marina sighed happily.

"They did. I can't believe how Albina has grown."

"She has, and I see it more now that I'm not living at

home. Lisa and Marco are happy, and his parents are happy for them. I can hardly wait for their wedding."

"One dove has left the nest and another one will leave sometime soon," Giorgio mused.

"May a dove bring peace on earth so people can be free to live their lives without fear."

"Amen!" She reached for Giorgio's hand.

*   *   *

"Oh, che freddo!" Marina moaned the day after Christmas as she swept away the early morning snow that had come as a surprise.

She turned at the sound of her elderly neighbor's voice, a kindhearted woman whose son was away at war. She was offering what Marina guessed to be a warm drink to the pale, young soldier posted at the corner of her home.

Looking quickly around, he refused in halting Italian. *"No, no. Io non prendere."*

Marina prayed that someone would be that kind to Gianni. Her heart went out to both of them. Something warm to drink would help him to bear the cold. The young soldier was more willing to bear the cold than perhaps bear the displeasure of his commanding officer.

She turned and went inside. A feeling of rebellion mounted in her at the injustice and the inhumanity of man. Since September 8, the Nazi Fascists had mounted a full-scale war against the people. Reports were that thousands of victims, mostly the elderly, women, and children had fallen to the atrocities of the now dreaded SS, the Black Brigades, and others. The Apennines, where the Germans had set up the Gothic Line, was particularly vulnerable.

The door opened, and Giorgio strode into the kitchen to warm himself in front of the fire. "I hope that we make it through this winter."

"If the wood lasts, maybe we will."

"I'm running out of nails, and the thought of having to go down to the valley isn't very appealing."

"Then go now. It's still early and the sooner you go, the sooner you'll be home." Marina squeezed his hand.

"Will you ever stop worrying?" He smiled at her fondly.

"Will I ever stop loving you?"

"I hope not."

"There you are." Marina stood on her tiptoes to kiss him.

After Giorgio left, Marina went to the *despensa* underneath the staircase and frowned. If food hadn't been abundant before, now it was much worse. Last year's jar of olives was down to half and they only had a small piece of cheese. Today she would have to bake bread.

There was a knock on the door, which opened, followed by a familiar voice. "Marina?"

"Amelia, what are you doing outside in this cold?" Marina drew her quickly inside.

"I can't live like a chicken in the coop. Giorgio is working?"

Marina drew two chairs closer to the fire. "He needed to go and buy nails, and I can hardly wait for him to return. I worry about him when he's out."

Amelia nodded, her expression serious. "I know. I still worry about him, too."

"Is there any good news to share?" Marina liked to spend time with her mother-in-law, who knew how to be close by if needed but far enough away to not meddle into her and Giorgio's life.

"I have news about Carla but it's not good, if it's true."

"I haven't seen her around for a while, but then I've had my own life to deal with."

"The talk is that she appears to be trying to flirt with the soldiers. So far, they have ignored her."

Marina frowned. Carla didn't know what she was getting herself into.

*　　　　　*　　　　　*

The year slowly drew to a close with food tightly rationed and electricity coming and going.

The day before the village feast of December 31st, Marina visited her family. Preparations, even if pale in comparison to other years, were underway for the celebration that honored the patron saint of the village for which the church was named. The New Year's Eve dinner that was always hosted by the family who owned the food shop, had been canceled because of the curfew. The dance that followed in the *piazza* was also canceled.

"It's so cold. In a way, it's just as well that we don't have anything going on tomorrow night." Daniela shivered.

"I know. I just wish that somehow we could get together." Marina pursed her lips.

"Why don't we have our feast at *pranzo?* That way you, Giorgio and Amelia can be here?" Lisa asked, her eyes bright. "Mama, what do you think?"

"The idea is good but it depends on what Giorgio wants to do."

"I'll talk to him." Marina liked the idea. "I don't think that there should be any problem. It will work out fine."

"Well," Nelsa said, "I used to cook at the shop for the feast. I'll cook here."

"Then it's going to be a good *pranzo*, for sure. I'd better go and pick up some food, but I'm getting really tired of buying only a few items and having to pay a lot more than we used to," Marina said glumly.

"It could be worse, *bimba mia.* At least we have something to buy and eat," Alda pointed out.

"I'm going. Stay as warm as possible." Marina opened the door to the sound of someone running away. There was no one outside save for the soldier who shifted his weight from one foot to another and smirked. Marina shrugged and passed by him.

*   *   *

"It will be a different feast tomorrow, but we'll still be all together." Giorgio smiled mischievously that night as they prepared for bed. "Then there's always the New Year's kiss to look forward to."

"Do we have to wait until midnight tomorrow night to exchange one?" Marina asked mischievously. She felt a longing inside of her that she hadn't felt for a long time. She realized with a burst of joy that she wanted something more than a kiss. Giorgio had been respectful of her wishes after the loss of the baby, but now she knew the time had come for a change. "It's been such a long time, Giorgio, that we… maybe we could… if you want…"

Giorgio took her in his arms before she finished speaking. Nothing more needed to be said.

*   *   *

The year ended and new one began with an intensification of the war. One afternoon, Marina was mending a sock by the light of the window, as the electricity had gone out. That had become a common occurrence, now. She raised her head at a droning sound. As she stared, shocked, the sock dropped from her hands to the floor. A formation of planes was flying north. Mesmerized, she didn't leave the window until Giorgio charged into the kitchen, out of breath.

"Giorgio, bombers are…"

"American bombers are heading north and also to

Germany," he gasped.

"I'm… I'm afraid."

"Of what?" He smiled wryly. "Germany is the one that should be afraid."

Marina brought her hand to her forehead. "There are bombings on the coast. Fighter planes are flying over the valley. What's going to happen to us?"

"We're here together. It's going to be alright." He said the words firmly.

His bravado didn't fool Marina. His hands shook as he spoke. That had never happened before.

CHAPTER ELEVEN

Marina snipped the last overcast stitch. The last of the four wide, hemp strips was sewn to the other three, making a new sheet for the bed. The finishing touches would be the hems and the monogram. Smiling, she looked with pride at the result of months of having her index finger pricked with the needle. There was more also to be grateful for.

Her eyes rested on Giorgio who poked at the fire, lost in his thoughts, a dreamy expression on his face. The sheet wasn't the only thing that she was grateful for. Last week Giorgio had been paid for the bedroom set that he had finished.

Tonight was the eve of the feast of the Epiphany. Excitement was high amongst the children in the village, but they were also thoughtful. The *Befana,* the little old lady, would arrive with her donkey during the night to bring gifts to those children who had been good.

"What are you thinking about?" Marina reached over and squeezed Giorgio's arm.

"Was it that long ago that I was a little boy eagerly waiting for this night?"

"How excited we were. I remember Mama would scoot us to bed if she heard a noise outside, saying '*E' la Befana!*' We didn't protest, but we couldn't sleep."

"I remember the morning I woke up to find a few oranges and a little hammer inside the door." Giorgio smiled broadly. "That little hammer was the beginning of everything."

"We used to leave water for the donkey and a little hay."

"I wish those days would come back."

"We can't have them back, but we can be grateful for what we have."

*   *   *

Marina woke up the next morning, giddy from a lovely dream where she saw Gianpaolo, happy and healthy.

Sitting up, shivering, she drew the covers up to her neck against the freezing cold.

Giorgio reached toward his nightstand and gingerly placed a little box in front of her.

"Oh, what is this?" Carefully opening it, she gasped aloud. Resting on fluff was a pair of gold earrings. With happiness and emotion, she turned to Giorgio, whose eyes twinkled. "Giorgio, I... *oh Signore!*" She kissed him, at a loss for words. "These cost a fortune."

"Do you like them?"

"I love them! Will you put them on for me?"

She gently touched them. She had never owned any-thing so fine. "I have something for you too. It's not dainty, but I think you'll like it." She got up and, from her dresser, took out her gift, wrapped in brown paper.

As Giorgio reached for it, and felt the contents, a smile broke over his face. Marina knew that he recognized what it was. A brand-new lathe.

"I could have given you something a little fancier, but the old one has seen better days."

"You've learned to read my mind. Thank you, *amore mio.*"

Marina snuggled under the covers a moment longer. Giorgio was excited at having been paid and realized that, even if a project wasn't always there for him, he wouldn't want to do anything else but to work with wood.

"Well, the bed is comfortable, but we have to get ready for church," Marina said and tossed back the covers.

Giorgio gasped at the sting of cold air. "You really want me out of bed!"

*   *   *

Excited children surrounded them at church where they told of discoveries of oranges, nuts, little handmade rag dolls. The *Befana* had been generous.

In the early afternoon, the little old lady went door to door, where people gave her freshly baked cookies, or maybe a flasket of wine. Later, before the curfew, she shared everything in the hall with the children. This had to replace the usual evening dance for now.

With the Christmas festivities over, January brought the sowing of the *orzo*-the grain that provided not only a refreshing drink, but could also be used in soups.

Even with Giorgio paid and life a little easier, the ups and downs of everyday life during the war continued. In Diecimo, in the Serchio River Valley, where the train station had been taken over, the German operations were especially evident. Since September, a flat area around the river had been mined against military vehicles or foot soldiers. Bridges were wired with dynamite. To help achieve their goal to hinder the advance of the Allies, the Germans had recruited older German soldiers, Polish prisoners of war, and older Italian men. Many of these, including the corps of engineer soldiers, by order of the German command, were housed in the homes in the village. The curfew was strictly observed.

Marina bemoaned the situation, because they were under curfew also, although they weren't required to house soldiers.

"Praise God that we haven't come to that point here," Giorgio said. "I don't know if I could handle it. When I think of the dreaded SS, who wear black uniforms like the Fascists but with lightning bolts embroidered on their collars..." He shivered.

"War!" Marina whacked a spider with an old broom that snapped in two.

Giorgio coughed to stifle a laugh. "You're dangerous, *carissima.* One whack and you're dead." He leaned against the wall, his arms folded across his chest. "Now I can look forward to the next project."

Marina looked at him, full of anticipation. "What it will be?"

"Maybe a baby's crib?"

She ran a finger along his cheek. "With our baby sleeping peacefully in it."

*   *   *

With a little more money to spare, Marina was happy that she could afford to buy something for her family. Even if she wasn't rich, she *felt* rich.

"You shouldn't have done this." Alda shook her head when she saw the small bag of flour on the table. "You need every lira you can get."

"Mama, if I couldn't do it, I wouldn't have."

"How are you feeling? Is there anything… new?" Nelsa asked, trying to sound casual as her fingers plied the flax that would become thread.

Her *nonna* was just as anxious for another baby as she and Giorgio were. "For now, there isn't. But we want a baby so badly. Giorgio wants to make a crib, but I don't know if I should encourage him or not, even if I should be pregnant."

"Why not?" Alda's eyes went wide with surprise.

"What if… if I lose this baby, too?" Marina frowned.

"*Bimba,* what happened was an accident. There is no reason why you can't bear a baby." Nelsa spoke with urgency.

Hugging herself, imagining the seed of life in her body, Marina couldn't ask for more than the tenderness and care that Giorgio had bestowed on her. Her musing was brusquely interrupted by Daniela who burst open the door and stumbled inside, gasping.

"*Mio Dio,* what is it?" Alda asked, alarmed.

"It's… it's Marco… his parents, Valentina… Bruno!"

"What happened?" Marina asked steadying Daniela.

"They… they've been taken hostage by the Germans. A..a soldier," Daniela gasped again, "has… been found wounded and unconscious."

"Are you sure?" Alda asked.

"The… the teacher's husband happened to be in the valley. He came home as fast as he could. That's all he knew."

Marina flew to the door. "I have to tell Giorgio!"

*   *   *

"Marco needs me," Giorgio said, pacing back and forth in the kitchen.

"What can you do?"

"Maybe nothing, but I am not going to let him face this alone." He clenched his fists. "If that soldier doesn't wake up and explain what happened…"

Marina had gathered a few personal items. "I want to see Marco and then continue to Mama's. I want to be there for Lisa."

When they reached Marco's office, there was no one waiting in the little hall. Giorgio knocked on the door of the exam room.

Marco opened to him, his face taut, his eyes wet with tears.

Marina hugged him. "We'll help you through this moment," she whispered against his cheek.

"They… were looking forward to coming up here to live… Now… who knows?"

Giorgio placed his hands on his shoulders. "They will be alright, my friend. We have to believe that."

Marco pressed his hands to his head. "I don't know… I don't know. I have to go… I have to go."

"I'm going with you." Giorgio nodded towards the door.

"I can't have you do that." Marco shook his head. "I… I don't want to place your life in jeopardy."

"You can't go alone. We're going together. Let's see what we'll need and then get going." Giorgio paced around the room.

"Please be careful, both of you," Marina pleaded and hugged them both. "I'm staying with Mama."

"Tell Lisa I love her," Marco whispered. "I don't know what… what's going to happen."

News of the plight of the hostages quickly made the round of the village. On the way to her family, Marina realized that she couldn't answer any questions because she really didn't know what to say. When she stepped into the kitchen, she found Lisa at the table, her head resting on her arms. "Why such evil? Why?"

Albina, Nelsa, and Alda were gathered around her and Daniela was seated next to her.

"You have to be strong for Marco," Alda said.

"Now that he needs me, I can't do anything for him." Lisa covered her face.

"Yes, you can," Marina knelt down next to her. "He needs you to be strong because if… if something should happen, you have to be his support."

Daniela drew Lisa's head to her shoulder. "Is there anything good anymore in this world? Everything is falling apart."

Her body tense, Marina shared Daniela's sentiment as the day dragged on. *Was* there anything good left in the world? Her heart went out to Marco, and she was worried about Giorgio. Lisa had sent word to the factory about what had happened even though she was convinced that those living in the Fegana valley already knew about it.

*   *   *

Dawn was a long time breaking. Wearily, Marina got up before anyone else to prepare something for breakfast.

She lit the fire and stared outside the window at the overcast sky. She turned at a soft footfall and Daniela walked into the kitchen, still half asleep.

"What a miserable night." Daniela moaned and sank into a chair.

Marina was struck by the dark shadows under her eyes. Daniela never descended the stairs without brushing her hair, even if she were in her nightgown.

"It seems that it's just one thing after another lately." Marina pursed her lips. "Come and have something for breakfast."

Daniela ate a cold piece of *polenta* and drank some milk. "I wish that I could be here," she said morosely.

"There's nothing that we can do except wait and pray." Marina joined her to eat a little breakfast. She glanced again at Daniela when she went upstairs to dress. She had the uncanny feeling that there was something more to her distress than worry over Marco's parents.

Alda and Lisa both came down from upstairs. Alda's brow was furrowed. "Daniela doesn't look good."

"I thought it was only my impression."

"She doesn't look good," Lisa said. "But then, I suppose that without sleeping, I don't look much better."

After a little while, Daniela came down. "I'd better go." She grabbed her umbrella and left.

Marina helped her mother and Lisa around the house. The morning was cold and dreary. After a while, they sat down in front of the fire, their spirits as grey as the day itself.

Alda turned to Marina. "Have you seen Amelia?"

"To be truthful, no."

"I'm concerned about her. She must not feel well."

"Shall I go and visit her?"

"Go. You can't do anything for me. What I need is to know that the soldier has awakened and that Marco's parents are freed." Lisa's voice trailed off. "Go and see her and go home. There isn't anything you can do here."

Marina got up wearily, wrapped her heavy shawl around her shoulders and left. Lisa and her mother were right. There was nothing that she could do. She hugged them tightly and left.

Amelia stood on her doorstep, but this time she didn't wave to her to stop by.

Marina climbed the steps and placed her hands on her shoulders. "Are you alright?"

"I'm alright, but this situation…"

"I know. Come and stay with me while Giorgio is away."

"No, I'll be fine." Amelia managed a smile.

"Amelia, please…"

"I'm alright, really. Go home."

Marina didn't argue, but raised her head to the overcast sky. "It looks like snow."

"Hopefully, it will cool some heads."

"Then it had better snow a lot!"

After seeing that Amelia was inside the warmth of the kitchen, Marina continued home. On her way, she saw Carla on the doorstep of her home, holding a bucket of water. "I heard about Marco's parents. I feel so bad for him."

"Giorgio has gone with him so that he won't be alone."

Carla turned pale. "He… did? I… I hope that he… that they'll be alright." Her expression hardened. "It seems as if it's one thing after another for Giorgio. First the assault and then losing the baby."

Something in her manner struck Marina as odd. She drew her shawl around tightly around her body. "I… I'd better go home."

"Yes, do. You don't want to give Giorgio more worry than he already has by getting sick."

Marina opened her mouth to retort, but thought it useless.

*   *   *

Theatrical snowflakes were falling fast the next morning when Marina looked outside the bedroom window. A lone sparrow chirped on the tree in her neighbor's garden. Her mind went back three months to the morning when she had lost the baby. But her *nonna* was right, she told herself. There was no reason that she couldn't bear another child.

After making the bed, she down on the edge, praying

fervently for a happy outcome for the hostages, for her family, for Amelia, for the baby they had lost.

She lighted the fire and was warming up some milk when there was a knock on the door.

She opened to Anna, who had a copper water bucket at her feet. "I have to go for water. Is there any news?"

Marina shook her head. "It's early, but at noon…"

"Don't say anything more. Is there anything that I can help you with?"

"I'm fine. It's a matter of waiting. How are the little ones?"

"Praise God they're fine for the moment. I don't have that much milk anymore, so I'm weaning Giorgio."

Marina smiled. "I don't think he's happy about that."

"He doesn't have much choice." Anna laughed, and then grew serious.

Sensing that there was something else she wanted to say, Marina took her hands. "Are you alright?"

Anna raised her eyes skyward. "Be wary of Carla. There's something that… that isn't right."

"What isn't right? Tell me!"

"Just be on guard!"

Anna left, leaving Marina leaning against the door as the old, creepy feeling took hold of her again.

*   *   *

The power went out again in early afternoon, but it had

stopped snowing, and the sun managed to break through the clouds. Sitting at the kitchen window, mending a sock in the silence around her, Marina jumped as the front door opened and she heard Giorgio calling her.

"Giorgio!" She flew into his arms. "You're safe. What's happened? Tell me!"

Haggard, unshaven, and shivering as he was, a smile broke across his face. "The soldier woke up. He… he said that he accidentally fell and hit his head. He'll be fine. Everyone was… was freed. Is there any warm water?" he asked composing himself, and wiping his face with his grimy sleeve.

Marina poured water into a pitcher, and followed him upstairs. Her heart ached, because she saw in his demeanor how the past hours had affected him. She waited until he was in bed before going back downstairs.

She sank down on a chair and Chicco jumped into her lap, his eyes staring into hers.

"We're fine, Chicco, we're fine."

To celebrate the release of the hostages and Giorgio's safe return, Marina baked *castagnaccio,* the chestnut flour cake, sniffing at the aroma of rosemary and *pinoli,* the pine nuts. She tip-toed upstairs to call him, but he was still sleeping soundly. Knowing that sleep would restore him more than a meal, she quietly descended the stairs and ate a little of the torte alone.

The evening went by, spent mending, knitting, or plying thread. She ended the evening praying the rosary, offering it in gratitude for Valentina and Bruno's release. Placing the rosary back in its little pouch, she stretched, finally feeling the weight of the past hours.

"I'm going to do the same," she murmured to Chicco, who was curled up in his box, fast asleep.

Pouring warm water into a pitcher, oil lamp in hand, Marina climbed the stairs. Winter time meant foregoing a leisurely sponge bath, but she could still enjoy the fragrance of the Palmolive soap bar that lingered on her skin. She slipped into bed next to Giorgio, turning towards him.

He stirred, smiling at her. "You smell so nice and fresh," he murmured.

Marina slipped her arm across his body. "My husband is home."

Giorgio drew her head to his shoulder. "I don't want to be anywhere else. You can't appreciate something until you have almost lost it."

"Marco must be spent from anguish."

"He confided to me that if his parents were spared, he wasn't going to waste any more time in proposing to Lisa."

Marina lay quiet. The soldier had waked up. Marco's parents were safe. Giorgio was home. But something didn't feel right. Why?

"Something's bothering you. What is it?" Giorgio asked.

"Nothing," Marina lied.

CHAPTER TWELVE

Marina stretched under the covers the next morning, grateful for their warmth.

"We have to get up, *carissima.*" Giorgio brushed a lock from her forehead.

"I know."

"Ooh." Giorgio shivered when he rose and opened the shutters. "It's stopped snowing, and the sun is shining. I'll go to the vineyard to see if Pallino has enough fodder and bedding."

"Go and visit your mother on the way." Marina pulled a purple cardigan over her head, and ran her fingers through her tousled hair. Her gaze met Giorgio's. "Is... is something wrong?"

"No," he answered softly. "I'll go light the fire."

Marina watched him as he went downstairs, humming to himself. Life was returning to normal.

After breakfast, Giorgio was ready to leave when there was a knock on the door.

Lisa stepped inside, and loosened the shawl wrapped around her head, letting her dark hair cascade to her shoulders. She hugged and kissed Giorgio. "Thank you for being there for Marco."

"Thank God that all went well." He smiled.

After he left, Lisa helped Marina peel potatoes. "Marco is keeping watch for a vacant house here for his parents. He doesn't want them in the valley any longer."

"I hope that he can find something soon because things are bound to get worse. I heard there is a German commanding officer who is terror itself." Marina shuddered.

"I haven't told Mama yet, but we want to marry in late spring. This episode nearly killed him, and it didn't do me any good either."

"I can understand that." Marina closed her eyes. Although the circumstances were different, the assault on Giorgio was always in the back of her mind.

"Do you mind if I… I turn to you for… counsel… for certain things? When we marry? I know it's not something to… talk about." Lisa lowered her eyes.

Marina contemplated her. She knew what Lisa wanted to know and felt privileged that she could help with her concerns. Not that their mother had ever refused advice, even though talking about delicate matters was, for the most part, unthinkable. But Marina remembered the moment that Lisa had stayed by her side when she most needed support, revealing the depths of her love. "You can turn to me for anything." She put her arm around her shoulder.

"Marina, what… what is it like for you when you and Giorgio…"

"I feel loved and respected. That's what makes the moment all the more beautiful." She was certain that Marco had Giorgio's tenderness, so she felt confident that Lisa would be just as happy.

"I would love to be able to have chil…" Lisa bit her lip. "I'm sorry. The wound is still fresh for you. I could have died the day you lost the baby, because there was nothing I could do to help you."

"Your love and patience were all the help I needed. I would love to become an aunt. How about trying for a boy? Like you said, it would be a welcome change."

Lisa burst out laughing.

The kitchen window rattled at the *whoosh* of wind.

Lisa washed her hands. "It sounds nasty out there. I'd better go home." She quickly wrapped her shawl around her head. "Thank you. This means a lot to me."

Marina stepped outside with her and caught sight of a uniformed officer at Anna's door. *"Oh, mio Dio."* She brought her hands to her face.

"What is it?" Lisa turned in the direction of her gaze.

After a moment, they heard a piercing scream as Anna collapsed into the officer's arms.

*   *   *

"Stefano, my friend… dead!" Giorgio gasped between

sobs, his face buried in his hands.

Marina stood behind him at the table, her hands on his shoulders. "Poor Stefano. Poor Anna. How happy we… were last year when his little boy was born." She raised his tear wet face. "I'm going to Anna to see if I can be of any help, alright?"

Giorgio nodded. "I'm coming in a moment, if I can pull myself together."

Marina's shoes crunched snow as she walked down to Anna's. She passed the pale faced sentinel at her neighbor's home. For a moment, a feeling of anger rushed through her. Stefano's death was because of them. But no. He was only doing what he was told to do. Perhaps he had a wife, too. She paused at Anna's door, praying for strength.

The door opened, and Anna's mother drew her inside. "Oh, please come in. I have to leave. I… I'll try to be back. Please stay for a while. I don't want her to be alone."

"I can stay," Marina answered, curbing her frustration. Not even a tragedy could reunite the families.

Entering the kitchen, she called softly, "Anna?"

"Marina!"

She opened her arms to the desperate young woman.

After a long moment, they sat down. Marina sat next to her, and took her icy hands in hers. "Giorgio is trying to compose himself. He'll be here, too."

Anna closed her eyes. "What's… to become of me? Of our children?"

"We'll take care of you. Remember that Giorgio and Stefano were like brothers. We won't abandon you."

"I know." Desolate, Anna looked around the kitchen. She walked to the fireplace where, on the mantelpiece, a picture of Stefano stood. He was smiling. Anna traced a caress across his face. "It was hard not having him home, but I was comforted by his letters. He was alive even if far away. Now, I... I have nothing to look forward to." She brought her hands to her face.

Marina's eyes dimmed. All she could do was to place her arm around her shoulders.

*   *   *

With little Giorgio asleep in her arms, Marina brought her finger to her lips when Giorgio arrived later. "I'm going to stay here tonight. I think Anna will be alone," she whispered.

Giorgio tiptoed to the table and sat down. "Her mother will be here, surely."

"I don't think so. She's probably afraid to meet someone from Stefano's family. You know how her husband feels about them."

"This is hardly a time for resentment." Giorgio spoke through clenched teeth. "Is Anna upstairs?"

Marina nodded. "She's trying to convince little Maddalena to come down and have something to eat. Ever since the officer came, she's been hiding in the bedroom. I think that she senses what has happened."

"She probably heard the officer and saw her mother cry."

Little Giorgio whimpered and Marina gently rocked him.

Anna came down holding Maddalena, whose face was buried in her mother's shoulder.

"Here's our girl," Giorgio said brightly. "You know what? I'll tell you a story. Would you like that?" He held out his arms to her.

Maddalena hesitated a moment, but then stretched out her arms to Giorgio.

Marina's lips curved into a smile. She tore her eyes from him and turned to Anna. "Shall I prepare something to eat for you?"

"My stomach hurts."

"Is it any wonder? What is it, little one?" Marina held little Giorgio up as he began to cry.

"I'll take him. There's not much left, but maybe he'll feel soothed." Anna cradled him in her arms and began to nurse him.

Marina shook her head. Here was a new life in a mother's arms. Somewhere was another life, lost.

Neighbors visited and offered muffled expressions of condolences with promises of help.

Darkness came quickly, adding to the darkness that already enveloped the home. Marina closed the shutters, and lighted the oil lamp on the mantelpiece. More neighbors came to offer condolences and promises of help.

When she and Anna settled down for the night, Stefano's family had not visited. Neither had Anna's mother returned.

*   *   *

Longer February days helped to banish the darkness of winter, but Marina couldn't rid herself of an anxiety that seemed to become worse. She finished pressing a pillowcase, smoothing out the edges of its crochet border. This was one of the first items that she had made for her dowry. She placed the small, heavy iron back on the hearth, and folded the sheet that she used to protect the table when she ironed. "That's done. I don't like to find myself with lots of laundry to press."

Nelsa had come to visit and sat mending a sock. "I don't like to iron, but I don't want my clothes to look like wrinkled prunes, either. Marina, I think that you'd better knit larger socks for Giorgio. Have his feet grown?" She stared chagrined at the hole at the toe.

Not even her *nonna's* sense of humor helped her.

"*Bimba,* what's wrong? You're not yourself."

"I don't know, *Nonna.*" Marina sat down, dejected. "I have this fear that I can't get rid of. The last time I felt like this, Giorgio was assaulted, and we lost Giada. Then I lost our baby."

"Feeling anxious doesn't mean that bad things happen.

144

I think that Stefano's death has affected you."

"It has, but I feel like this all the time. Am I normal?"

"Is anyone normal these days?" Nelsa raised her arms to heaven. "If the people who governed us had reasoned with their heads, instead of their... ooh!" Nelsa covered her mouth.

"Nonna!"

"It's the truth."

Marina pondered her words. Maybe her grandmother was right. Good things had happened too. "I have a loving family, a wonderful husband, a home of my own." She looked at Chicco who swatted a ball of yarn across the kitchen floor, only to bump his head on a chair leg as he chased it. "I also have that little creature."

"Good. Hold on to those thoughts." Nelsa cupped Marina's face and kissed her on the forehead.

Marina turned to Giorgio who came in from outside, pale and shaky. "Are you alright?" Alarmed, she led him to a chair.

"I... I don't know." His hand shook as he ran his fingers through his hair.

Nelsa poured a little wine into a glass and gave it to him. "Drink this."

"What happened?" Marina took his hands, alarmed.

"You won't believe me." Giorgio shook his head.

"What happened?" Marina insisted.

"I... I was cleaning out the stable and Pallino was outside. I heard my name... turned around." His eyes filled. "I… I saw… saw Gianni."

Stunned, Marina stared at him, hardly daring to breathe.

"You saw Gianni?" Nelsa asked in a choked voice.

Giorgio looked from one to the other. "I know you don't believe me, but I know who I saw, even if he was unshaven and ragged. He spoke a secret word that we used as children."

Marina blinked back tears. "Wh-what did he say to you?"

"Nothing. There was the sound of voices. He… ran behind the stable, where the chestnut tree is. After a moment, I went to look for him, but he was gone."

Marina rose, a determined look on her face. "He might be hiding somewhere there. I'm going to see if I can find him."

"You're not going alone. We'll both go." Giorgio got up.

"Nonna," Marina placed her hands on her shoulders. "Don't mention this to Mama or the girls yet."

Nelsa nodded. "I won't, but don't you be a doubting Thomas, alright? Giorgio saw him, and you will, too. Remember, good things happen."

Her grandmother's words stayed with her every step of the way to Giorgio's vineyard. That Gianni was alive seemed almost like a dream. So many soldiers had died.

In the vineyard, the bleakness of winter showed in the naked vines bereft of their lush, green foliage, their twisty branches barely showing the first hint of buds. A few dried grape pips on the stems provided food for the sparrows. The apple and fig trees stood stark against the blue sky.

"Where would Gianni stay if he was really here?" Marina stood in front of the stable. In the shadier areas where the sun's rays didn't shine as much, patches of snow covered dead grasses. "Where would he be? How did he get here? Why was he afraid to be seen by other people?" She turned to Giorgio.

"I don't know, but I have a feeling that he either deserted or something happened to his unit."

"He's living like a fugitive, if he deserted." Marina brought her hands to her face. "Could... could he have joined the Partisans?"

"I wouldn't put it past him. He longs for the day that Italy will be free."

Marina walked around the stable, listening to Pallino's movements inside. Giorgio followed close behind her. She turned to him. "There's no way that he could hide anywhere around here, except in an abandoned stable or a barn. Could he hide in a *capanna delle foglie*?" The little barns held leaves to use for bedding for cows. They were located here and there close to where people had stables with animals.

"He could... yes." Giorgio's face lit up with a smile, and followed her gaze. Then he frowned. "The problem is, which one? There's one on the hillock behind us, one in the chestnut grove over there."

Marina groaned. "Who knows?" She hugged herself

against the brisk, icy wind that began to blow. "It's too cold to stay out. Let's go home."

Later that evening, Marina lingered a moment before going to bed to finish winding the plied thread into a ball. Her happiness that her brother was still alive was overshadowed by the fear that he was living like a fugitive. She put down the ball and let hot tears run down her face.

*   *   *

Marina waited a day to visit her family. She didn't know how she could approach them and not say anything about Gianni. The soldier nodded to her as he always did. From the roof, water dripped from the melting snow and formed puddles on the ground.

She turned the key in the door. The warmth of the kitchen enveloped her. She saw her grandmother at the stove in her nightgown, wrapped tightly in a shawl. Daniela and Lisa sat at the table, looking ghastly.

Nelsa turned around. "Marina," she said in a voice hoarse from a cold. "Don't come in. We're all sick."

"*Oh Signore!* What happened. Mama? How bad is she?"

"Sneezing and coughing like the girls and I. You don't want this, trust me."

"We have to call Marco. I feel so miserable," Daniela moaned.

Lisa stared at her aghast. "No!"

"Why not? We're all sick." Daniela protested.

"You forget that we're going to marry. He can't see me in a nightgown."

Daniela sneezed loudly, and blew her nose. "This isn't the time to act like a pru…" She caught herself. "I… I mean…"

Marina exchanged a glance with Nelsa whose cheeks puffed. Marina covered her mouth and cleared her throat. "Thank God, I came. I… wasn't able to come yesterday. I had no way of knowing that you were all sick. I'll go to the vineyard to be sure the rabbits have fodder."

"*Bimba,* who knows that this wasn't meant to be?"

Marina went downstairs. The all too familiar sickle was in its place alongside the gunny sack. She was grateful for her winter clogs as she headed out to the old, familiar path. The blackberry bushes twined through the weathered wood railings. The path that led down to Giorgio's vineyard brought a smile to her face. How many times she and Giorgio had met there to talk and to dream together. She continued along the mule path where the imprints of a donkey's hooves and the first signs of spring grass told her that life continued. Her clogs sank a little into the soft earth as she walked down the path into the orchard. She stood under the bare peach tree, her back to the little stable where the rabbits were. All around her was pure silence.

"Psst!"

Marina frowned, not sure what she had heard.

"*Fuoco!*"

Fire? Marina turned around slowly, her heart in her throat. No one else knew, not even Giorgio, that secret word. No one except herself, her sisters, and Gianni. It was the word they shared as children when they knew they were in trouble. Her eyes met those of a man, a little older than her. He wore a short beard, his dark hair was in disarray, his clothes were ragged, but there was no mistaking his eyes, or his tentative smile. She swayed, and her legs buckled.

CHAPTER THIRTEEN

When Marina regained consciousness, she was aware of the pungent odor of the stable and the rabbits scampering about. Bent over her, concerned, was her brother. She raised her hand and touched his face. "Gianni?"

His eyes glistened with tears as he helped her to sit up. "Marina."

She grabbed his arms, desperate to keep him with her. "How… how did you get here? Did you ever receive our letters?" There were many questions that she wanted answers to.

He sat down next to her. "After I was released from the hospital, I rejoined my unit. Two months ago, we were attacked."

"Were you injured? How did you get help… what did you do?"

"No." Gianni shook his head. "By God's grace I was spared along with another soldier. We outsmarted the enemy by playing dead until it was safe to move."

"The others… died?"

Gianni's voice grew husky. "Yes, even our doctor.

Many were so badly wounded that there was nothing we could do to save them. They couldn't survive in the freezing cold. You go through so much together, you become like brothers, and… and you have to leave them behind." He turned to Marina. "I have nightmares and feel terrible remorse that I had to leave them there."

"Where did you go, you and the other soldier?"

"We traveled from town to town to try to reach home. The other soldier is from this area, too. Wherever we went, there was always someone to help us, so here I am. We… we wanted to help free Italy." His eyes clouded. "We heard about other soldiers joining the Partisans to help the Allies."

"You didn't join them, did you?" Marina asked quickly.

"Yes." Gianni's expression hardened. "I'll do anything to free Italy from the Nazis and the Fascists."

"*Dio mio,* you're putting your life in danger. The Germans will kill you."

"They have to catch me first." He laughed.

"You're just as bad as Giorgio," Marina moaned.

"What is he up to? We didn't get a chance to talk when I saw him."

"Why did you run away?" She touched his face. "You've always been like brothers."

"I know, but it was risky to be seen together. Never mind me." He smiled at her and put his hands on her shoulders. "Tell me about everyone, about you." He fixed his gaze upon her. "Wait a moment. Aren't you expecting a baby?"

Marina lowered her head.

"Marina?" Gianni cupped her face, and raised it.

"You didn't receive the letter about my miscarriage," she said softly. Well, with what had happened to his unit, it was impossible. She sighed, and explained everything to him.

"*What!?* I'm so sorry." He hugged her, his eyes full of sorrow.

"There's good news, too." Marina smiled. "*Nonna* is living with us, and Lisa is engaged to be married to the new doctor in the village. Daniela is tutoring children. Oh, Gianni, please come and see Mama and the girls. Better yet, leave the Partisans. Come home!"

"I can't, Marina. Not as long as Italy is under the Nazi Fascists. When we are free, then I will."

"But at least come home just to visit." She clutched his arm. "I'll help you, even at night, if you're afraid to be seen."

"With the curfew?" He shook his head, scowling. "No. When I come home, I don't want to have to leave again." He got up and helped Marina to her feet. "I have to go now." He still held her close. "Tell everyone at home that I love them. Tell Giorgio the game of *briscola* is on."

"Tell me where you're going." She held on tightly as he tried to free his arm. "I'll find a way to get to you."

"No." He gently pried her hands free. "That would be dangerous for both of us. They could kill you for helping a

Partisan, and I don't want to find myself dead. But then, rather than being deported to some hellish place, being shot dead might be preferable." He kissed her on the nose. "I love you. Be happy with Giorgio, and make me an uncle."

"Gianni, I... I love you, too." She threw her arms around him. She couldn't let him go, she couldn't.

He disengaged himself from her arms. "I have to go."

Before Marina could say anything more, he was out of the door. She stood helpless. "God be with you." she whispered.

*   *   *

Marina wrestled with the idea of telling her family about Gianni. She sat on a sack of sawdust, confiding her fears to Giorgio. "What am I going to do? If I keep quiet, Mama won't know that he's alive. If I tell her that I saw him and that he joined the Partisans, it will mean more worry for her."

Giorgio put down the lathe. "If you don't tell her anything and, God forbid, something happens to her, you'll live with the regret that she didn't know that her son was alive."

"Oh no." She clasped her hands tightly. She hadn't thought of that...

He wiped his hands. "Let's go, Marina. She has to know."

Marina's mind was a whirlwind as she tried to find the right words to break the news to her family. Giorgio held her hand tightly as they approached her home. "Everything will be fine."

When they entered the kitchen, Alda knew immediately that something had happened. She looked from one to the other. "Something's wrong. What is it?"

Marina took a deep breath. "Mama, you… you'd better sit down."

"I don't like this," Lisa said.

"I don't either," Albina whispered.

"We… we both saw Gianni." Marina turned to face the window.

Lisa gasped, and a sob escaped Alda.

When her mother calmed down, Marina spoke cheerfully. "He looks good, even if his hair is messy and he has a short beard. Actually, it doesn't look bad on him."

"Why… why didn't he come here?" Alda found her voice.

"He told me that when he comes home, he wants it to be for good." Marina made her voice firm.

"He also wants to help free Italy," Giorgio added.

Lisa's eyes widened. "Did he join the Partisans?"

Marina nodded. "Yes. That's why he's in hiding."

Alda lowered her head, her expression sorrowful, worried, but with a hint of relief.

Marina knelt at her knees. "Mama, I know it's hard. But he's alive. We didn't know that before." She held her mother's hands tightly.

Albina hadn't spoken a word, but now she began to laugh. "He's alive! Can't we understand that? He's alive."

Her outburst relieved the tension of the past two years. Even if Gianni had joined the Partisan cause, there was reason to hope that he would be home one day soon. They had to cling to that.

When Marina and Giorgio returned home, she walked to the table and gripped its edge. She wasn't able to hold back her emotions any longer and her tears marked the wood.

"It's alright. It's alright." Giorgio took her in his arms.

*   *   *

On the last Sunday of *Carnevale*, in February, before the beginning of Lent, Marina prepared *cenci fritti*. Her hair secured with a bright bandana, she prepared a mixture of eggs and flour, along with a little olive oil and sugar. There wasn't much to work with, but she wanted to celebrate Gianni's return.

She kneaded the dough until it was smooth and elastic. Rolling it out, she sliced it into long, thin rectangles that she fried in hot oil made from the olives in Giorgio's vineyard. When they became puffy and golden, she carefully lifted them out, and placed them on yellow absorbent paper, made from straw, and used also for wrapping food. After arranging them on a platter, she dusted them with a pinch of sugar. Elated, she presented the platter to her family, Amelia, Marco, Valentina and Bruno.

After the first bite, Valentina sighed happily. "Marina, this is heaven."

"If heaven is as beautiful as this is good, I have a lot of work to do to get there." Bruno raised his eyes heavenward.

There was another good reason to celebrate. A refugee family had moved out of the village, leaving a house free for Valentina and Bruno.

"In the midst of all the bad, we have much to be grateful for between Gianni and the house." Giorgio cheered, and bit into the puffy delicacy. "I totally agree with Bruno. This is more than good, Marina."

Marina was thrilled that her first attempt to make the *cenci*, had turned out well.

Valentina could not restrain her excitement. "I'm so happy, so grateful to be alive. I can hardly wait to settle in here."

"You may have second thoughts with the lot of us." Giorgio laughed.

"We're not *that* bad," Marina protested.

"No," Giorgio said, "but we've had some moments."

Everyone contributed to the gaiety. Marina's exuberance slowly faded when her gaze fell on Daniela, who sat quiet, and almost sullen.

*   *   *

Marina moaned as the blustery wind pierced her clothes the next morning. Even if spring was not that far away, the wind that whipped snow into the air on the crests of the Apennines, the *cavallone,* as it was called locally, suggested otherwise. She winced as the gusts bit into her face, and she was helpless to protect herself with the bucket full of water balanced on her head. If nothing else, her feet were nice and warm in the wool socks she had knitted.

"Let me help you." Giorgio helped her to lower the bucket onto the counter in the kitchen. "You feel like an icicle! Go and warm yourself. I'll bring up some wood."

Marina rubbed her hands together in front of the fire. She scooped glowing embers into the burners to prepare some hot *orzo* that she had to measure carefully, as the tin was almost empty.

"Why is it that I can never get used to the cold?" Giorgio brought in an armful of wood.

"When summer comes, you'll be saying that about the heat." She laughed.

He sat down, puzzled. "Have you seen Carla lately?"

"No. Why? Is something wrong?"

"I don't know… it's something I feel."

"Eh?"

"Every time I see her, she acts as if she possesses me. She asks me questions and gets too concerned about my well-being. It gives me the chills."

Marina poured the steaming drink into a wineglass and handed it to him. She remembered Anna's words, but tried to make light of it. "I get overly concerned, too."

Giorgio looked at her with a hint of exasperation. "You're my wife. She's not. Your concern, I don't mind. Hers, I do."

Marina felt mischievous. On impulse, she took the glass from his hands and sat in his lap. "I'm glad that I'm your wife," she murmured.

"So am I."

A tingle coursed through her. Maybe Carla wasn't to be trusted. If she had any designs on a man, Marina was more than determined that it wasn't going to be *her* man.

*   *   *

The Lenten days grew a little longer and warmer, and the buds were now visible on the fruit trees. On a sunny afternoon in early March, while Giorgio was in the valley purchasing some supplies, Marina helped her family with a few outside chores. Twigs that had fallen from the cherry tree because of the snow were gathered up into a bundle. Marina paused at Giada's little grave. How she missed her.

"How are you feeling?" Lisa asked. "You must be better, if you're here."

"I... I feel fine.' She looked at Lisa, puzzled. "It's everyday life as usual."

"Are you really alright?" Lisa frowned. "Giorgio confided to Carla that you weren't feeling well, and of course, she *would* have told Mama."

"What?" Marina frowned. "Why would he say that?"

"I don't want to upset you."

"I'm not upset. I'm just surprised that he would say something that isn't true."

Lisa rolled her eyes, clearly vexed that she had said anything. "Marina, he might *not* have said it."

"I'll talk with him about it when he gets home." She frowned. "Talking about someone not being well, is it just me, or is Daniela acting a little strange?"

"A *little?* She goes by fits, lately. One moment, she's happy, the next, she's as sour as bad milk. Here she comes."

Daniela came smiling into the garden, as if she didn't have a care in the world. "The teacher gave me a few of her books to read."

"That's nice of her. What are they about?" Marina asked.

"Geography. I love to read about places in the world that I know I'll never be able to see. I better go and see if I can help Mama with anything."

Marina raised her eyebrows at Lisa who, in turn, raised her shoulders.

*   *   *

On her way home, Marina called on Anna, who was sweeping the kitchen. "You can see that little Giorgio not only crawls but likes to chew on bread at the same time." Anna pointed to scattered breadcrumbs on the floor.

"I'd love to see him when he does that!"

"Sit down. We haven't visited for a while."

"Are the children sleeping?"

"Yes. They're so full of energy that once they touch the pillow, they're in dreamland."

Marina saw the toll that the past few weeks had taken on Anna. Dressed in black, shadows under her eyes, Anna was obviously getting little if any sleep. With her hands, she brushed back the thick, brown hair that fell to her shoulders. "I lost my black hair comb. I… I don't know what happened to it."

"When you least expect it, it will show up. Do you need help with anything?"

A tear rolled down Anna's cheek. "No… I'm alright. I just wish that I could have my Stefano… home." Her voice trailed off. "How are you feeling?"

Piqued, Marina felt warmth rise to her cheeks. "Fine. Why?"

Anna's expression grew troubled. "Carla has been saying that you aren't well."

"I feel perfectly fine. What's with her? Lisa asked me the same thing. Oh, how I want to give her a piece of my mind!"

"Don't talk a lot with her, Marina. I've never told this

to anyone, but when… when I gave birth to my little boy, she questioned whether he was Stefano's child."

Marina sat stone still, shocked. When Stefano left for the war, Anna had found out that she was pregnant. How could anyone even think that the baby was the result of a betrayal?

She remained with her for a while until the children woke up.

"Come upstairs. They'll want to see you," Anna said.

Marina delighted to see little Giorgio on his hands and knees in the crib, as Maddalena showed her a little picture book. She contemplated them, especially the little boy. He had just begun his life, and already he was facing the cruelty of gossip.

"Don't dwell on what Carla said about your baby." Marina consoled Anna as she left. "It will only upset you, alright?"

Anna nodded. "I have other concerns, but believe me, it's not easy."

Incensed at how low a person could stoop by spreading vicious gossip, Marina hurried home, flung open the kitchen door and slammed it shut, gasping.

Giorgio whirled around, startled. "What's wrong, what's happened? You look like a thundercloud ready to burst."

"The nerve of that woman!" She raised her arms in exasperation. Then she turned on him. "Have you told Carla that I wasn't feeling well?"

"*I* told Carla you weren't feeling well?"

"It's made the rounds of the village."

"Marina, I never said anything to Carla." Giorgio's voice was firm, his jaw set. "Although I'd love to be able to say that you're not feeling well because you're expecting a baby."

She, too, would be happy to say that she was going to have a baby. Taking a deep breath, Marina calmed down. Her face felt tight. She refrained from telling him what Carla had insinuated about little Giorgio. When Stefano left for the war, Giorgio had made it a point to watch over Anna. When she found out she was pregnant, his resolve grew stronger. Any talk about Anna was just as bad as if it was about her.

"Let's just avoid Carla as much as possible." Marina sighed.

Giorgio gave her a crooked smile. "Like trying to avoid the stones on the street."

*   *   *

The week before Holy Week was a busy time in every household. The blessing of the homes by Don Antonio was underway. The homes were carefully cleaned, not only for spring renewal, but for the renewal of the soul as well. This was the time that Don Antonio met on a more personal level with his flock.

Marina and Giorgio welcomed Don Antonio in to

receive the first blessing of their home. When the prayers had been recited, he sat down to relax a moment, having only a few homes left to visit.

"This home is a little nest." Don Antonio gazed with admiration around the kitchen.

Marina warmed at the compliment. She had done her best to have everything looking as fresh as possible. "We have to thank his father." She nodded towards Giorgio. "We wouldn't be here without him."

"He bought a house, but both of you have made it a *home.*"

"We hope that it won't be two of us for long," Giorgio said. "We want to have a baby so much."

"Sometimes God's ways are mysterious." Don Antonio nodded and smiled. "Is there anything that you need to talk about?"

"For the moment, no, but if the need should arise, we will. We haven't forgotten how you helped us through our trial when we lost our baby." Giorgio glanced at Marina.

"Especially me," Marina said softly.

Don Antonio nodded. "Well, I'd better go. This chair is getting too comfortable for me."

Marina gave him a couple of eggs as a gesture of appreciation for his visit. "It's not much."

"It may not seem like much to you, but for me, each one of them is a dinner. Thank you."

When Don Antonio left, Giorgio turned to Marina. "Our home is blessed. May we always live in peace."

*   *   *

The most sacred time of the year, Holy Week, brought the *Triduum,* the three days commemorating the last hours of the Lord before His crucifixion, and culminating with the celebration of His resurrection.

From the crenelated tower, the bells rang out the glory of Easter.

Walking hand in hand, Marina and Giorgio paused a moment at the top of the church steps. The fields were dotted with fruit trees just beginning to bloom. Wildflowers grew alongside the paths. Directly below, the Fegana River tumbled over rocks.

Marina's gaze fell on the Serchio River Valley to the southwest. "Such a view. Who could believe what is happening down there?" she asked softly, her dark hair barely visible through her white lace veil.

Giorgio nodded soberly. "We haven't seen anything yet. The Allies have landed in Anzio, in the south. The coming months are going to be brutal for sure."

Marina dreaded the thought. She shook herself. She wasn't going to allow dire thoughts to ruin the most beautiful and sacred day of the year.

"Ehi, wait for me!"

Marina turned to Lisa as she hurried up the steps, *"Buona Pasqua!"* she gasped, out of breath.

"Happy Easter to you." Marina kissed her.

Lisa glanced down to Marco who was climbing up after her alongside Valentina and Bruno. "We've set a tentative wedding date. We have to talk with Don Antonio, but there shouldn't be any problem. We want to announce it at *pranzo,* with everyone present."

"How wonderful," Marina exclaimed.

Giorgio grinned. "Marco is one brother-in-law that I'm not going to be cheated out of if I can help it."

*   *   *

This was going to be a good day, Marina thought to herself when later she walked down the street, carrying the almond torte she had baked. Today, the Easter meal would be at her family's home.

Savory aromas of broth, bread baking, and roasting chicken, helped her to forget the cares and worries of the war for one day. She turned at what sounded like footsteps behind her, but saw no one.

The sentinels were about their usual routine. Marina almost felt sorry for them. They only knew orders and nothing else. There had to have been Easters, and Christmases for them, too, before the war.

Marina fell immediately in step once in her family's kitchen. She donned her favorite apron, which was a little worn but still her favorite.

"How nice it is to have all of us here together. If we could have Gianni, it would be a perfect day," Albina said.

"God is good. We know he's alive." Alda placed her low rimmed copper baking pan with the rice torte that she had baked on the kitchen table.

Pressing lightly with her finger, Albina tasted the rice topping.

"Is that proper?" Alda stared, shocked.

"It was too tempting, Mama."

"Thank you, but *don't* do that again."

Alda smiled and shook her head when Albina kissed her on the cheek.

The meal was simple but good, and everyone was in good spirits, including Daniela.

Marina was happy that *Nonna* Nelsa was as witty and spry as ever. She noticed a sparkle in her mother's eyes, and didn't doubt for a moment that it had to do with Gianni.

When everyone had eaten, and the last of the serving trays had been taken away, Lisa raised her eyes to Marco. "I think it's time to tell them," she whispered.

He stood up. "Lisa and I have… something to announce." He smiled at her and continued. "We still have to meet with Don Antonio, but we plan to marry in early June."

"Bravi!" Giorgio cheered above the clapping of hands, and echoes of good wishes.

Alda rose, and made her way to Lisa, who stood up to hug her.

"I'll never be that far away, Mama," Lisa assured her

with a big smile.

"I just want you to be happy."

"Now is the time for the tortes." Marina swallowed a lump in her throat and disappeared into the kitchen.

"And, the wine." Giorgio followed her. "Are you alright?"

"Yes. I'm fine." She turned to a burst of laughter. "What a difference when we announced our marriage."

"Do we love each other any less than they do?" Giorgio asked.

Sitting in church later for Vespers, Marina found it difficult to listen to the ageless Psalms being sung. Her mind wandered to Gianni. He would have joined Giorgio in cheering Lisa and Marco, but not without a little sadness. Only Daniela and Albina would be left to tease, but Daniela knew how to put up a good fight, which he had discovered once, to his dismay. She thought back to that moment when she saw him in the vineyard. Wherever he was, she fervently prayed that he was safe.

CHAPTER FOURTEEN

Easter Monday, *Lunedi dell'Angelo,* or *Pasquetta,* was dedicated to the Angel who announced the Resurrection. In early afternoon, if the weather permitted, villagers celebrated the day with a *merenda,* a picnic, usually at a shrine farther down the hill. Here, they shared food, and there were games for everyone. Afterwards, Don Antonio would gather his flock inside the small church.

Marina and Giorgio decided to forego the usual gathering and treated Anna and the children to a more intimate one, in a clearing in the chestnut grove that belonged to Amelia.

Maddalena was full of questions as they walked the path to the grove. Little Giorgio's eyes were wide as he looked around him. Giorgio carried him, pointing out a bird or a flower that peeked up from the earth.

When they reached the clearing, Giorgio walked around surveying the area while Marina and Anna spread two tablecloths on the ground. Warm sunshine shone down on them as they sat down to talk a while.

"Mama, I'm hungry." Maddalena exclaimed.

"Let's eat then," Giorgio said and reached for the basket.

"I'd better tend to my little man," Anna smiled when little Giorgio whimpered. She gathered him in her arms and walked over to the edge of the grove to nurse him. "Marina, look at these daffodils."

Marina got up and walked over to Anna, ignoring her twinge of jealousy at how she contentedly nursed her baby boy. "Who on earth tends these flowers?" She knelt down and gently touched a full, yellow bloom.

When Anna finished nursing, she held little Giorgio to her shoulders, gently patting him on the back. Anna apologized for him when he responded with a loud burp.

Marina laughed. "I think he's satisfied."

She and Anna joined Giorgio and Maddalena, who were already eating. They exchanged memories of happy times with Stefano and Gianni, especially Giorgio. "What a happy bunch we were." His eyes filled.

Maddalena played with her little doll for most of the afternoon while Marina walked around with little Giorgio in her arms. He squealed with delight at a butterfly that zigzagged around him or when, held by Marina to toddle on his feet, he touched a flower.

Anna and Giorgio sat on the blankets. Anna was concerned for her future. "I have to see if I can find work in the statuette factory in the valley. I can't keep the land going without help, and you know that my family and Stefano's aren't on the best of terms. Hopefully, Mama or my sister can watch the children."

Giorgio looked at her, pensive. "I can't do very much, but I'll try to keep the vines tended to for you."

"No." Anna smiled. "You have your vineyard, you're helping Marina's family, plus you have your own work."

"I have room to stretch a little," Giorgio declared and mimicked an accordion's expansion.

Anna giggled and her gaze fell on Maddalena who had laid down on the blanket, her eyes heavy. "I think I'd better go." Anna gently placed her hand on her little girl's head.

Giorgio rose and walked over to Marina. "We'd better go home. Maddalena is sleepy."

"Little Giorgio is falling asleep, too." Marina looked tenderly at the little boy who rested his head against her shoulder.

They reached Anna's home, and when the children were tucked into bed, she extended her hands to Marina and Giorgio. "I can't thank you enough for this day."

"We enjoyed it," Giorgio said.

Marina walked hand in hand up the street with Giorgio. The sun's rays played with the shadows between the homes. She was reluctant to have the day end and looked up at Giorgio, whose expression was melancholy.

When they entered the *soggiorno,* Giorgio trudged into the kitchen.

Marina followed him quietly. Something was amiss.

When he stood looking out the kitchen window, Marina

wrapped her arms around his slender body, pressing her head against his back. "Something's bothering you," she said softly.

He turned around. "I loved seeing little Giorgio in your arms."

Marina nestled in his embrace. "I loved holding him and hearing him laugh." She lifted her face to his. There was the dreamy look again. "What are you thinking?"

Instead of answering her, he smiled wistfully and held her close to him.

Marina wasn't fooled by his embrace.

*   *   *

The harshness of winter ceded to warmer days. The vineyards and the fields came to life. Pruning the vines, clearing debris, tending to the barley that had sprouted and to the first vegetables, which had been sown during Holy Week, were now the everyday tasks.

Marina enjoyed this time outdoors when she could help her family in the vineyard more than ever, because Gianni had met her there. The stable was no longer just a shelter for the rabbits, but a haven where they had reconnected. There was also another reason to keep her mind occupied.

Giorgio was busy in his vineyard, working alone. Marina noticed a subtle change in him. She attributed this to worry over his mother. Lately, Amelia had been feeling tired, and her appetite, which had always been good, had dwindled. Even this, though, wasn't really a reason. She had to be truthful. Since the picnic, something had changed.

"I hope that Amelia will listen to you."

Alda broke into Marina's thoughts. "Yes… yes, I hope so. I don't like to see her like this."

She and Giorgio had agreed to meet at Amelia's home later that morning to convince her to go and see Marco.

Marina curbed her irritation when she arrived at Amelia's and Giorgio barely greeted her.

Amelia was rinsing out a stockpot and turned to her. "He wants me to go to see Marco. I'll be fine when the weather warms up." She shrugged her shoulders. "I've been inside for too long."

"Mama, it's for your own good," Giorgio pleaded.

"Let's wait a bit and see what happens."

"*Wait* a bit? You're not eating. So help me, you're going, even if I have to carry you," Giorgio fumed.

Amelia glared at him. *"Provaci!"*

"Try it? You better believe that I will." Giorgio slammed a chair against the table.

Marina was astonished at his tone of voice and manner. Even if his mother was stubborn, he could be a little nicer. She took Amelia's damp hands in hers. "Amelia, we love you. Let us help you. Just think how happy you'll be when you can do your chores without feeling tired and enjoy your meals again. Won't you do it for me?" Marina caressed her face.

"Oh, all right," Amelia ceded. "Only, because of you. But as far as *he's* concerned," she glared at Giorgio, "I'll deal with him later. Carry *me*, will you?"

"I'll talk to Marco." Giorgio turned on his heel and went to the door.

Amelia stared at him, and back at Marina. "I'm not the only one who needs a doctor," she muttered.

Marina didn't answer.

*　　　　　*　　　　　*

Marina and Giorgio accompanied Amelia to Marco's later that day. When the exam was finished and Marina walked out to the waiting area with Amelia, Giorgio rose and voiced his concern. Marco reassured him that he didn't think it was serious. "We have to consider the things that happened last year that were traumatic for her. She was stoic, but now, I believe she's feeling the effects. Her heartbeat is slow, which is what is probably causing her fatigue. Nevertheless, a specialist won't hurt."

"If I had died that day…"

Marco placed his hands on Giorgio's shoulders. "Let's not go there."

On a drizzly late April morning, Marina and Giorgio took Amelia to the heart specialist in Lucca that Marco had referred her to.

The appointment went better than expected. Amelia's heartbeat was strong, even if slow. A medication was prescribed to help bring her heartbeat to normal, as well as something to help perk up her appetite. In a month, she was to return for a follow-up.

"All in all, Amelia, you're alright." Marina placed her arm around her thin shoulders when they left the office.

"It makes me mad that I can't get everything done that I want. I'm not *that* old!"

Good, Marina thought. She still had fight in her. "A lot has happened, and sometimes things get the better of us. You do what you can and that will be fine."

Giorgio walked ahead of them.

Amelia stopped. She looked squarely at Marina. "What's happened? Something is bothering him. I don't like fish, and I smell a bad one."

Marina sighed at her mother-in-law's words. She had no answer to give her. "I don't know. But this isn't the moment to talk about it. Now, we're going to get you home, and I'm going to prepare something nutritious for you."

When Marina and Giorgio left Amelia later that day, the sun was out. She raised her head at the drone of Allied fighter planes flying north. Again, Giorgio walked ahead, alone. A sense of dread overcame her, and it wasn't just because of the fighters overhead.

*   *   *

Marina visited Amelia again the next morning. She

turned the key in the door, and stared surprised at the cups, saucers, a tureen, various odds and ends, and utensils on the table. Amelia stood on a chair in front of the *credenza*. She let the decorative strip of yellowed white paper that formed a border across the top shelf fall to the floor.

"Amelia! You shouldn't be up there," Marina protested and held her by the waist. "Get down and I'll do that."

"I knew I couldn't get away with it." Amelia rolled her eyes and got down. "I haven't done this in a long time."

"I'll help you. Have you taken your medication?"

"Yes. What's that son of mine doing this morning?" Amelia asked, frowning at a filmy wineglass.

"I..I don't know really," Marina said lamely.

"You don't know?" Amelia pulled two chairs away from the table. "We have to talk. I want to know what's wrong."

Marina sank down on a chair. "That's just the problem. I don't know what's wrong. I keep asking him, and he keeps saying that everything is alright. First, it was me over the baby. I'm handling that better now. Now, it's him. How do you get a man to talk when he won't?"

"Corner him and threaten not to cook anymore. That should get him talking."

Marina couldn't help laughing.

"Seriously, talk to Marco. Something has to be wrong," Amelia urged.

"I already thought about that. Come," Marina rose. "Let me help you here."

Since she didn't know where Giorgio had gone or when he would be home, Marina helped Amelia to redo the *credenza* with odds and ends of clean paper. She cut two decorative borders from white paper for the shelves. When they had put everything back in place, she closed the polished glass doors.

"Stay for something to eat?" Amelia asked.

"I'd better go. I have to take the thread I plied to the loom, and I'm not comfortable about being out without Giorgio knowing anything."

Amelia wrinkled her nose. "Did he bother to tell *you* anything?"

Marina hugged her mother-in-law and left. If things didn't change, she might shrug her shoulders from now on.

*   *   *

May brought the countryside to life. Lush foliage quivered in the breezes, especially on the vines, where tiny grapes were visible. Bees buzzed around the wildflowers in bloom. Marina and Giorgio headed out to his vineyard one afternoon. This time he walked along by her side. She stopped short and turned to face him. "Giorgio, are you alright?"

Before he could answer, a roar reverberated farther down the valley.

"What was that?" Marina gasped, startled. She wondered if it was in Diecimo.

Giorgio shaded his eyes with his hands, and peered into the distance. He grinned from ear to ear. "I think the Germans have gotten an unwelcome visit from the Allies."

Marina watched, breathless, as fighter planes swooped over the mountains in the distance, and disappeared into the horizon. "Could they have killed the Germans?"

"If they were rigging a bridge, that's a certainty."

For a moment, they stood quiet. Marina repeated her question. "Are you alright?"

"Yes, why?"

"Something isn't right, Giorgio. Lately, you're not you. If there's a problem, I want to know. I...I have to know."

"Is it possible that you always have to think in terms of bad?" he asked, peeved.

Marina rolled her eyes, irritated. She decided against going with him to the vineyard, turned on her heel, and left him alone on the path.

*   *   *

The weather was unpredictable, but between sunshine and showers, preparations for Lisa's wedding went ahead. It was going to be a simple wedding followed by a small, intimate reception with family and close friends. Lisa wanted to have it, as Marina had, in her unfinished home.

Everyone helped to clear cobwebs, and wash windows. On her hands and knees, Lisa scrubbed away dirt and grime from the old terra cotta kitchen floor with Marina and Daniela at her side. Albina finished the scarves for the dresser and the nightstands and placed them folded on the bed upstairs. Giorgio replaced windowpanes that threatened to fall out at any time and a wobbly kitchen table soon had a new leg.

A lock of hair danced on her forehead as Lisa eased herself from the floor to a chair. "That's it, people. What's done is done." She winced and rubbed her sore knees.

Daniela looked around the kitchen. "I think we did a good job."

Marina stood at the kitchen window that looked across to the store, a step away. "Lucky you. Marco's office is up the street and the food is next door."

Lisa smiled wistfully. "I'll miss shopping with you. You haven't been married a year, and now I'm getting married."

Daniela wrinkled her nose as she held up a filthy floor rag by a corner. "This is of no use anymore."

"Toss it." Lisa gestured.

"I think that we can go home now. Anything left to do can wait until tomorrow." Alda gathered buckets and brooms.

"Thank you, all of you. Marina, would you stay a moment longer?" Lisa lowered her voice. "I need to talk to you, if you don't mind."

"I'm going home, Marina," Giorgio said.

Marina pursed her lips as she stared after him. "I'll be there in a little while." When they were alone, she sat down with Lisa. "What is it?"

"It's not about me. It's… it's about Daniela."

Marina straightened up, every fiber in her body alert. "What's wrong?"

"I don't know. I was going to the basement a few days ago when I saw her trying to converse with the soldier. They were laughing softly. I wanted to see what was going to happen, and lingered at the kitchen door. They… they entered the old empty shed that faces the junction. A few minutes went by. I was growing concerned, but then they came out. I stepped back and… and saw Daniela button… button her blouse."

Marina would have been happy if her heart had stopped beating. "Lisa, are you… you sure that you saw what you saw?"

"Would I be making this up?"

"Of course not." Marina sat back against the chair. Fury mounted in her. "Has she gone mad?"

"What are we going to do?"

"I have to talk to her immediately. Thank you for telling me this." She squeezed her hands.

"I hope I did the right thing."

"You did."

"Marina," Lisa's eyes filled. "I'm… I'm afraid for her."

"So am I."

This news was crushing. Marina hurried out the door and nearly bumped into Carla in front of the food shop. In her arms were two small bags and a small loaf of bread.

Not wanting to betray the turmoil inside of her, Marina managed a smile and asked how she was doing.

"I'm fine. What's happening with you?"

"We're preparing for Lisa's wedding, so that's keeping us busy."

A sly smile appeared on Carla's face. "Isn't it nice to do things without any rush?"

Marina clenched her hands so hard that her nails dug into her palms. "Goodbye." Carla's words made her walk all the faster to her home. To her relief, Daniela was alone in the kitchen, still in her dirty clothes.

"Can we talk?" Marina asked, without preambles.

Apprehension showed on Daniela's face. "Yes... of course. Let's sit down."

"What's happening, Daniela?"

"Nothing. Why?"

"Is there anything that you want to talk about?"

"No."

Marina's resolve to tread gently, dissipated when Daniela clenched her hands. "Well, then, I'm going to talk to you. Leave the soldier alone."

"I don't know what you're talking about."

Marina detected an almost defiant tone in her sister's voice. "You know what I'm talking about, and I know what you did."

Daniela frowned. "How do you know anything of what I've done, if I did anything?"

Marina didn't want to involve Lisa. "Someone saw you,

and this person was concerned and told me. You're treading on thin ice, and I don't want to see it crack under your feet. I also don't want to see people getting hurt. You don't know how his commander will react to this. It's dangerous."

Daniela's eyes filled. "I've heard of other women falling in love with the enemy. Heinrich is good. He… he doesn't like being a soldier."

"I'm not saying that he isn't good, but this isn't love. If you really care about each other, you will respect your boundaries, and time will prove it."

"I hate war," Daniela blurted out.

"What else is new? We all do."

"He must have parents, a brother, a sister. He wants to be free. He… managed to tell me that… that he and… and another soldier want to desert."

Marina gasped. "Don't you *dare* do anything to help them." She clutched Daniela's arms in fear.

Daniela shook her head. "I won't, but I won't hate him just because he's German."

"No one is talking about hating, although there's plenty of reason to with what is happening around us. Please, Daniela, please!"

Daniela nodded as a tear trickled down her cheek.

"I'm going home now. But, I trust you to do what is right." Marina cupped her face. "Be a good girl, and remember that I love you."

"I love you, too," she whispered.

At the door, Marina heard rapid footsteps, but no one except the soldier, Heinrich, was outside. He looked past her with a quizzical expression on his face. When he turned and his eyes met hers, he lowered his head.

Marina hurried home. She felt tired and out of sorts. The day had been long. At the bottom of the garden steps, the pot of freshly sprouted mint lay on its side. Pursing her lips, she descended the steps to right it. She noticed that the workshop door was open. Maybe Giorgio was still working. She called out in what she hoped was a cheerful voice. *"Amore mio,* isn't it time to come up?"

There was no answer. She stepped inside, but he wasn't there. It was odd that he hadn't closed the door when he finished for the day. The workshop was untidy which didn't surprise her. They had been too busy with outside chores. Tomorrow she would have to help him tidy up. She picked up his work jacket that lay across the table, and shook the dust from it. She put her hand into the pockets to turn them inside out, and felt an object, and a piece of paper. She removed them, and froze. It was a black, hair comb. In neat print, she read: *All I can do is to give you this.*

*   *   *

Marina sat at the kitchen table, her mind a whirlwind of if's and but's. That Giorgio would betray her was unthinkable, and for Anna to betray their friendship was unthinkable, too. Yet, the evidence proved differently. Anna couldn't remember where she lost the comb. They could have met in the vineyard. He was alone there. They also could have met in the workshop, but Giorgio wouldn't have been so careless as to leave his jacket lying around with the comb and note tucked in a pocket!

The door opened, and Giorgio walked into the kitchen, wiping perspiration from his forehead. "It's warm out today. Is there any water for freshening up?"

"Yes." She rose and poured warm water into the pitcher on the counter.

"*Ehi,* you're prettier when you smile, you know." He placed his arm around her.

Marina fought the urge to accuse him. She would bide her time.

"What's happened? Tell me!" He turned her towards him and held her by the shoulders.

The comb was foremost now in her worries, but she hadn't forgotten about Daniela. "It's Daniela."

"What's wrong with her?"

She told him what was happening.

Giorgio drew a deep breath, his expression concerned. "You have to talk to her."

"I did. I hope it had some effect."

"Everything will work out." Giorgio held her in his arms and caressed her hair.

Giorgio couldn't possibly hold her in his arms and betray her at the same time. She didn't want to believe that.

That night, she lay wide-eyed in the dark. Giorgio had turned on his side. They talked little, and the intimate moments had dwindled.

Marina dared not think of the future.

CHAPTER FIFTEEN

In the first week of June, Lisa was busy with the final touches to her new home. Marina crossed the *piazza* where a few pre-school children played hide and seek under the watchful eyes of their mothers. She remembered how many times she had sought out Giorgio in the game.

Dark rain clouds floated in the sky.

When she arrived at Lisa's to help her with a few tasks, she saw that what had once been a home to spiders and mice was now a home in the true sense of the word. On a kitchen wall hung the plate rack filled with plates, cups and saucers, some of them from her *nonna*. The stone sink under the kitchen window had undergone a thorough scrubbing. From here, Lisa could see the other end of the village to her right and the woods with the public wash area, directly in front.

"You know, now when you have to go to the *pozzo* to launder something, I can see you." Lisa smiled.

A moment went by before she heard Lisa talking to her. "I'm sorry. What did you say?"

"I said that now when you go to launder something, I can see you."

"That you can." Marina smiled at her sister, whose eyes were luminous.

The sunny morning disappeared as the clouds had gathered to release a fine drizzle. Marina found a certain beauty in the wisps of clouds that floated around the hillock.

She helped Lisa to give another scrubbing to the floor of the small dining room.

"If this isn't clean now, it will never be." Lisa looked with approval at the red terra cotta tile.

Marina placed the sopping wet, dirty rags in a metal bucket.

"I… I can still turn to you for that advice that we once talked about, can't I"

"Of course you can."

"What's wrong? You haven't been yourself lately. Tell me." Lisa took Marina's hands in hers.

Marina didn't have the heart to tell her sister. She didn't want to burden her with her problem with Giorgio. It would spoil everything for her. "I… I think of Gianni a lot." It wasn't a total lie.

Lisa's eyes filled. "When he comes home, we'll have so much to make up for… birthdays, Christmases."

Marina looked out the window again. The drizzle had turned to rain. "I'd better go and visit Mama." Marina hugged Lisa tightly and left, before her sister could see the tears that welled in her eyes.

*   *   *

A steady rain was falling when she arrived at her family's home. She immersed herself in the tasks at hand, one of them being tiding up the basement. Working alongside her mother, she told her mother about the children.

"At least they don't see the horrors of the war here." Alda sighed.

"Giorgio says that the Allies are getting closer every day, and the Germans fear that they are losing."

Germany was desperately trying to halt the advance of the Allies in Tuscany. They worked to fortify the lines of defense along the Apuan Alps that overlooked the marble quarries of Carrara on the coast to the west, as well as along the Apennines, which were bordered by Tuscany and Emilia Romagna to the north. Desperate to use to the maximum the Gothic Line, they formed a ring of fire around the partisan lines and indiscriminately and brutally attacked the people.

Marina gathered up pieces of bark and put them into a gunnysack. They would come in handy as kindling for the fireplace.

"We're finished here." Alda straightened up and shook the dust from her apron.

They went upstairs and enjoyed a slice of *castagnaccio* that Albina had baked the day before.

The door burst open, and Giorgio rushed in. His face

shone with joy. "Rome… has… has been liberated."

Albina clapped her hands.

"Santo Cielo!" Alda exclaimed.

"Italy will be free in no time. Today is June 4th. I have to mark it down." Giorgio fumbled for the pencil that he always kept in his pants pocket.

His happiness gave Marina one more reason to worry. He had narrowly escaped death once. The followers of Mussolini and his ideals wouldn't give up the fight so easily.

*   *   *

Giorgio and Marina acted as witnesses for Lisa and Marco's wedding the week after Rome had been liberated.

If for nothing else, Marina was grateful for the lovely morning after the unpredictable weather of the past week. Marco was handsomely dressed in a dark blue suit. Lisa wore a long sleeved pink dress with a matching jacket that hugged her slim body. On her head, she wore a white hat adorned with a rosette, and wore white pumps.

After the wedding Mass, while the bells rang for the happy occasion, a procession of family and close friends made their way from the church to Lisa's new home down the street.

Albina and Daniela helped to arrange the almond and rice tortes, bottles of liqueurs, and pots of hot chocolate on the dining room table. Marina had lent her the same white, rose patterned tablecloth that she had used for her reception.

Don Antonio looked with appreciation at the collection of books of geography and works of renowned authors that Marco was showing him.

Bruno and Valentina chatted amiably with friends and family.

Marina leaned her head towards Giorgio. "Isn't this lovely?"

"Yes it is," Giorgio sighed and moved towards the guests.

Marina's face flamed with irritation and she closed her eyes a moment to compose herself. When she opened them, her gaze met Lisa's puzzled look.

The reception slowly wound down in late afternoon. Giorgio left for home with the last guests while Marina remained behind to help tidy up. She prayed that Lisa wouldn't ask any questions. The last thing she wanted was for her family to suspect that something was wrong.

"Thank you so much." Lisa hugged each member of her family. "Mama, the biggest hug is for you."

Alda held Lisa tightly. "Big or small, I'll always want your hug."

When Marina left, she wished that she could go any-where but home. What had happened between her and Giorgio and when it *had* happened she didn't know, but she couldn't continue like this.

Giorgio sat in front of the fireplace. His shirt was

unbuttoned at the collar and his tie hung loosely. His face wasn't that of the man that Marina knew. She stood behind him, trying to find the words to discover something, anything. Whether he sensed her presence or not, she didn't know, but he turned around.

Giorgio spoke in a low voice. "We… we have to talk."

Marina inhaled deeply. Good or bad, the truth had to come out. She would be calm, but firm. "Yes, we'd better. What's happening with you, Giorgio?"

"I'd rather die than admit it."

Marina dragged a chair to the plate rack, kicked off her pumps, lifted up her skirt, and stepped onto the chair. She reached for a little box, got down, and smacked it on the table. "Are you admitting to this? Are you? I… I… want the truth, Giorgio. Is this why you're no longer you? Open it."

Giorgio slowly reached for it. When he opened it, he gasped. "Whose comb is this? *Che diavolo?*"

"Maybe the devil is in this, but I want an answer, now!"

"Where… where did you get this?"

Marina rolled her eyes. "Anna lost her hair comb. I was shaking the dust from your work jacket, and turned the pockets inside out. Read the note."

Giorgio hastily read the note, and slowly raised his eyes at Marina. "Oh no," he shook his head. "You… don't think that… *ahi*, Marina!"

"What *am* I to think?" Marina's resolve to be calm flew out of the window. "You've changed. Today, you… you practically cast me off at the reception. You're… you're in a world of your own. What am I supposed to think?"

Giorgio's face grew dark. "I swear on the grave of our baby that… that I never betrayed you, and… and that Anna never betrayed you, either. Even… even if I did, do you think me so stupid as to leave… this lying around for you to find it?" Giorgio slammed the comb on the table. "Someone put it there for you to find."

Marina nodded. He was right, he would never have been that careless. "Then what's wrong, Giorgio? Once, and for all, tell me!"

Giorgio's eyes welled with tears. His voice was above a whisper. "That day at the picnic, your face was like a sunbeam with little Giorgio in your arms. Since then, I've… I've been crippled by the doubt that maybe I'm… I'm to blame for our not having a baby yet. I… I know how much you want one. Maybe something's wrong with me. I love you so much. but…" his voice broke, "but I don't have the heart to… to show it anymore."

Marina stared, speechless. She'd never dreamed… Whatever hurt she felt crumpled at her feet. "Oh, Giorgio, no! I… saw that… you weren't the same, and… then… then I found the comb…" She took a step over to him and cupped his face. "Do you think I would love you any the less for this reason? Why didn't you tell me your fears? Why?"

"Why didn't you tell me yours when you found the comb?" He shot back in irritation and hurt.

Marina slowly withdrew her hands. "I've ruined my marriage…"she mumbled. "I… I…"

Giorgio gathered her in his arms before she said anything more. His fingers locked into her hair, his cheek, against hers, was damp with tears. "No… no. We were both wrong."

Marina cupped his face again. "I feel so stupid for not telling you about the comb when I found it. I… I hurt you and… and I'm so sorry." Hot tears of embarrassment and relief ran down her face.

"I should have told you my fears. Now I see that I was an *idiota.*"

Marina giggled. "I want to grow old with this idiot."

For a long moment, they clung to each other and then Giorgio kissed her. "It's getting dark outside. Let's close the shutters before we light the oil lamp."

Marina felt drained from the emotion of the moment. "If you don't mind, I'm going to change and go to bed."

"All alone?" Giorgio asked casually.

Marina smiled mischievously, took hold of his tie, and began to walk away, gently pulling him towards her. "Not if I can help it."

*   *   *

Marina and Giorgio were in no hurry to get up the next morning. They hadn't realized until now the toll that the past few weeks had taken on them. They rediscovered the beauty of their love as they promised to each other to never hold back anything that could affect their happiness as husband and wife.

"Whoever did this, spied upon me and took advantage of a few minutes of absence." Giorgio reflected. "This person was determined to ruin our marriage."

"Anna must never know about this. Let's let her believe that she lost the comb."

"I agree. You know what I was thinking, *carissima*?"

"What?" Marina smiled inwardly as she turned in his arms. Never had that endearment sounded so good.

"Lisa and Marco are enjoying their honeymoon at home. Why don't we enjoy a couple of days to ourselves? I'll see that Pallino has enough fodder, and the workshop can stay closed for a few days. Let's just be selfish." Giorgio kissed her temple.

Marina slid her arm over his body. "I'd like that very much."

*   *   *

"I can't believe what has happened between you two." Amelia finished peeling a potato and dropped it into boiling water.

Marina had explained to her what had happened. There had been no use hiding it because Amelia had noticed the change in Giorgio as well.

"I could give him a good spanking for not confiding in

you. And that comb…"

"We don't want Anna to know anything. This would kill her."

Amelia's expression was serious. "May God take me now, if I say anything. Has Giorgio calmed down over the liberation?"

Marina laughed. "He still has moments of euphoria." She watched with pleasure as Amelia bustled about the kitchen, almost herself again thanks to the medication.

"I don't like what's happening around us. These accursed SS are barbarous."

"Giorgio has called this a summer of horror." Marina shuddered.

On June 17th, the supreme commander of the German troops in Italy had ordered that all means available be used to quench any support for the Resistance. The harshest methods were to be used. Commanders, who went beyond what was considered "normal" would be protected. Now, more than ever, she feared for Gianni. In a way, he had been right when he said that he would rather be shot than end up in "a hellish place". Terrible as it was, she would rather know him dead than that he was in the hands of the SS.

In those areas that extended to the coast, the Nazi Fascists had caused nearly two-thousand deaths. Around Lucca, the SS had their 16th Division. Many buildings had been converted for use in the repression, and an elementary school was now a prison and a horror chamber.

There was also the *rastrellamento* to deal with. It hadn't happened in the village yet, but many poor souls had been rounded up in other towns and villages and sent to labor camps or concentration camps.

Marina stayed a little longer to help Amelia with a few tasks and then went home. She heard Giorgio sawing in the workshop. She descended the steps and paused on the doorstep. He had his back to her. He straightened up a moment and then continued working, unaware of her presence. She felt a tingle of happiness because ever since they'd opened up about their fears, he'd taken up his craft with renewed enthusiasm.

Giorgio finished and wiped perspiration from his forehead with his sleeve.

Marina stepped inside. "*Ehi,* how are we doing?" She smiled and placed a hand on his shoulder.

Giorgio kissed her, stretched out his overworked arm, and winced. "That piece was a tough one."

"Take a little break."

"I might just do that."

"Marina! Giorgio!"

"It's Daniela. We're down here," she called from the door.

Daniela hurried down the steps and brought her hand to her chest. "Giorgio, you... you have to run... run away!"

Giorgio grabbed her shoulders. "What are you talking about?"

Daniela gasped. "I... Heinrich... told me that there's

going to be a *rastrellamento* this week. Please," she placed her hands on his shoulders. "Find somewhere to hide!"

"Daniela, what did you do?" Marina voiced the ugly suspicion that came to her mind.

"I swear that I didn't do anything." Daniela's eyes pleaded. "He stopped me when I came back with water. He told me on his own. Marina, I didn't do anything, believe me."

"I can flee to the next village. I'll find a stable, something along the way where I can hide." Giorgio paced back and forth.

"You're not going anywhere. You have typhoid fever."

They whirled around at Marco's voice.

"Let's go upstairs, quickly," Marco said.

Dumbfounded, Marina, Giorgio, and Daniela followed him upstairs.

Marco proceeded to tack the notice on the front door of their home. "The only way to spare you was to invent typhoid fever. Marina, you'd better play along with this, too, just to make it more realistic."

"How did you find out about the *rastrellamento*?" Daniela asked.

"After you left, Lisa visited your mother. She hurried to the office and told me."

"How long will this charade last?" Giorgio asked.

"The duration of the disease is usually three weeks."

Marina shook with tension. "Will… will it work?"

"The Germans shy away from contracting any disease.

They'll stay away from here. I just wish to heaven that I could spare every able-bodied man in the village." Marco shook his head sadly.

"You can only do so much." Giorgio rubbed his hands together. "I would love to see their faces when they find out that we've outsmarted them."

"So would I. With the backup of an Allied soldier," Marco said.

Daniela reassured Marina that she would tell the family and Amelia what was happening.

After Marco and Daniela had left, Marina brought her hands to her face. Here was a new crisis to deal with. Giorgio ran a hand through his hair. "Well, we had a couple of days to ourselves." He smiled grimly. "Now we have three weeks."

CHAPTER SIXTEEN

Giorgio stood at the open, kitchen window and breathed deeply of the fresh air of early morning. "How much longer is this going to continue? It's been almost three weeks. What's happening out there?"

"Who knows? Marco hasn't visited for a few days. He's our only means of communicating with anyone." Marina pursed her lips. She was used to being in and out of the house, busy with her chores. The rays of the sun that rose over the mountains across from them illuminated the kitchen. She wrapped her arm around Giorgio's waist, grateful that they could enjoy these moments as much as possible. She longed for the days that they could turn on the light when the evening shadows fell, but now all of that had changed. The power plant was no longer in use. Now, for their safety, they had to close the shutters before lighting the hurricane lamp. The Allied bombers that flew overhead at night could mistake any hint of light for German activity. At the familiar knock on the door, she quickly opened it to Marco. "Thank goodness. What's happening out there?"

"The *rastrellamento* has been called off. Apparently,

more than one person has been infected…" Marco smiled slyly.

Giorgio burst out laughing. "We did it!"

Marco placed a small bag of rice on the table, as well as a few tomatoes.

"What is Daniela doing?" Marina felt guilty for thinking the worst of her sister in regard to Heinrich.

"She told me to tell you that she's fine. The family is well. Lisa has been visiting them almost every day. Amelia is taking good care of Pallino. Did I leave anything out?" Marco asked, all in one breath. "To play it safe, give yourselves another week or so to 'recover.'"

"Another week?" Giorgio protested. "What am I going to do? Being sick is one thing, playing sick is another."

"Learn how to cook." Marco laughed.

Marina brought her hand to her forehead in dismay at the suggestion. Giorgio was hopeless in the kitchen.

"You two figure it out," Marco waved his hand. "I'm going home."

"Marco," Marina kissed him on the cheek, "thank you."

"You're more than a brother-in-law. You're a friend." Giorgio hugged him.

After Marco left, Giorgio looked glumly at Marina. "Another week?"

Marina looked at him keenly. "Am I too much to put up with?"

"No." Giorgio shook his head vigorously and then smiled. "You know better than that."

"We'll be fine." Marina reassured him. "Before you know it, everything will be back to normal."

"You're happy, and I'm happy." Giorgio brushed away a lock from her forehead.

"I want us to be happy together."

*   *   *

Marina sat outside on her family's balcony in early afternoon. July had arrived with its summer beauty, even if undecided about whether to settle on sunshine or rain. The sparrows chirped in the branches of the cherry tree, and the rambling rose once again bore its clusters of red blooms. As she drank in the peaceful setting, Marina couldn't help but recall what had happened a year ago when she had sat here with her sisters. Mussolini had been arrested. She brushed away this thought and focused on something else, something beautiful. There had been a change in her body, but she didn't want to say anything yet, until she knew for sure.

Alda sat down next to her and fanned herself with her handkerchief. "I'm so relieved that we have been spared the *rastrellamento*. But I am worried about Marco. He risked a lot in doing what he did."

"I pray that the Germans don't find out the truth."

A roar echoed from the other side of the mountains that faced them.

"The Allies must have fired upon the German trucks

that are heading north." Marina turned to Giorgio, who came to the balcony. He was beaming. "Giorgio?"

"The Partisans have been more active in the valley. The Allies have reached Pistoia and are in a position to penetrate the Gothic line." He rubbed his hands together in satisfaction. "The Germans are really worried, and will do anything to keep the Allies from doing so." His enthusiasm slowly waned. "There is talk about a *sfollamento* of Diecimo and the entire valley, though."

"Why do they want to evacuate the people?" Marina narrowed her eyes.

"They no doubt want to blow up the bridges and whatever else they can to halt the Allied advance."

"Where are these people to go?" Marina clasped her hands.

"I heard that they are to walk toward Pistoia. From there, they will board trains that will take them to northern Italy. And then, who knows? The resident priest there encouraged the people to flee to the nearby villages in the mountains, rather than face God knows what."

"Could Gianni have participated in the Partisan activities?" Alda asked quickly.

"I don't know." Giorgio smiled. "But I'm convinced that in some way, he's out there watching over us. If the Allies can penetrate the Gothic Line, it won't be much longer that they will be in the valley. Oh, what a day it will be."

Marina squeezed Giorgio's hand. She shared his

enthusiasm. Pistoia was not that far from Lucca. The battle with the Germans was sure to be fierce, but oh, the heady prospect of liberation.

*   *   *

The talk about the *sfollamento* had become reality. In mid-July, the people of Diecimo and the surrounding villages had to evacuate.

"When that day comes, will we be able to get used to the idea of being free?" Nelsa reached up over her head and lowered the first of the faggots of kindling wood. By summer's end, they would again be stacked almost to the ceiling.

"It's like a dream… returning to living a normal life." Marina lowered her faggot, removed her dusty bandana, and ran her fingers through her hair. "Let's sit down a moment on the steps outside where it's cooler." She fanned herself with her hand. The air felt stuffy beneath the low ceiling.

"*Nonna,* it's been almost a year that you have been with us. Do you have any regrets?"

Nelsa shook her head as she smiled. "No, I don't. I can't ask for more than being with all of you."

Marina cherished this moment with her *nonna.* They never seemed to catch up with each other, one on one.

"Things are going better for you and Giorgio now?"

"Yes." Marina nodded as she smiled. She had confessed

to her family about what had happened. "We've promised each other not to be secretive about anything that we feel could harm our marriage. We've learned our lesson."

"That's what marriage is about, *bimba mia*. It's not always roses without thorns. One of these days, you'll be telling us that you're expecting a baby." Nelsa's voice was eager, joyful.

Marina hugged herself and decided to confide in Nelsa. *"Nonna,* I need for you to keep a secret again."

"It better be good this time."

"I think I'm expecting a baby."

Nelsa gasped aloud. "I won't tell anyone, I promise. Oh, I hope that it's true. Giorgio doesn't know, then?"

"No, I haven't told him, but I'll have to when I make an appointment with the midwife in Lucca. I don't want to go alone."

"Alone? Giorgio must go with you."

The noise of thunder rolling in the distance told Marina that another summer storm was on the way. She rolled her eyes. "What else is new? I'd better go."

"Go." Nelsa waved her away. "The faggots will still be there waiting for us."

Marina hurried down the street as light rain began to fall. Before she reached Amelia's home, she saw Carla standing under the balcony.

"Hurry home, Marina, you don't want to catch a cold, and be sick," Carla urged. "You're *so* delicate."

Marina didn't bother to answer, but draped the well-worn apron that she wound to balance objects on her head, across her head and shoulders.

She crossed the *piazza* and was almost past Anna's home when she heard Anna call her.

Marina turned quickly. "Anna, I have the laundry out," she gasped.

"Come and see me when you can."

"I will." Marina rushed home and into the *soggiorno*. Hanging on the rail of the little balcony were the almost dry hemp sheets. She gathered them and draped them across the dining room chairs, then sat down to catch her breath. The house was quiet, save for Chicco's movements inside his box as he played with his small ball of yarn. Giorgio was probably upstairs resting. Today, he had had the messy chore of cleaning out the stable. She sat for a few minutes and then went upstairs to freshen up. Giorgio was fast asleep on the bed, snoring gently.

She dropped her dirty, wet clothes to the floor next to his dirty ones. After she freshened up, and dressed, she quietly descended the stairs.

From the kitchen window, she looked out at the valley. Behind the hills to her right the Serchio River flowed towards Lucca. She didn't know how long it would take for the Allies to reach Lucca, but their determination to free the people was just as strong as the Germans' determination to prevent it. They lost no time, bombing bridges and roads after the evacuation of the valley. Many houses were destroyed and obstacles were placed to halt the advance of the Allies on the two major roads.

*   *   *

The storm passed as quickly as it came. It was still early in the day, so she decided to visit Anna.

"Come in." Anna drew her inside.

"I'm sorry that I haven't been to visit you lately. How are the children?" Marina sat down with her at the kitchen table.

"They're fine." Anna smiled. "Little Giorgio is upstairs napping, and Maddalena is at my sister's."

"Mama!" His high pitched call came from the stairway.

Anna shook her head. "He woke up earlier than usual today. Come up with me."

Marina followed her upstairs. Little Giorgio pulled himself to his feet inside the crib.

"You're awake." Anna lifted him, and kissed him tenderly.

Little Giorgio pointed to the floor.

"What is it, *amore mio*?" Anna looked down. "Did you lose your little toy? Let's see if I can find it."

"I'll hold him for you." Marina took him in his arms.

"What's this?" Anna held up the toy as well as her black comb.

Marina dared not breathe. She had found the comb.

"It was under my nose all the time." Anna looked at Marina quizzically. "Is something wrong?"

"No, oh no!"

"Something's wrong. What is it? Tell me!"

Marina fidgeted. Getting out of this without revealing everything seemed impossible. To her relief, she heard the kitchen door open downstairs, and a voice calling out, "Anna?"

"Maddalena is back. I'll take him now. Come, little one." Anna reached for little Giorgio, who squealed with delight.

When they were downstairs, Maddalena ran to her mother.

"Aren't you coming in?" Anna asked her sister.

"No, I can't. I left a pot on the burner. I'll come by tomorrow and visit. *Ciao,* Marina."

Marina greeted her as she offered a silent prayer of thanks for the timely visit.

"Maddalena, aren't you saying anything to Marina, who came to visit us?"

"*Ciao, tata.*" Bashful, Maddalena hid her face in her mother's apron.

Marina reached out for her. *Tata.* The endearment used among close friends filled her with joy. She cupped Maddalena's face and kissed her on the top of the head. She would have stayed a little longer, but she was anxious to get home and tell Giorgio what she had found out.

She hurried up the street and came face to face with him just as he was going out of the door. She gently pushed him back inside.

"What's this?" Giorgio stepped back, bewildered.

"The comb that I found in the jacket wasn't Anna's!"

Giorgio stared blankly at her. "What… what did you say?"

Marina told him about her visit with Anna. "She found the comb stuck between a bed leg and the wall."

"I burned the comb along with some wood shavings. But, if the comb wasn't Anna's then whose was it?" Giorgio opened his arms wide.

Marina raised her shoulders. "I don't know. This is… is unreal, and… and… what about the note?" Vexed, she pursed her lips. "We have a war to deal with, my brother is a Partisan, and now there is someone who passes off a comb as belonging to a helpless window, plants it in your jacket, and almost costs us our marriage."

Giorgio shrugged. "In the end, it doesn't really matter. What matters is that nothing can come between us."

Marina walked towards the kitchen and suddenly turned around. It didn't matter and now Giorgio had to know that it really didn't. She took a deep breath. "Giorgio, I… I think that I'm… I'm expecting."

Giorgio stood looking at her, transfixed. Slowly, her words sank in. Before she knew what had happened, he'd grabbed her in his embrace and kissed her soundly.

*   *   *

The following week, Marina visited the midwife. She walked out of the exam room floating on air.

Giorgio waited in a side area, pacing back and forth. He rushed to her side. "Are… are you…?"

"Yes!" Marina threw her arms around him.

When they reached home, Giorgio had Marina go upstairs to rest. "We… we have to be careful. I'm going to tell the family."

"Giorgio, I don't need to lie down. I'm fine," Marina protested.

"Just lie down a little while." He took her by the shoulders and gently had her sit on the bed.

"Alright." Marina resigned herself to his insistence. "I'm so happy and most of all, I'm happy for you."

Giorgio sat down next to her. "You can't believe what I went through with the doubts that I had about myself." He kissed her forehead. "You relax now. I'm going."

Marina clasped her hands in joy. Giorgio whistled a tune all the way out to the front door.

*   *   *

"I knew it. I just knew that you were going to have another baby!" Nelsa hugged Marina the next morning. "There was no reason that you wouldn't." Her eyes sparkled as Marina offered her and Amelia a glass of *orzo*.

"Everyone is so excited. I'm… I'm a little afraid, *Nonna.*"

"Don't be. You just have to take a little extra care of yourself. We're all here for you, *bimba.*"

"I'll have to finish the baby sweater that I began last time," Marina said excitedly and went into the *soggiorno* to fetch her basket of handiwork. She showed Amelia the beginning of a tiny sweater and did a mental count at the same time. "The baby will need this for sure in early spring."

"The girls are already planning who is to make what. You can be sure that between all of us, the baby won't lack for clothes," Amelia assured her with a big smile.

"What is most important is that my little he or she be born healthy." Marina held the little sweater to her tightly.

Later that morning, Marina crossed the *piazza* to go visit her family. She didn't pay attention to the group of people standing together speaking in low tones, their faces grim. No doubt it was some aspect of the war news. She stopped short as a man's voice reached her.

"I knew one of those killed. The Partisans don't stand a chance with these people."

Her heart beating fast, Marina edged closer to the group. "What happened? Who's been killed?"

The villager turned to her. "The Germans shot a group of local Partisans down in Fegana. I knew one of them... a fine man..." The villager's voice broke and he couldn't continue.

Marina brought her hand to her heart. Her first thought was Gianni. She turned around and rushed home. She quickly descended the garden steps to Giorgio, who was in the workshop.

Giorgio dropped the lathe when Marina burst inside the door, in tears. "Marina!" He held her tightly by the shoulders. "What's happened?"

"A… a group of Partisans have… have been shot in the Fegana valley." Marina fought hysteria.

"Sit down." Giorgio led her to the gunnysacks in the corner. "Who told you?"

"In the *piazza* people are talking about it. Gianni… could… could he have been… killed?"

Giorgio ran his fingers through his hair. "No, oh no." He wiped his hands on a rag. "I'm going to see what I can find out."

"But how, where…"

"Someone has to know something, especially where these people were from. You go upstairs and lie down." He shook his head. "You didn't need this now."

"What of my family? If word reaches them about this, it will kill Mama."

"I'll go to them first. Go, *amore mio*. Please."

"Be careful," Marina whispered against his cheek.

*   *   *

After eating a frugal meal of a slice of *polenta* and a little cheese, Marina stepped outside into the street. She guessed that Giorgio wouldn't be home until late afternoon. Added to the worry about Gianni, now there was Giorgio. The Germans would probably patrol the valley road after this incident and she raised a fervent prayer that they wouldn't see him. She heard someone running up the street, and cried out as Giorgio ran towards her.

Relief and concern flooded her soul, as he stopped for a moment in the street to catch his breath. He raised his head and smiled at her. Before she could say anything, he put his fingers to his lips and nodded towards the sentinel who paced up and down past the houses. When Giorgio approached her, he took her in his arms. "It's alright. He's fine," he whispered.

Inside the *soggiorno*, Giorgio sank onto a chair. "Gianni's fine. Something told me to cut through your family's vineyard to go to the Fegana. That's when I saw him." He took a deep breath.

Marina clasped her hands, delighted. "You *saw* him?"

Giorgio grinned from ear to ear. "This time I made sure that he wouldn't get away without a word. I ran so fast, grabbed him so hard that we both lost our balance and fell to the ground."

"Thank God!"

"He wasn't exactly thankful until he recognized me. When he did, we both laughed and cried at the same time. We went into the hayloft and… caught up with two years."

Marina hardly breathed, so anxious she was to hear every word. "Is… is he with other Partisans around the area?"

"He has been with a group from other villages, but after

what happened, I think that he's having second thoughts about everything. He's still fighting for the cause, but I have a feeling it won't be all that long before he'll come home."

"I hope that you're right." Marina cupped his face. "Thank you for doing this. You were ready to put your life in danger."

"It all turned out well. Is there anything for me to eat?" Giorgio got up, rubbing his stomach.

"Left-over *polenta* and some cheese?"

Giorgio frowned. "You're going to need more than this with the baby."

"Knowing that Gianni is alive and having you back home safely, is worth more than food for me now. God will help us with everything else."

*   *   *

Marina cried out and stretched out her arm towards Giorgio the next morning, but instead of his torso, she felt the pillow. Alarmed, she lifted herself up on her elbow.

"Marina! It's alright. I'm here." Giorgio took her in his arms.

"Giorgio, thank goodness."

"You had a bad dream."

"It was a bad dream." She smiled. "But it was only a dream. Everything is good."

"Stay down a little longer. I'm getting ready to take

Mama to her appointment with the cardiologist."

"I'm getting up." She rose and quickly dressed. With a burst of happiness, she realized that her skirt felt a little snug at the waistline.

"I like it better when you're happy," Giorgio said smiling.

"I'm slowly growing." Marina touched her belly.

Giorgio kissed her on the forehead. "Good. I hope that I can feel the baby kick soon."

"Our baby. Can you believe that? If it's a boy, I hope that he looks like you."

"Are you sure about that? I'm not a dashing person, you know."

Marina wrapped her arms around him. "You're dashing to me," she whispered.

"I'm going to forget what I have to do this morning if I stay here with you," he told her between kisses.

Marina felt mischievous. "Is that such a bad thing?"

"You're a sorceress!"

Marina giggled and let him go. Their day had begun.

*   *   *

Marina went for her usual little walk along the mule path later that morning. Giorgio had left, and her mother and *Nonna* Nelsa were down in the valley shopping in town. Daniela was helping a refugee child deal with reading. Albina was at home to mind the kitchen.

Not wanting her to take any chances with the pregnancy, Giorgio, as well as Amelia and her family had all asked her not to go to the vineyard anymore.

The day was clear and warm sunshine shone down on her bare arms. Above and below, the villagers were busy with their outdoor tasks. The vines were lush, the potatoes had sprouted from the ground, and down at the Fegana River, Marina saw her family's patch of hemp.

She passed a hedgerow to her left. Below it, a large snowball bush bloomed, and from somewhere within its branches, a sparrow chirped. Below that was her neighbor's terraced vineyard. She stopped a moment to enjoy the view that looked so peaceful. Immersed in her thoughts, she jumped at a voice.

"Fuoco!'

Marina whirled around. She peered at the bush Gianni's voice had come from.

"Marina, it's me."

Her heart in her throat, Marina saw him crawl towards the path, his fingers to his lips. The bush was just a few feet down from her. Carefully, she walked down. Gianni stood up and took her hands, helping her to step off.

Marina threw her arms around him when they were out of view of the road. "Giorgio told me everything. I… I thought that you were… among those…"

"It's alright." Gianni held her tightly. "Thankfully, my group never met up with them."

Marina held on tightly to him. "You took a chance on being seen."

"I wanted to see you. Giorgio told me that you usually go for a walk, so here I am. Besides, there has to be more to the world than a stable." He laughed.

Marina smiled through her tears. "Gianni, did Giorgio tell you that I'm pregnant?"

Gianni cupped her face and kissed her on the forehead. "He did. He told me everything that's been going on. Lisa has married." He sat down on a jutting rock and had her sit in his lap.

"Yes. She married Marco, the new doctor in June. Another little bird has left the nest."

"I can hardly wait for this war to be over. I'm aching to see all of you, and to begin living my life again."

Marina studied him carefully as he spoke. His face was gaunt. He looked tired, and she feared he was sick. "You're not well."

He shrugged in his characteristic way. "I'm alright, but I just wish that I could have some of Mama's *polenta* to help cover my ribs."

"Gianni, come home. Please," Marina pleaded.

"We'll soon be free." His voice grew soft. "When that day comes, I haven't forgotten where my home is."

Marina wanted to make sure that he wouldn't forget. "I'm bringing you some food. No arguing."

He grabbed her shoulders. "Listen to me. I can't deny that I'm hungry, but I won't have you put your life in danger. If you're discovered helping me... I... I... can't replace my sister." His voice broke.

Marina got up, and placed her hands on her hips. "That's a chance I'm going to have to take." Come what may, this was her brother.

"No, Marina, I can't…"

"I said that I'm bringing you food. *Hai capito?*" She had never spoken like that before, but then she never faced a situation like this either.

Gianni let her go and shook his head, smiling. "I heard you." He laughed softly. "Are you like this with Giorgio when you want your way?"

"Oh… you…" Marina smacked him gently on the arm. "Don't go anywhere, alright? I'll be back as soon as I can."

Marina placed a hand over her pounding heart. Gianni helped her onto the path. She glanced up to see if there was anyone walking about. Eager as she was to bring food to him as quickly as possible, she forced herself to stay calm. When she got onto the mule path, she hastened her pace.

The fastest way to bring food to Gianni was to go to her family. The tricky part was not to let on about what she was doing. If something should go wrong, she wanted to be the sole person responsible for her actions.

At the junction, Heinrich walked back and forth. Marina got the impression that he was bored. He smiled shyly as she approached. Maybe he felt awkward about the *rastrellamento,* and maybe Daniela was right about his having second thoughts about being there.

Enough! There was Gianni to think about. She took a deep breath and entered the kitchen.

Albina stood at the table, kneading dough for bread. "*Ehi,*" She smiled warmly. "How are both of you doing?"

"Fine. Giorgio went with Amelia to her appointment."

"I wasn't referring to Giorgio," Albina laughed.

"Oh," Marina touched her belly. "We're both doing fine. I didn't make any bread. Do have any, just for dinner?"

"Yes. Look in the *madia.*"

In the dining room under the staircase was a large wood storage chest for bread and flour. Marina sliced a few pieces of bread that would hold Gianni over for a couple of days.

"There's also *polenta* if you want. Mama made more than usual."

Marina smiled. Perfect. She placed a few slices of *polenta* and the bread on a small plate. "May I take a napkin to cover it?"

"Need you ask?"

Marina would have lingered a moment or two, but she was worried about Gianni. "I'd better go. I'm sorry that I can't help in the vineyard anymore."

"Don't worry about that. Are you leaving already?" Albina wiped her floury hands on her apron.

"I promise to come and visit tomorrow." Marina hugged her tightly and left.

Again, Heinrich smiled faintly at her. She went on her

way, conscious that she was taking a big risk, but in life, there were moments when risks had to be taken.

She tried not to rush to Gianni. When she approached the snowball bush, she sighed with relief and called out softly as she stepped onto the path. There was no answer. Concerned, Marina carefully went down the path.

Gianni sat on the ground, leaning back against the outcrop, fast asleep. Tears filled her eyes as she knelt down to gently rouse him. "Gianni."

He started, and blinked. A smile lit up his face when he saw the little bundle in Marina's hands.

"This will hold you for a day or two." Marina lifted the edge of the napkin.

"Thank you," he whispered, and helped her up. "You'd better go home now. I pray that no one saw you because I'll kill myself if something happens to you."

"Be good, Gianni." Marina cupped his face. "Don't do anything that… that will endanger the people. We've heard about the new Major from Austria."

Gianni scowled, and raised his hands. "Don't even mention him."

Marina nodded. He had probably heard more about him than she cared to know. "Eat now and rest. Can you make your way back to the stable in the vineyard?"

Gianni nodded. "I'll stay there until tomorrow morning. With this infernal curfew, things are more complicated."

"I love you." She hugged him.

Gianni nodded. "I love you, too. Thank you," he

whispered against her cheek. "Take this back." He gave her the plate. "We don't want Mama to find out that it's missing."

Marina stared in disbelief. "Don't you have bigger concerns? How are you going to carry the food?"

"There won't be that much left to carry, trust me." He cupped her face. "You take care of yourself, alright?"

Marina nodded and ran her fingers along his cheek. She turned around and went up the few feet to the mule path. She had to look at him one more time. He was keeping an eye on her. A tear trickled down his cheek.

On the mule path, a chill ran along her spine when she spotted Carla who stood just beyond her. A feeling of dread filled her, but Carla turned quickly and left.

Marina breathed a sigh of relief and hurried on home. Although she was happy to have helped Gianni, she didn't fool herself. The danger that something would surface because of her action was real. Her family had to remain out of this, but she had to tell Giorgio.

She went into the workshop immediately. "Giorgio, I have to tell you something."

He stopped sanding, and wiped his dusty hands on a rag. "Something's wrong. I can see it in your face. Are… are you feeling alright?"

"I'm fine, but I have to talk."

They sat down on the gunnysacks, and Giorgio let her pour out her heart, his face grave with concern. When she finished, he didn't reprimand her, but smiled instead. "I'm rather proud of you.”

“I know that there could be consequences, but he looked so gaunt. I didn’t have the heart to not help him.”

“No one can blame you.” He squeezed her hand. “If Carla did see something, we’ll find out soon enough. If she should ask you anything, don’t answer. Tell her to talk to Gianni. That should quench her curiosity.”

Marina giggled. “Now that would be something to see.”

*   *   *

July ended with a village feast. In the *piazza*, Marina and Giorgio attended the dance along with her family and Amelia. Alda was there, too, as well as *Nonna* Nelsa, whose foot tapped to the music.

“*Nonna,*” Marina squeezed her hand, “I think that you’d like to dance.”

Nelsa raised an eyebrow. “And make a silly fool out of myself? Go dance with your husband, who can’t seem to sit still with the music.”

“I don’t know…” Marina hesitated. “I’m afraid for the baby.”

Giorgio was thoughtful. “I won’t argue that.”

Marina glanced at Albina and Daniela who sat on the bench next to theirs. She sensed their eagerness to dance. “Dance with my sisters,” she said to Giorgio. She didn’t want to take any chances with the pregnancy, but at least they could enjoy the evening.

Without hesitation, Giorgio got up and went to Daniela. He promised Albina the next dance.

Daniela hesitated and gave Marina a quick look.

"Go and dance." Marina pointed to the dance floor.

Marina watched them, delighted. As Giorgio led Daniela out to dance, she saw her burst into laughter at something that he must have said. Daniela quickly picked up the rhythm. She was a graceful dancer. They waltzed around and around, and whirled by Lisa and Marco. She noticed Carla keeping her eyes on them as they waltzed, and when they whirled towards her, Carla moved a little towards them, and suddenly sank to the floor as in a faint. Marina couldn't be sure if it was real or a tactic and rose to go and see for herself.

Giorgio knelt down in concern while the other dancers moved away. "Carla, Carla!"

Someone brought a glass of water that Giorgio dampened his handkerchief with it, and placed it on Carla's forehead.

"This is a ruse." Marina voiced her suspicions to Daniela in a low voice.

Daniela looked at her in surprise. "What do you mean?"

"Trust me. Was it just coincidence that she moved towards you and Giorgio and fell faint in that instant?"

"Maybe it was a coincidence. Aren't you being a little hard on her?" Daniela raised her eyebrows.

Marina rolled her eyes.

Carla opened her eyes and smiled sweetly at Giorgio,

almost slyly. "Giorgio. Thank you. Would you help me to sit up?"

Giorgio helped her while Carla placed her arm around his neck for support with her face close to his cheek.

Marina saw Giorgio frown. His jaw tensed. He disengaged himself from Carla and stood up quickly. "You'll be fine." Then he spoke just loud enough for Marina to hear. "Don't think of trapping me."

His words brought a few chuckles from the onlookers.

Marina's spirits soared as he placed his arm around her waist, took a stunned Daniela by the hand, and led them back to their place.

*   *   *

The weather continued to be unpredictable and the war raged. One night, around mid-August, Marina stirred and sat up in bed, not knowing what had awakened her.

Alert, she heard what had become a familiar sound in the night hours. Allied planes were flying over the valley. The Partisans had been able to have radio equipment from the Americans smuggled across the German lines with the help of the population. To avoid being discovered by the Germans, they set the equipment up in remote places or houses. They were able to send information to the Allies regarding the movements and the locations of the German troops. Marina prayed that if Gianni wanted to help the Allies, that he would be decent about it.

She didn't want him to be like those Partisans who did more harm than good. They raided villages and homes for food and provisions. The people didn't like them. They also harassed the Germans, who punished the nearby villagers in retaliation by taking hostages and killing them. The situation was made worse with the new Austrian Major. Dangerous, and with no sympathy towards civilians, he made sure that anyone caught helping the Partisans was killed on the spot.

Marina rested her elbows on her legs, and brought her hands to her forehead. Trying to sleep now was useless. How she wanted to convince Gianni to come home.

CHAPTER SEVENTEEN

The next day, Marina stopped by Lisa's home for her usual 'good morning' on her way to the food shop. She had left Giorgio busy in the workshop doing little jobs. Although she tried to keep a positive attitude, she prayed that something more than little jobs would come along.

At the door, Lisa took her hands and quickly drew her inside. "I think I'm expecting a baby," Lisa exclaimed with a burst of happiness, before Marina could say anything.

"How wonderful! We're both expecting," Marina cried out.

Marco has made an appointment for me with the same midwife that you went to. Will… will you come with me? Sit down."

Marina held Lisa's hands, feeling elated for her younger sister, who was excited and apprehensive at the same time. "Of course, I'll go with you. Have you told Mama yet?"

"Yes." Lisa nodded. "If I am, I'd be so happy, even if the world isn't the happiest place now."

"It won't always be like this." Marina reassured her. "Focus on your health and the baby."

"I'll turn to Mama and to you for advice."

"You're better off with Mama." She laughed gently. "For the moment, I don't have much advice to offer."

"You *do*. I want to know how you feel, *what* you feel with the baby."

"I'm still in the learning process. But when you know that you're expecting, nothing equals that happiness," Marina said warmly.

"I can just see our little ones playing together."

Marina remembered a holy card of little Jesus playing with John the Baptist. They were little cousins, too.

"I'm going on home now. You take good care, alright? Let me know about the appointment." Marina kissed her on the cheek.

"I can hardly wait to know for sure."

On her way home, Marina's happiness for her sister was crudely quenched by the ugly reality of the war. She entered the *piazza* and came upon a group of people, some of whom were weeping, in front of the little chapel. Her first thought was that a loved one had died. She quietly approached them. "What's happened?"

"The SS…" One of the women gasped the words out between her sobs, "massacred over five-hundred people in Sant'Anna in Lucca. Old men, women… children… machine-gunned. Just gunned down."

Sant'Anna was closer to the coast, and she had heard

that the occupation was especially brutal in the area. "Wh… what did these poor souls do? The… children?"

"Someone did something." An elderly man clenched his fists. "The SS found out that some of the people were helping the Partisans… giving them food and maybe sheltering them. They… they accused the people of helping them to help the Allies." The poor man closed his eyes tightly while tears trickled down his face. "They… didn't know who it was, so… so they gathered the people in the square. A priest tried to intercede and… and… was gunned down, too. Dear God!"

Marina turned away, sick to her stomach. Her heart heavy with sorrow, she walked slowly home. She raised her head to the sky and asked aloud who was to blame for this. She couldn't begin to imagine the scene. Especially the children. The Partisans, in their zeal to help the Allies, could have been in part responsible. Or whoever had informed the SS. It was a sad day. She shivered because her greatest fear now was that it could happen here, too, and she could be responsible for it.

*   *   *

The shock of what happened in Sant'Anna lingered, yet everyday life had to continue. Marina and her family, Giorgio, Amelia, Valentina and Bruno, gathered in the kitchen at Lisa's home the following week, the day after the appointment.

"I can't believe this! Me! A father," Marco exclaimed.

"Praise God for some happy news. Heaven knows that there hasn't been much of it." Alda raised her eyes heavenward as she helped Lisa to set the kitchen table. Even if the meal was simple, they were celebrating the news of both pregnancies.

"What a gift I'm receiving from my wife." Marco's excitement filled the kitchen.

"It'll be a long wait." Lisa laughed. "It won't come for eight months."

"But oh, when it comes." Marco finally relaxed into a chair at the table.

"I can add my voice to yours, my friend," Giorgio said.

In spite of the general gaiety, what happened in Sant'Anna wasn't forgotten.

Marina turned to Giorgio. "What should I do? Should I tell them about Gianni?"

Giorgio nodded. "I think you'd better."

Everyone grew quiet when she mentioned Gianni. "I don't want to ruin this day…" She looked from one to the other. "But, I can't…"

"Marina," Alda fixed her gaze on her. "What about Gianni?"

"Please forgive me, but I… I helped Gianni the other day. I… I brought him food."

Albina narrowed her eyes. "Is… that why you asked me for bread?"

Marina nodded. "I should have told you, I know. But…

but if something was going to happen, I wanted the blame to be mine alone. He looked gaunt and admitted that he was hungry. He… he didn't want me to help him. He… he was afraid for my life. But, I didn't care. He's my brother." Marina covered her face.

Alda rose from the table and walked over to her. She gently pressed Marina's head to her body and kissed the top of her head. "You risked… but I love you all the more for this!"

"We all do," Daniela cried out. "I… I would have done the same thing."

Valentina dabbed at her eyes. "If… if you should have any problem, we're at your side! I know that I'd be happy if someone helped Marco if he needed help."

"Count on us," Bruno said firmly.

"Let's take it day by day." Marco swallowed hard. "No one knows that he's a Partisan, so it should be alright."

"We have to believe that it will be. Now…" Giorgio rose. "Can we toast these babies who are to arrive?"

*   *   *

That night, Marina envisioned the little things she could make not only for her own baby, but for Lisa's, too. Tiny sweaters, booties. She would also make a nice shawl for Lisa, especially if she could find her favorite color. This could be her opportunity to show her love and appreciation to her sister.

Giorgio stirred. Marina turned towards him and gently brushed back a lock of dark hair from his forehead. She mused on the features their baby might have.

"Are you awake?" Giorgio murmured.

"Yes."

"Good. I'm so happy."

"I can't believe all this. Seeing Gianni, my pregnancy, and now Lisa's."

"I can't believe it, either." Giorgio yawned.

"We've got to sleep."

Giorgio took her in his arms. "I can't think of a nicer way to fall asleep than this," he whispered.

Marina smiled and nestled against him.

CHAPTER EIGHTEEN

The latest news was that the Allies had broken through the German ranks at the Lima River, by way of Pistoia to the east. This meant that the longed for liberation of the Serchio River Valley was near. For Marina, especially, it meant that Gianni could soon come home.

Giorgio emptied a sack of potatoes in a corner of the *cantina.*

Marina knelt down to spread them out. "Our lives will be more disrupted now with the Allies advancing. But— and I sound selfish—I can only think of Gianni finally coming home." Smiling at the image of him walking in the door for good, Marina filled a small sack with potatoes to bring up to the house. She rose and offered a prayer of thanks. It wasn't a plentiful crop, but she felt grateful for whatever they could have.

"You're not selfish. You're reasoning like a sister." Giorgio folded up the sack. "It will be like old times."

"I'd better go and bake bread."

"Do you feel up to doing that, with the nausea?"

"I don't mind baking bread. It's just cooking that

bothers me. But it's worth it." Marina touched her belly, and smiled. "How much has happened since last year. Sunday, we have another feast with the dance." A shiver coursed through her body. *"Oh mio Dio,* that was the night that you were assaulted."

"And here I am," Giorgio said brightly, smiling at her. "I don't know what I would have done without you. I wouldn't have made it."

"That's not true." Marina shook her head. "Don't forget about your mother and Marco."

"I know, but you gave me the extra push." He looked at the potatoes neatly spread out. "I think that's it. Can we invite Don Antonio for *pranzo* on Sunday? Except at church, we never see him."

"I'll talk to him." Marina like the idea. Don Antonio brightened a room wherever he went.

They walked up the garden steps to where Pallino was tethered to a ring in the house wall.

"I'm going to take you back down to the vineyard. *Fermo, fermo."* Giorgio gently steadied Pallino as the donkey sidled restlessly.

Of the many things that she loved about her husband, this was one of them. The little donkey wasn't treated as merely a beast of burden, but as a creature who served them well. At Giorgio's gentle smack, Pallino clipped-clopped down the street.

When Marina had kneaded the dough and had placed the loaves on a special board to rise, she decided to take a walk. Maybe she would meet Giorgio on the way.

She passed in front of Anna's home where she heard the happy chatter of Maddalena with her mother and a squeal from little Giorgio.

Down in the *piazza* a few men talked about the Allies and the liberation of the valley. At Amelia's home, Chicco's mother lay stretched out at the railing, fast asleep.

She continued on past her home and thought it best not to call as her mother was probably resting. Along the path, a gentle breeze rustled the grasses. Clusters of grapes in their rich colors of dark blue or red peeked through the leaves on the vines. The *vendemmia* would soon be upon them.

Marina mused on how different her circumstances were from last year, and felt a tinge of sadness. One minute, she had been expecting her first baby. The next, for reasons she still couldn't understand, it had all been over

Just as she thought, she met Giorgio on the mule path at the top of his vineyard. "You haven't taken Pallino down yet?" Marina's gaze fell on what used to be the wood railing. A post had snapped at the ground. Part of the rail lay against a blackberry bush. "What happened here?"

"I think the years took their toll. I'm going to have to make a new one. I'll go down. Will you wait for me a moment?"

Marina fixed her gaze on the sweep of the valley to her right. The coming months would bring more action. Her concern was for Gianni and that what had happened to the Partisans in the Fegana could happen to him.

*   *   *

As the curfew during the summer months was extended, the traditional candlelit procession from the church once again wound through the village. Marina took part in it, arm in arm with Lisa. Marco and Giorgio helped to carry the statue of the beloved saint this year.

Gathered in church with the other villagers on Sunday morning, she sensed more excitement in the air than at this time last year. The idea that liberation was so near, gave her people new hope. After Mass, Don Antonio stopped to greet a few of his parishioners under the center nave in church. Marina lingered with Giorgio to greet him.

"Don Antonio, at your convenience, we'll be waiting for you."

"Thank you, Marina. I'll join you soon." The priest gave her a warm smile. "How are you feeling?"

"I feel fine, and I'm so happy."

"I knew that when the good Lord willed it, your dream of a baby would come true."

Marina left them and stopped at the top of the steps, enjoying the warm, morning sunshine on her arms. In that moment she stood alone, she savored the sounds of nature around her. It might have been her imagination, but she had the sensation of something or someone behind her. In a flash, her mind went back to the morning when she had fallen down the steps into the garden and lost the baby. She turned around quickly, just in time to see someone disappearing around the corner. At that moment, Don Antonio came out of the church, followed by Giorgio.

Marina frowned, shaking.

Her perturbation didn't go unnoticed by Giorgio. "Are you alright?" He took her hands. "You look shaken."

Marina managed a smile. "Yes… yes, I'm fine. Let's go home. I have to put a meal together." She took a deep breath and descended the steps. Giorgio put his arm around her shoulder. On impulse, she kissed him soundly on the cheek. Giorgio turned to her, his eyes wide with surprise.

Marina turned to look back. Someone had stood behind her. She wasn't crazy.

Once at home, Marina changed her dress and put on a crisp white blouse and a skirt. She secured her long hair with a comb, and tried to focus on what she had to do. She wasn't about to ruin a festive occasion with her doubts and fears. As she bustled about between the kitchen and the *soggiorno,* where she had adorned the table with her best tablecloth, she heard a familiar footfall on the stairs.

Giorgio entered the kitchen and rolled up his sleeves. "What can I do?"

"Would you put the potatoes in the oven and make sure the chickens are roasting and not burning?"

Giorgio chuckled. "Is there a difference?"

Marina rolled her eyes. "You're impossible! Here." Marina handed him the pan of potatoes.

"My mouth is watering," he said, sniffing the aroma of rosemary and garlic.

"Good for you." Marina groaned and turned away from the savory aroma. "I'm happy that we invited Don Antonio. We haven't had him with us for such a long time." She arranged two pink roses from the garden in a narrow vase and caught Giorgio's gaze on her. "What?"

"Nothing." Giorgio smiled tenderly and headed to the door.

His smile sent a thrill through her. He was saying much more than he let on.

*   *   *

When the family was finally together, Marina delighted in the contented chatter around the table. Today, everyone talked about their hopes and dreams for the days after the liberation. *Nonna* Nelsa was trying to work out a plan so Gianni could have his room back. Bruno and Giorgio were commenting on the weather's unpredictability and its effect on the outcome of the wine.

Lisa and Marco were overjoyed at her pregnancy.

Don Antonio sat back in the chair, his face beaming. "Marina, thank you as always." He sipped his Rossetto wine. "You look especially happy today."

"I'm excited like everyone else and rejoice with Lisa."

Marina touched her belly. "I pray that Gianni is well and will come home soon."

After consulting with Giorgio, she had confided to Don Antonio that she had seen Gianni and that he was a Partisan. He had promised secrecy.

"I pray for him and all the men in the village who are at war." A shadow crossed Don Antonio's face. "I feel bad that we lost Stefano."

"I do, too." Marina nodded sadly. "Anna seems to be getting on a little better. We try to be as close to her as possible."

"She told me. It's good of you to do so." Don Antonio pursed his lips and took another sip of wine.

Something in Don Antonio's manner made Marina uneasy. "Is… is something wrong?"

"No, no. Nothing's wrong." Don Antonio smiled warmly. "We have a lovely gathering of family, good food. What else can we ask of the Lord?"

Marina wasn't convinced. "Would you come with me into the kitchen? I need your opinion on a bottle of wine."

Don Antonio's eyebrows arched. "Yes, of… of course."

Giorgio, who sat next to Marina, glanced quizzically at her.

Marina drew Don Antonio to the far end of the kitchen, out of earshot of everyone. "Something's wrong, Don Antonio. I can tell. What is it?"

"*Ahi,* Marina," he groaned.

"Don Antonio?" She placed her hands on her hips. She

wasn't about to let him leave until he explained himself.

"I… found out about… the comb."

Marina gasped aloud. "The… *comb*? How did you find out? This was only between Giorgio and I and our family."

Don Antonio sighed deeply. "A few women lingered after Mass this morning. You know that my upstairs window faces the church door. While I was getting ready to come here, I… I overheard them talking, and you know how it goes. They connected Anna to Giorgio, and…"

"And assumed that they are lovers." Marina rolled her eyes. "What else is new? But how did they find out about the comb?"

Don Antonio raised his arms and let them fall. "I don't know. Marina, please tell me that everything is alright between you and Giorgio."

"Everything is fine." Marina stomped her foot. "But it won't be for whoever is responsible for all of this. I can promise you that. If Anna finds out…"

Don Antonio placed a hand on her shoulder. "Let God handle it."

When the meal was over, the men walked out with Don Antonio. Marina, with the help of her family, Amelia, and Valentina tidied up the kitchen and the *soggiorno*. They would all go to the *piazza* for the games later in the afternoon.

Giorgio had offered to help with the games. Marina and her family, Amelia, and Valentina joined in the fun watching the men in a tug-of-war with a rope, pole climbing to reach a prize at the top, and children of various ages hopping along in a sack race. Other men enjoyed a game of *bocce.* Marina winced at the colorful expressions of frustration when the *boccia* either missed the little ball completely or didn't get close enough.

A real treat was provided by slices of watermelon, served from a stand in a shady corner of the *piazza.*

The evening ended with the dance. Although Marina and Lisa didn't dance, Giorgio and Marco made sure that Daniela and Albina did.

"I can't believe how Albina has grown." Lisa commented to Marina as Giorgio led her onto the dance floor.

Marina didn't hear. She had tensed when she saw Carla enter the hall and look around. She met Carla's gaze and smiled at her. Carla turned her head away. A shiver ran along her spine when Giorgio whirled by with Albina and Carla's expression hardened. Carla stood looking at them for a moment and then left the hall. The nagging thought of the comb never left her, nor the fear that Anna might find out. And then there was that strange happening on the church steps that morning.

"Marina, are you off somewhere?" Lisa asked her.

"I'm sorry. I got distracted by Carla's manner."

"What did she do?"

Marina told her. "Trouble is ahead with her, I feel it."

"How about just enjoying this evening?" Lisa rolled her eyes. "Can we just forget about the war and Carla for once?"

"You're right," Marina said firmly.

The evening went happily by.

*   *   *

German activity picked up in the Serchio River Valley. The combination of the 92nd Infantry Division and the 1st Armored Division were slowly inching closer to Lucca, but traversing swollen rivers and streams was difficult because of the unpredictable weather.

As far as the villagers were concerned, if the weather didn't help the grapes, it fostered the growth of the coveted mushrooms. Weather permitting, people set out in early morning or in the afternoon to their favorite places in the chestnut groves to seek the chubby *porcini*.

Giorgio didn't stand by watching. One late afternoon, he brought home a handful. "Here's to luxury."

Marina carefully cleaned them with a damp cloth. She took a small twig and skewered the little mushrooms on its branches to dry outside or in the house. When needed, they could be reconstituted. It was a small, insignificant thing, but this was one of the little pleasures of life that made her realize how blessed she was. Soon they would have the *vendemmia* and preparations for it would be underway in the *cantine* in spite of everyone's skepticism as to the outcome of the wine.

*   *   *

August ceded its lush green of summer to September with its hint that autumn was just around the corner. The leaves of the chestnut trees once again turned into yellow and russet, and the clusters of burs hinted at a good crop.

On the morning of September 5th, Marina helped in the *cantina.* On the low concrete shelf that held flaskets and small demi-johns, Giorgio had placed a large metal tub filled with water so Marina could rinse them out. She straightened up and winced.

"Rest a moment. We're almost finished." He frowned at the large demijohns on the dirt floor. "Who knows if we'll need these, judging by the way the grapes look."

"Whatever we get, will be a blessing," Marina said softly.

"It's good to see you so positive." Giorgio gently brushed away a lock of her hair from her forehead.

"I'm trying to be, but there's a lot going on. Ooh!"

"What is it?" Giorgio's eyes went wide with alarm.

Marina took his hand and held it to her belly. "Do you feel it?"

Giorgio grinned from ear to ear. "A kick! I felt a kick!"

"That's our baby," Marina said softly.

After *pranzo,* Giorgio went to help Alda prepare her *cantina.* Marina busied herself with her usual everyday tasks. She had almost finished sweeping in front of the *cantina* when she heard shouts and whoops of joy down the street. She dropped her broom, quickly climbed the steps, and walked down into the street. The shouts of jubilation from her neighbors reached her. Among them was Giorgio who waved to her.

He ran up the street to her, ignoring the sentinel who frowned at the commotion. "Marina! Marina! It's happened! We're free!"

Marina stared open-mouthed. Before she could say anything, he grabbed her in his embrace, laughing and crying at the same time. He let her go, and all she could do was to keep on staring at him, stunned. His words slowly sank in. "Wh… what did you say?"

"The Americans have arrived in Lucca. Bless the Buffalo's!" He kissed her soundly.

"The *who*? How did you find out?" Marina asked as she followed Giorgio inside the house.

"Let me catch my breath." Giorgio sat down at the table and motioned for Marina to do the same. "The Buffalo soldiers are the Black soldiers of the American infantry and regiment. I saw Don Antonio. He had gone to Lucca early in the morning. When he got there, he got caught up in the excitement over their arrival that he forgot what he went there for. He took the next bus back."

"But… but how did they get past the Germans? They… they had rigged the bridges to blow up to halt the advance."

Giorgio grinned from ear to ear. "Ha! It's simple. The Germans miscalculated. They didn't think of the possibility that the Allied forces could follow the Lima

River from Pistoia. They found the Allies practically at their backs. Plus, a group of Partisans did their part, too, and opened the door to the Americans. *Amore mio, we're… free."*

Caught off guard, the Germans pushed back their line, but in doing so they destroyed bridges, roads, and railroad tunnels in the area where the Serchio River Valley separated from the Lima Valley. Even in the next valley town over, a concrete bridge had been blown up.

Excitement ran high over the Allies in Lucca as well as dismay over the destruction that wreaked havoc on the people.

*   *   *

"The Germans won't give up." Giorgio smacked his hand on his leg in frustration the following day.

With the arrival of the Americans in Lucca, reports were that the Germans had spread out towards the outlying areas, machine gunning and firing cannons at the Allies and the partisans.

"I'm aching for the whole valley to be free, but how many people will be wounded or lose their lives?" Marina asked.

"I hope that by the time our babies are born, this nightmare will be over." Lisa was visiting and she sat in front of the fireplace, where a cheerful flame warmed the kitchen. She placed a hand on her rounding belly, barely noticeable beneath her loose-fitting dress. I also hope that with the Americans' arrival, Gianni comes home now. He has no reason to continue with the Partisans.

"I hope so, too," Marina said softly. She pictured the day when he would return home and smiled at how much they all had to catch up with.

"Mama wishes that she could see him. She doesn't care what he looks like." Lisa breathed deeply.

"Trust me, Gianni wants that more than anything. When the time is right, he'll come home. He promised," Marina said confidently.

*   *   *

The *vendemmia* had arrived. The clip-clop of donkeys and mules had become a familiar sound in the village as the villagers went to and from their vineyards.

"Thank you for helping me," Anna told Marina and Giorgio one early morning in mid-September. Pallino stood tethered outside Anna's *cantina.*

"Giorgio will have to pick the grapes on his own this time," Marina said.

"Let me help you."

Giorgio shook his head. "You and Marina stay here. "I'll be fine. It will take me longer, but I have an early start. Let's just hope the weather holds. Marina, I have to go up to the workshop a moment to find a tool that I need here. The key is in its usual place?"

"Yes. In the meantime, we can rinse these out." Marina took an armful of flaskets and followed Anna up to the kitchen. "It's so strangely quiet."

Anna laughed. "I know. Maddalena and little Giorgio are quite a pair. I doubted that we'd be able to do much with them here, so they're with their aunt today."

Marina had learned to pay attention to the sensations of something not feeling right. Anna's laugh sounded empty. She finished rinsing out the flaskets and placed them on a towel on the table. She turned to her. "Anna, is something wrong? Are you alright?"

Tears suddenly appeared in Anna's eyes. She gripped the edge of the stone sink and leaned forward. "Oh, Marina... I..." She broke into a sob.

Alarmed, Marina placed her arm around her shoulder. "Anna, what's wrong?"

"The... the comb. You... you had to... to know... to believe... that it wasn't mine!"

Marina gasped. Fury mounted in her. "How... how do you know about the comb? Giorgio and I didn't want you to find out because we knew it would hurt you."

"I just found out. You know how talk goes around." She turned a tear wet face to her. "That day that I found it under the bed... I... I don't understand it... if my comb was under the bed, then whose comb..."

Marina pursed her lips. "We don't know, but I never doubted you." She didn't have the heart to tell her that it had almost cost her and Giorgio their marriage.

"I would never do anything to harm you or your marriage," Anna said softly. "But I would like to know *whose* comb was it that you found?"

"So would Giorgio and I. Someone is up to mischief. But let's not talk anymore about it. You have your children to think of, and I have my baby to think of."

Anna nodded. "My little boy is a year old now. How am I going to raise him without a father? I had talked about finding work to do. Like it or not, I'll have to."

"Giorgio can't replace Stefano, but he will help you and be there for the children." Marina reassured her. The thought warmed her heart. Anna's children could be their adopted ones, even if not on paper.

"God knows that he's done more than his share already."

They rinsed out the flaskets and stepped out into the street to go to the *cantina,* when they heard the roar of aircraft engines overhead.

Anna shuddered. "Will it ever end?"

It was early afternoon when Giorgio brought up the last of the harvested grapes. "There's just the last two rows, but I can do those early tomorrow morning. When those are done, I'll help Alda, and begin my vineyard." As he spoke, he lifted the last *bigoncio* and poured the grapes into the small, hand cranked press that squeezed them. Then, he poured the dark red juice into a vat.

"Done," Giorgio said, satisfied.

"What can I say?" Anna opened her arms to both of them.

Back in the street, Anna's sister was coming to the house, holding the hands of Maddalena and little Giorgio. Maddalena let go of her aunt's hand to run to her mother. In that moment, there was another roar overhead.

"Mama!" Maddalena cried out.

Before Marina could say anything, the little girl ran up to them, but stumbled on a stone and fell. Frightened by the noise and the bruise on her knee, she burst into tears.

"It's alright, *amore mio.*" Anna knelt down, and took her in her arms. "It's alright."

That night in bed, Marina thought of Maddalena.

The little girl would hear much more frightening noise in the coming days. She also thought of her little brother. He would do well, with Giorgio's help.

She turned to Giorgio, who was sound asleep and contemplated his still-boyish face. He had matured so much since last year. She kissed his shoulder, rested her head against it, and slowly drifted off to sleep.

CHAPTER NINETEEN

arina stretched under the covers as she wakened next morning. She turned to Giorgio, who lay staring at the ceiling with a look on his face that was at once concerned and sad.

"Ehi," Marina caressed his cheek. "What's wrong?"

"Maybe I'm tired. I don't know." He turned to her and smiled. "How are both of you doing this morning?"

She took his hand and placed it on her belly. Ever since she had told him that she was expecting, Giorgio had made it a point to include the baby in his good morning or good night. "We're good. You have to finish picking those last two rows in Anna's vineyard. Then you have your grapes to pick."

Giorgio sighed deeply. "I know. I'd better get up. Last night it had clouded over. If it starts to rain again, the grapes may rot. The harvest isn't the best this year."

"It seems that nothing has been the best for a long time now. Can these be the lean years?"

"I could testify to that." Giorgio smiled wryly and ran a hand down his side. "I can count my ribs."

Marina burst out laughing. "I'm filling out a little with the baby."

Giorgio bit his lower lip, rolled over, and sat on the edge of the bed.

"What's wrong?" Marina scooted over behind him and placed her hands on his shoulders.

Giorgio shook his head sadly. "Not having any work at this moment isn't good. I need something more than little jobs to do. What rations we can buy seem to cost more every day." He ran his fingers though his hair. "I don't want to deprive you of anything, especially now with the baby. We've been married for almost a year, and it has been nothing but worry and toil." He caressed her cheek. "Some anniversary."

"Oh shush!" She wrapped her arms around his neck, placing her cheek against his cheek. "Things won't always be like this. Let's go down and have breakfast. *Nonna* provided us with eggs. Our breakfast will be rich this morning."

"You have a way of making me a better man, *carissima.*"

Marina lost herself in Giorgio's intense yet tender kiss, and breakfast was forgotten for the moment.

*   *   *

"I'd better go and do what I have to do." Giorgio frowned at the menacing dark clouds beyond the kitchen window.

"Finish your breakfast and go. I don't want you and

Pallino to get rained on." Marina sipped her *orzo* thoughtfully. "You know, I wish that we could keep him closer to home. There has to be a place where we can keep him." She loved the gentle creature, and if he was close by, she could also tend to him.

"I know. But where?" He took his cup and plate to the sink, stepped to the other window, opened it, leaned over and looked down. "If I don't cut down that vetch growing up the house wall, it'll come up to the window. It's a wonder that old shed is still stand… *Mio Dio*—that's it." He brought his hand to his forehead, and turned around.

"What is it?" Marina looked up, alarmed.

"The piece of land below. Why didn't I think of this before? The owner let Papa work that land for his own use. I remember that he would plant vegetables there and Mama had planted a couple of roses there, too. There is something in the law that says that unless otherwise agreed, Papa would have become the owner of it after twenty years. The owner had no relatives here, and he died shortly after Papa did. I'm going to find out about it. If I can have it, I can turn that shed into a stable for Pallino, maybe even enlarge it. There's enough space to grow vegetables, and… and you can even have a nice flower garden, too."

Marina caught Giorgio's enthusiasm. "I like the idea. It would be so much easier for you, and… and we can even raise a few chickens of our own."

Giorgio rolled his eyes. "Yes, but it's going to take

money to make that shed decent. Let's hope that I can find something to do that will bring in enough money to make this a reality. "I'm going."

Marina finished eating, pensive. His craft was their livelihood. After he had finished the bedroom set, he had earned a little money with small jobs here and here. She wasn't interested in having luxuries. All she wanted was to be able to live within their means. Giorgio was right that rationed food wasn't cheap. She hadn't considered going back to work, and even if she wanted to, she wouldn't take chances with the pregnancy. She bit into a slice of bread to swallow the unwelcome lump that had formed in her throat.

*   *   *

By noon, the sun had broken through the clouds, and the last row of grapes in Anna's vineyard were picked. After *pranzo,* Giorgio would begin on the family's vineyard.

"Come up and eat," Marina called down to Giorgio in the *cantina.* She had Amelia join them for *pranzo,* as she had offered to help pick the grapes for her family. Today, the meal was a real treat. The corn meal *polenta* was enriched with a savory sauce thanks to a little meat that Amelia had bought at a hefty price and had shared it with her. Marina had added a touch of the *porcini* mushrooms to it.

Amelia sank into the chair at the table.

"Mama, are you sure that you feel up to helping me?" Giorgio asked her as he placed a basket of bread on the table.

"I'm fine. If Alda's vineyard is anything like the others, there isn't much to pick between the weather and the birds." Amelia turned to Marina. "You're not eating enough, *bimba.*"

Marina paused with a forkful of *polenta* at her mouth. "I'm happy today with my appetite. The nausea seems to be going away. I didn't mind cooking, either."

"I got some interesting news from Daniela today." Giorgio smiled.

"I hope it's good." Marina raised her eyes to heaven.

"The soldier, Heinrich, told her that a new commander is taking over the encampment. The present one isn't well and has to leave."

"We haven't caused problems for the present one, and I don't foresee us causing any for the new one, so it's really of no importance to us." Marina shrugged.

A little later, Giorgio took the lead rein and patted Pallino on the neck as he stood tethered to the ring in the wall. "Come. Hopefully, you'll soon be closer to home."

Pallino shook himself, jingling the little bells on his bridle, as if happy at the prospect.

Marina descended the garden steps to see if the little rosemary bush that her mother had started for her had taken root. Standing at the waist high wall, she could see part of the vineyards and the chestnut groves that had begun to turn color. Her gaze rested on what, hopefully, would be their property. In her mind's eye, she pictured the stable for Pallino, a hen house to the side, vegetables and flowers. She shook herself. Daydreaming was nice, but she still had things to do in the house. She climbed up the steps to the street. At the top step, she paused, thinking back to the incident on the church steps. If it hadn't been for Don Antonio and Giorgio... A shiver ran along her spine.

*   *   *

The grapes were picked, the wine made, and mushrooms were still found. One morning towards the end of September, Marina and Daniela trudged along the path from their favorite spot in the chestnut grove beyond the village. They had found a small basket of mushrooms. Giorgio had gone to the Commune House to inquire about the land.

Marina frowned at the fine drizzle that had begun to fall. "We should have known better than to look for mushrooms today. It was bound to rain."

"But look at what we found." Daniela held up a chubby mushroom. "Have you ever thought that as the seasons come and go, we simply get older?"

Marina stared wide-eyed at her sister's serious expression. "Mercy! You're only seventeen."

"Maybe it's the war, but I feel older." Daniela pulled her shawl closer around her shoulders. "Let's hurry home before we really get rained on and get sick."

At her sister's sad tone, a surge of tenderness washed over Marina. Her younger sister had had her own little trial, mistaking infatuation for love. But by having warned Giorgio about the *rastrellamento,* she had played a crucial role in sparing him who knew what fate. Marina placed an arm around her shoulder and kissed her on the cheek.

*   *   *

Marina quickly changed her clothes and dried her hair in front of the fireplace. She looked at the clock on the mantelpiece. Hopefully, Giorgio would be home soon. The days were a little shorter and she was happiest when he was home before dark. All too soon, the hours for the curfew would change. "Marina!" The front door opened and Giorgio called her name ecstatically.

She rushed to him. He had a broad smile on his face. "I'm going to begin clearing our property."

"It's ours? Oh, I'm so happy!" Marina threw her arms around his neck.

"Papa is happy, too," Giorgio said wistfully. "Let me see what I can do."

"I'm coming down. It's stopped raining."

Wrapping a shawl around her shoulders, Marina followed him out the door.

At the far end of the garden wall, a low, wrought iron gate hung between it and the retaining wall of the property. "What a tangled mess. How are you going to get through that?" Marina stared in dismay at the briars that had woven themselves around the bars.

Giorgio didn't waste any time. He climbed on the wall and lowered himself on the other side. "*Ahi!*" He winced as a prickly briar hooked onto his pants. With a few solid whacks of the sickle, he freed the gate and cleared a swath to the shed.

The old shed, once used for tools, could easily hold Pallino. Giorgio tested it here and there with his fists. "Believe it or not, it's still pretty solid. Tomorrow, I'm going to clear more space around it."

"Would you clear the grass around these rosebushes?"

Giorgio knelt and cut down the weeds around them. "There we go."

Marina gingerly walked to them. She touched a little red rose bud on a thin stem. "Here's the beginning of my flower garden. Beauty in the midst of chaos."

*   *   *

"What irony," Marina exclaimed to her mother when she paid her a visit in early October. She was helping Alda to sew new gunnysacks. "The people of Diecimo had to evacuate because of the *sfollamento*. Now they've returned to their homes and have found themselves in the middle of fierce fighting."

September had come to a close with the exciting news that the Buffalo Soldiers had liberated Diecimo. Then, on October 1st, Bagni di Lucca, the lovely little city known for its thermal baths on the other side of the mountains facing the village, had been liberated, too.

"The Germans have been outwitted and they're not happy about it. Praise God for the Americans, but our problems aren't over yet."

Marina remained for a little while and then left. Giorgio had begun to work on the shed and she was anxious to see how he was progressing. She found him working on the shed's door. "How are you doing?"

"Not too bad." He raised his head and looked at the roof. "The roof needs new tiles. The beam will have to be replaced in time, but for now it'll hold."

Marina walked to the retaining wall to the left of the shed. Giorgio joined her. "Now I can look out to the valley and smile." He shaded his eyes. "Marina, look."

Marina looked in the direction of his finger to the valley directly below them. What appeared to be military trucks were heading up the valley. "Could it be the Americans?"

"Yes. Now we can finally see our liberators."

"It doesn't seem possible," Marina whispered. "Maybe the German soldiers will leave the village now."

"I don't think they'll stay much longer." Giorgio put his arm around her. "The Americans aren't a dream. They're real."

"I wonder if Gianni is somewhere nearby to see them." Marina hadn't seen him for a long time now and neither had Giorgio.

"Ehi, ragazzi!"

They both turned to Amelia, who was walking towards them.

"Mama, what do you think of it?" With a sweep of his arm, Giorgio presented their property.

Tears filled Amelia's eyes. "Your father loved this piece of property." She walked to the rosebushes that Marina had now staked erect. "I'm glad that you saved them. I still have the last rose that he picked for me before he died. It's all dried out, but for me it's as if he picked it that day.

"Then they're even more special for us." Marina smiled tenderly at her.

Giorgio looked at this pocket watch. "I'm going to the valley to buy some supplies." He looked around and smiled satisfactorily. "We've done a lot."

*　　　*　　　*

Giorgio got up the next morning and groaned when he opened the shutters. "It looks like rain again. I'd better go to the vineyard and check on Pallino." He pursed his lips. "I hope that some money comes in soon. I need to get him up here before winter comes. What are you going to do?"

"I have to ply some thread." Marina wrinkled her nose.

"It's an annoying task, but it has to be done. Anna offered to come and help me, which will be nice."

"Well, if we don't get up, nothing's going to get done." He kissed her on the forehead and rolled over to the side.

Marina rose and pinned her hair on top of her head. She poured a little water in the washbowl and splashed some on her face. As she dried herself, she met Giorgio's contemplating gaze. "I know I look better when I'm dressed," she said meekly.

"You've never looked lovelier," Giorgio murmured and went downstairs.

*   *   *

Anna came by later that morning to help Marina. "This is the perfect job for this weather. If we continue like this, we'll have moss growing on our backs." She brought a chair close to the fireplace.

"I keep the wardrobe doors open all the time right now to let some air circulate."

Marina and Anna chatted as they each plied thread. They talked about their hopes and dreams when the valley would be finally liberated and the war come to an end. Most of all, they wanted a future for their children.

Marina looked at her reddened finger tips. "Let's stop. My fingers are sore."

"So are mine," Anna said. "If we wanted to make

money, these sheets would come with a hefty price tag considering all the work that goes into them."

"The way things are going for a lot of us that might not be a bad idea. I'm going to make us some *orzo*. How are the children?" Marina hadn't visited Anna lately and missed seeing them, especially little Giorgio.

"They're good. Little Giorgio is learning how to walk, and he never tires of exploring the world around him. Maddalena likes to use the small whisk broom to help sweep the floor. I can't believe how fast they're growing." Anna's voice took on a sad tone. "I just wish that… that Stefano could have come home to see them."

Marina's heart ached, and she felt at a loss for words. Only God knew how many more wouldn't come home.

"I'm sorry." Anna smiled up at her, blinking back tears. "We should be talking about happy things. You and Lisa are sharing so much in this moment."

Marina sat down and gave Anna her glass full of the steaming *orzo*. "I can hardly wait for our babies to be born, but I'm afraid that we're making Mama dizzy with our questions. She has a lot to handle being that it's the first time for both of us…" Marina bit her lip. "At least it is for Lisa.

"Don't say anything more. You're doing fine, and Gianpaolo is fine."

"I know. He's our little angel."

"Have you thought of a name for the baby?"

"If it's a boy, we'll name him Andrea, after my father.

If it's a girl, we haven't decided yet."

"Hopefully, you won't face any rude gossip like I did when my little boy was born."

"Carla had better be careful." Marina tightened her lips. "We can't prove that she was behind a lot of things that have happened, but Giorgio is getting suspicious.

Anna shook her head. "We all grew up together as children. Why do we have to act petty amongst ourselves? You and I have been through good and bad times. Would you believe that talk is still going around because of that stupid comb?"

"What? That's over with, and it wasn't even your comb."

"Go tell some people." She shook her head. "I suppose that all that matters is that you, Giorgio, and I know the truth."

"Yes," Marina replied. "And the nicest part is that we're having a baby!"

*   *   *

Marina felt in good spirits after Anna left. *Pranzo* would be a little later. As she bustled about to prepare something to eat, she hummed a favorite tune.

The door opened, and Giorgio burst into the kitchen waving a letter. "Marina!"

"What is it?" Marina stared, surprised. Giorgio's face beamed like a ray of sunshine.

"The… the lady from Lucca, for whom I made the bedroom set. She… she's so happy with… with the work that I did for her. She… she wants a few pieces of dining room furniture." Giorgio exclaimed. "A hutch, a small side table, and… and maybe a dining table." His words tumbled out in excitement as he read the letter. "She would like me to take the measurements as soon as possible."

Marina clapped her hands at this welcome news. "How wonderful. I'm so happy for you."

"I'm happy for both of us. This is a blessing from heaven!" Giorgio kissed her soundly.

"When are you going?"

Giorgio thought for a moment. "As soon as I can. In the meantime, I can go and pick up some supplies tomorrow morning. Let me see what I have downstairs."

Before she could tell him to sit down and eat, Giorgio raced into the *soggiorno* and was out the door.

Marina closed her eyes, grateful for this answered prayer. God was good!

*　　　　　*　　　　　*

The sun broke through the clouds in early afternoon. Giorgio went down to work on the shed, and Marina tidied up the kitchen. She heard the key turn in the door and then the soft voice of Albina.

Marina smiled warmly. "Come in."

"I have to go for water, but I wanted to drop these off

for you. I couldn't wait." She smiled shyly as she handed Marina a soft packet. "I also have one to give to Lisa."

Marina opened it with a cry of delight. "Oh, Albina. How precious." She held two tiny light blue booties, each threaded with the same color ribbon.

"I'll make pink ones, too, even if Mama thinks that you'll have a boy."

"That will make Lisa happy." Marina recalled how Lisa had told her that a boy would be a welcome change.

"I can hardly wait to become an aunt." Albina kissed her. "I'm going, otherwise I may get rained upon."

When Giorgio entered the kitchen a little later, his gaze fell upon the packet on the table. "What's this?"

Marina placed the booties in his hand. "Albina made them. She says that she'll also make pink ones in case it's a girl. Aren't they pretty?"

Giorgio couldn't speak as he looked at the tiny items in his palm. "What a miracle. *Amore mio,* you're carrying a miracle!"

"You're an important part of it, you know," Marina said softly, recalling what Don Antonio had told her.

Giorgio nodded. "I have a feeling that things are changing for the better. We'll have money coming in. We have a baby on the way. The Americans have arrived. All we need is for the war to end and for Gianni to come home."

"I wonder if he's been to the vineyard anymore. Now that the Americans are here, I want him to come home. I want him to see the babies born," Marina said wistfully. "Stefano can't, but he can."

Giorgio's eyes welled with tears as he remembered his friend. "I still hurt when I think of Stefano. I wish that Anna could have some closure, even if it's only getting his dog tags back."

Later in bed that night, Marina prayed for all those who had lost their loved ones in the war. She smiled at Giorgio's gentle snoring. Yes. God was good.

*   *   *

"What miserable weather," Amelia moaned one drizzly afternoon in mid-October. "Summer was bad and before we know it, it will be winter." She lifted a white linen napkin from a half-filled basket of chestnuts on the table.

"When you boil them to make *ballocci,* you won't even remember the rain." Marina's eyes sparkled at the plump reddish brown *marrone* chestnuts that were sweeter, and when boiled, were filling. As much as she had wanted to help Amelia find them, bending over wasn't easy anymore. She was also afraid of getting sick because of the rainy weather.

"Thank you for the *minestrone.*" Amelia sniffed at the aroma emanating from the still warm vegetable soup in the saucepan.

"I thought that you might like to have something ready for dinner." Marina placed her hand on a chair and eased herself to the floor in front of the fireplace. "I'm going to light the fire. You're going to catch a cold."

"No." Amelia waved off Marina's concern. "I'm a tough old bird. I'll be fine."

Marina laughed. Amelia was just as spunky as her *nonna*. "Ooh!" She eased herself back up onto her feet and brought the chair with Amelia's jacket hung from it closer to the fire to dry out. The crackling fire sent a flurry of sparks up the chimney and soon filled the little kitchen with warmth.

Amelia frowned at the damp, tattered jacket that she wore for outdoor tasks. "I suppose I should throw that away. It's seen better days, but it was a gift from Paolo," she said with a note of sadness.

Filled with tenderness Marina gently squeezed Amelia's hand. "I don't think that he would want you to wear it like that." She saw a faraway look in Amelia's eyes, as if she was lost in time.

Suddenly, Amelia smiled. "I know what I'll do. I'll put it in Rosa's box for her to sleep in."

"There you go." Marina nodded in approval. The precious jacket wouldn't be tossed and Chicco's mama could sleep in luxury.

"Sit down a moment." Amelia patted the chair next to her. "How are you feeling?"

"I'm over the nausea, thanks be to God. It makes being in the kitchen a little easier."

Amelia looked at her fondly. "You look good, and

you're glowing."

"I'm so happy and Giorgio is up in the clouds. I'll have to grab his feet to get him back down." She laughed and then became serious. "Anytime that something happens and I become frightened or upset, I touch my belly and keep telling our little one that everything is alright."

"Just keep reassuring him or her that it will be fine." Amelia's eyes twinkled. "Hopefully, when the baby is born, this accursed war will have ended."

"I really hope so. Reports say that the rains are hindering any actions on the part of both the Allies as well as the Germans. Thankfully, the Americans have arrived in Bagni di Lucca. From the garden, Giorgio and I saw a line of army trucks heading up the Fegana valley. People in the area have said that they have set up a bivouac."

Amelia smiled with satisfaction. "I've noticed that there aren't as many soldiers in the village as before."

"I have, too."

"I wonder how Mussolini is doing with his republic." Amelia's tone was caustic.

"His quest for the glory of Italy has crumbled into pieces. The more the Allies have advanced north, the more demoralized he has become." Marina got up and looked out the window. "It looks as if it has stopped raining. I'd better go. I don't want to be out late."

"I'll walk you home." Amelia rose and reached for the shawl that she always kept handy.

Marina shook her head, and hugged Amelia. "No, I'll

be fine. Enjoy the *minestrone.*"

Amelia wrapped her arms around Marina with a mock grimace. "This isn't easy to do anymore, *bimba mia.*"

"Giorgio says the same thing." Marina laughed. "But I wouldn't have it any other way right now." Marina left Amelia and strolled up the street, listening to the drip, drip of the eaves. A ray of sunshine broke through the late afternoon clouds and shone upon her, warming her body for a moment. She let out a contented sigh. *We're fine, little one, we're fine.*"

*　　　　　*　　　　　*

"Marina, Marina!"

Wiping her floury hands with her apron, Marina quickly opened the doors to the balcony in the early afternoon the next day.

Giorgio was down below and waving his arms excitedly. "Look above the church."

"What is it? What…" The drone of planes was nothing new, but these were not fighters flying north. This was a battle between what looked like an American fighter plane and a German one in the sky above the bell tower.

Marina stared transfixed with Giorgio and their neighbors at the scenario unfolding in the cloudless sky. A few children jumped up a down rooting for the American fighter.

A cry of dismay escaped everyone when the American

fighter plane was hit.

Marina offered a prayer for the man whom she knew was now a casualty, but after a moment, she gasped as a ghostly image emerged from the black smoke of the plane. As the fighter spiraled downward, a parachute became more visible. The parachute floated lazily towards the mountains to their left. Marina rushed outside, and, along with Giorgio and the neighbors, she hurried towards the public fountain where there was a better view of the valley. From the valley, she made out flashes of light, like mirrors catching the sun's rays.

"The Americans are signaling the pilot." Giorgio said excitedly.

With the wind in his favor, the American pilot slowly but surely landed in their camp.

"Aha, bravo!" Giorgio clapped his hands enthusiastically.

His enthusiasm transmitted to Marina, who joined in the excitement of the happy outcome.

In a matter of minutes, a *boom* echoed through the valley. A thick, dark column of smoke arose from where the fighter plane had crashed. A group of men and boys hurriedly started down a small path that led down to a grove of chestnuts.

"Pallino! I pray God that the stable was spared. I'm going, too," Giorgio said, hurrying after everyone else.

Marina walked back home. She pictured Don Antonio, wide-eyed at what was happening above the church. She finished preparing the bread and decided to visit Amelia.

In the *piazza*, she came upon a group of animated, disheveled youngsters who were describing their close encounter with the fighter plane. On the low wall flanking the chapel sat an elderly man. He had been widowed for several years, and was a pillar in the village, always giving a helping hand when needed. Marina's heart went out to him as he looked and no doubt felt miserable. His face and arms bled from being pricked and scratched. His daughter sat next to him, gently dabbing at the wounds.

"We… were playing down in… in the field when… when we heard a loud noise and looked up…"

"And I saw the plane come down fast!" A dark-haired boy added his input, interrupting the young girl. "We… we ran in every direction!"

"He got the worst of it," another boy said, nodding towards the elderly man.

"Curses to this war and those who started it!" The elderly man shook his fist in anger. He had made sure the youngsters had safely fled before he had launched himself into a hedge of briars. "*Al diavolo, la gloria!*"

The glory could indeed go to hades as far as he was concerned. Marina found out later that he had developed a fever and had to be hospitalized.

*　　　　*　　　　*

Marina couldn't understand the feeling of uneasiness

that weighed her down the next morning. The fighter plane had crashed in another vineyard, so Pallino was safe. Giorgio was at his mother's to help her pour wine from a demi-john into flaskets. The work on the shed was progressing. He had received a down payment to begin the work on the furniture. It was the second day in a row that the sun was shining, and she took advantage of it by visiting her family. When she reached the junction, Heinrich wasn't there, but she didn't think anything of it. With the arrival of the Americans, many of the soldiers had left, disheartened by the Allied gains.

Marina turned the key and entered the kitchen.

Nelsa sat in front of the fireplace, stirring the bubbly white milk that would soon produce cheese.

"*Bimba,* sit down. Your mother is at the shop."

Marina sat down contemplating her *nonna*, whose bandana always managed to be a little askew on her grey head. "Albina?"

"She's paying a visit to a neighbor."

The door burst open. Albina stumbled inside followed by Giorgio, gasping. He removed the key from the door and quickly closed it behind him.

Stunned, Nelsa looked at them with the big slotted spoon suspended in the air.

Marina looked from one to the other. Before she could say anything, Albina, on the verge of hysteria, sank down on a chair.

Giorgio found his voice. "Heinrich... and... another

soldier have deserted."

Marina sucked in her breath and looked at Albina. "Daniela… *oh Signore!*"

Albina raised her head. "They've taken… taken her hostage," she cried out. "Giorgio… saved my life but… but he has to save his!"

"Giorgio…" Marina looked at him in desperation, feeling sick.

Nelsa jumped up from the chair. "What is this?"

Giorgio gasped. "I was at Mama's. There was shouting and… I… I went to see what was happening. A neighbor screamed that the Germans were rounding up anyone they could find to put together ten hostages. People were… were fleeing. I ran back to Mama's. I saw two soldiers and their commander coming down the street with five hostages. Daniela was among them. I waited until they had disappeared and ran here. On the way I saw Albina." Giorgio placed his hand on Marina's shoulders. "Everyone who can is fleeing to safety. I'm going, too."

Marina's knees buckled, but Giorgio grabbed her in time. "I have to save my life for our sakes."

"No, oh, no!" Marina sobbed. She wrapped her arms around his neck. She wouldn't let him go, she wouldn't!

"Please, Marina!" His voice grew desperate. "I have to go!"

Tears flowed down Nelsa's face. "Marina, he's right. He has to save his life!"

"What of Mama?" Marina cried out. "She's out there!"

Giorgio shook his head. "I don't know."

At the pounding on the door and a woman's desperate voice, Nelsa opened to Alda who entered frantically. "What's happening?" she cried out.

Giorgio managed to disengage himself from Marina's embrace. "I have to go. I love all of you. I love you!"

Before Marina could cry out to him, Giorgio quickly opened the door and fled.

CHAPTER TWENTY

awn had barely broken when Albina set a frugal breakfast on the table and turned to Marina who sat listless, staring at her plate. "Try to eat something and then go and lie down. You tossed and turned all night."

"I don't know if I'll survive this," Marina said softly and then touched her belly. "But I have to, for the baby." She brought her hands to her face. "Could Daniela have helped Heinrich to escape? Was she playing a game with me, with all of us, and did the unthinkable?"

"No, I won't believe that of her. She may have been infatuated with him at first, but that was over."

"I don't know what to believe anymore. My sister is a hostage, my husband is God knows where, and Gianni? Where is he?"

Alda trudged into the kitchen.

Marina's heart ached. Gone was the sparkle in her mother's eyes and the brisk step. In a matter of hours, she had aged.

"Mama," Albina said softly, "come and eat something." She took her gently by the arm.

"I prayed to God when I went to bed that he would take me and let Daniela live. But this morning I woke up, instead." Alda unsuccessfully blinked back tears.

Albina sat down next to her and frowned at the flickering flame of a candle. "We can hardly see each other in here."

"Now, more than ever we can't open the shutters. We have to let them think that no one is home."

Marina looked at the clock. "What's going to happen? If they do as they did in other places, the deadline is noon. It's barely six o'clock in the morning."

"Do you have your rosary?" Albina asked softly.

"Yes. Let's pray." Marina took the shimmering rosary from her pocket and kissed the crucifix.

That was their only hope.

*   *   *

"Mama! Albina!"

Marina dropped the clothes that she was folding in the dining room. She rushed to the door followed closely by Albina. "It's Daniela!" Marina quickly opened the door.

Marina opened it and Daniela stumbled inside, disheveled, laughing and crying. Marina grabbed her hands.

Alda held her tightly and kissed her over and over. "I can die happy now."

When Daniela had regained her composure, she straightened up. "A soldier... not Heinrich... returned. He wanted to desert to the Americans in Bagni di Lucca, but changed his mind. We've all been released."

Marina held Daniela by the shoulders. "Daniela, you… you had nothing to do with…"

Daniela shook her head. "No! Nothing!" She looked at Marina as tears welled in her eyes. "Did you really believe that I could have?"

Hot tears ran down Marina's face. "Giorgio had to flee… you were taken." She frowned. "If you didn't do anything, why… why would you have been a hostage? The soldiers had escaped. Their commanding officer wouldn't have known about you."

"Marina, I swear by everything that's dear to me, I had nothing to do with this."

"You didn't, but someone did for sure," Albina said.

"Never mind. She's safe. Now I just want Giorgio home." Marina closed her eyes.

"Giorgio is right here behind you!"

Marina whirled around. In their excitement, they had left the door open.

Disheveled, with dark circles under his eyes and his clothes smelling of hay and goats, Giorgio stepped inside the door.

"Oh, thank God! Thank God!" Marina laughed and cried as she held him tightly and kissed him. "Where… where did you go?"

"I wasn't that far away. I hid in a barn just outside the village and kept the goats company." He sniffed at his shirtsleeve and wrinkled his nose. "But you figured that out already. I had told our neighbor where I was going. He let me know that the hostages were released."

"Shall we go home?" Marina asked.

Giorgio could only nod in assent.

Marina and Giorgio had barely passed Amelia's home when Giorgio stopped short. "I smell smoke."

Marina felt amused. "I suppose that after the smell of goats it's a welcome change."

"This isn't wood smoke from a chimney." Giorgio narrowed his eyes.

They both turned, startled, at a scream behind them. It was Albina running towards them, crying hysterically.

Marina hastened towards her. "Albina! Albina!" She managed to grab her. "What's happened?"

"The… the soldiers are… are burning our home!" Albina broke away from her but Giorgio was quick and grabbed her, holding on tightly as she fought him, beside herself.

Frantic, Marina tried to rush up the street as fast as she could.

Amelia came out of the house at the commotion and quickly took in the situation. She tore her gaze from Giorgio and Albina, who had sunk to her knees on the ground, to Marina. "Marina! Wait!"

With an effort, she reached Marina who was already half-way to her former home and managed to hold her back. "Don't go any farther!"

Marina choked and coughed in the cloud of smoke that enveloped them.

"No, oh no," Marina sobbed. "Mama! Daniela!" She watched them stumble down the street towards them. Her *nonna* sank down on a low wall, sobbing.

CHAPTER TWENTY-ONE

Marina still couldn't believe what had transpired. She sat dazed while Giorgio stoked the fire and cursed under his breath. The same fire that could warm a home could also destroy it, or a good part of it.

"I'm going back to the house." Giorgio rose with an effort. "The neighbors are keeping an eye on it, or what's left of it." He placed his hands on Marina's shoulders. "It's… it's hard now, but we will survive this."

Marina felt beyond tears. "How much more can we handle?" Her voice broke into a sob.

Giorgio took her in his arms and cupped her face. "One day at a time, we'll survive this. Take a deep breath. We have a baby to think about. We have Daniela and Albina here with us and your mother and *Nonna* are with my mother. They all have a roof over their heads."

"I know." Marina nodded. "Go and see how your mother is feeling, and I'm also worried about Lisa." Marina dried her tears with her apron.

"I'll take care of it. I love you." Giorgio kissed her tenderly and left.

Daniela descended the stairs as Giorgio closed the door behind him. Her face was taut, her eyes swollen from crying.

Marina's heart went out to her. She couldn't begin to imagine her terror when she was rounded up with the others as a hostage, and then seeing the soldiers torch the house... She opened her arms to her. For a moment they clung together without speaking. Marina held her at arm's length. "I know we've lost something dear, but it will be alright. You're here with us. We'll make it all right."

"Marina," Daniela said softly, "I swear that I didn't do anything to encourage Heinrich to desert. I didn't!"

"I know you didn't. Losing the house is nothing compared to what would have happened to you, had the other soldier not returned."

Albina entered the kitchen. Daniela turned a tear-wet face to her. "What's... what's going to happen... to us?"

With their arms around each other Marina cried along with her sisters, but also reassured them that if they had managed to survive today, they would survive tomorrow, too.

*   *   *

A week had gone by since the fire. Marina stepped outside on the balcony one early afternoon and called out to Pallino, who was down at the stable with Giorgio. Pallino shook his head, jingling the bells as if returning the greeting. She raised her head at the ominous clouds that hovered above her. The respite from the rain wouldn't last long.

Daniela was at school and Albina had gone to visit Alda and Nelsa. Heartbreaking as it was to have lost their home, Marina couldn't help but feel grateful that they were all safe. Don Antonio had visited to offer any assistance. Neighbors had visited with offers of help, especially Anna, who was crushed at what had happened. Marina hadn't seen Carla, but she really didn't care. Carla could be unpredictable. What she did care about was whether or not Gianni knew about the fire, and where he was.

She felt a drop on her arms. She called down to Giorgio, "It's beginning to rain, Giorgio. You had better come up."

Giorgio quickly went into the *cantina* for an old blanket that he always kept handy for Pallino. He steadied him and placed the blanket over his back. "I'd better take him back down to the vineyard. I hope that it won't get worse. God, I can hardly wait for the stable to be ready."

Marina watched him as he led Pallino down the street and felt the blood drain from her face. She sucked in her breath. A tall, German officer was walking towards Giorgio. She watched, hardly breathing. The officer spoke a few words, smiled, patted Pallino, and continued up the street. Marina quickly stepped inside and closed the balcony door. Since the round up, they always removed the key from the front door. To her relief, she heard his booted footsteps pass the house.

Marina walked into the kitchen, pensive. The officer's countenance hadn't been frightening. His smile and that pat for Pallino were a sharp contrast to the behaviors of others of his kind. She had never seen him before. Maybe he was the new replacement for the old commander. Nevertheless, she still feared. Too many things had happened.

Daniela arrived, threw her books on the table in the *soggiorno,* and flew upstairs.

Marina exchanged a glance with Albina who had just returned.

"Something's wrong," Albina said.

Marina didn't waste time and rushed upstairs with Albina close behind her. In the bedroom, they saw Daniela sitting on the edge of the bed, tears streaming down her face.

"Daniela! Wh-what's happened? Why are you crying like this?" Marina sat down next to her and placed an arm around her shoulders.

"It's all my fault!" Daniela cried out.

"What are you talking about?" Albina kneeled at Daniela's legs, her hands clutching her skirt.

"When… when I got out… there was a group of people standing near the school… I… I heard one of them call me a whore when I passed by. They… said that… that because of me people would have died. I wish I could die! I'm not going back to school," Daniela sobbed.

Marina felt crushed. She drew her sister to her body, and held her head against her shoulder to let her cry out her anguish. "You're not a whore. Don't ever, ever believe that."

"Who were they? I'll tell them a thing or two!" Albina got to her feet, incensed.

Marina looked up at her and shook her head. She cupped Daniela's face. "Listen to me. You know how people are. Nothing happened. Everyone is safe." Marina brushed back Daniela's hair from her face. "Wash your face, and come downstairs to have a little something to eat, alright?"

Daniela straightened up. "I don't understand it. Did the soldiers burn the house because they found Heinrich's uniform in the basement?"

"Yes," Marina said.

Daniela sprang to her feet. "Did Heinrich flee naked?"

Albina gasped. "Where did he get the clothes to flee? They certainly weren't Papa's."

Marina sat stunned. The scenario grew murkier.

*   *   *

"I said that I didn't want to go back to school, but I won't let myself be put down by people's talk." Daniela poured hot milk into her cup of *orzo* and sat down to her breakfast the next morning.

"Good girl. That's the only way to fight all of this."

Marina sighed with relief. She had feared that Daniela would withdraw into herself. She sat down next to her and dunked a thin slice of bread into her milk. It was going to be a good day.

"If I don't pick up my life, I'll go crazy!"

Albina joined them in the kitchen. "I'm going to help you ply thread, Marina, but first I want to visit Mama and *Nonna*."

"I'd really appreciate that."

Giorgio brought in an armful of wood. A little smile appeared on his face. "May I join you?"

Marina patted the empty seat next to her.

Giorgio looked at the faces that sat around the table. "I don't know if I can get used to being surrounded by women."

"As long as it's us, I don't mind," Marina said mischievously.

"We'd better begin the day. Albina sighed.

Daniela rose. "Thank you, Marina for having us with you."

"You know that where Giorgio and I are, you'll always have a home." Marina smiled and tried to swallow the lump in her throat. "You stay focused on the children. Albina, tell Mama that I'll go visit her later in the day."

Giorgio followed the girls with his gaze. He turned to Marina. "How are you feeling?"

"Fine, but I'll have to buy a larger size wool dress and a cardigan. I'm growing!"

"We have some money now. The problem is, you'll have to go on your own to see what you need." He got up. "I'd better go to the house and see what has to be done."

"We had our little treasures on the dressers. Now… who knows…"

"I'll get a basket. Whatever I find, I'll bring home, alright?" He kissed her on the forehead and left.

Marina went upstairs to do the rooms. The girls had made the bed. The room was neat. Suddenly, she realized that they only had the clothes they wore. She had given them her nightgowns, but they would need clothes. They would also need the more important things like identification booklets. She sat down on the edge of the bed. The fire had turned their world upside down. She opened the bedroom windows, welcoming the fresh air, and descended the stairs.

She took a broom from the balcony and began to sweep the strewn damp leaves from in front of the house. She turned quickly at the sound of heavy footsteps and came face to face with the German officer, who inclined his head.

"*Buon giorno.*" He smiled as he greeted her in perfect Italian.

"*Buon giorno a lei.*" Marina used the traditional form of greeting for strangers or in deference to a person's position.

Marina studied him for a moment. He was tall and solidly built with a well-proportioned body and perhaps in his mid-forties. His facial expression was open and friendly. His eyes were brown as, well as his hair. His uniform was, as they all were, spare and military, but there was something about him…

If she studied him, she sensed that he studied her, too, with a tender expression. *"Tu abiti qui?"*

Marina nodded. She lived here.

"Tu mi ricordi mia figlia. Lei e' giovane come te," the officer said wistfully as tears filled his eyes. *"Posso chiedere come ti chiami?"*

He clearly missed his daughter who was her age. Instead of the enemy, Marina saw a man who longed for his family. She smiled and gave her name when he politely asked it of her. *"Mi chiamo* Marina."

"Marina". He repeated softly. *"Bello."* Then he frowned, and looked quizzically at her. *"La tua casa di famiglia e'… e' stata… bruciata?"*

Tears sprang to her eyes as she nodded. Her family home had been burned. She surmised that perhaps he had heard her name mentioned in regard to the house.

The officer closed his eyes and shook his head sadly. *"Io sono arrivato due giorni fa'. Mi dispiace."* He sighed deeply and hastily cleared his throat. *"Io devo andare."* He inclined his head again, and continued down the street.

She watched him as he turned the corner. He had arrived only two days ago. Her lips curved into a smile. Somehow, she felt relieved that he hadn't had anything to do with what had happened.

She was about to enter the house when Don Antonio called out to her, "Marina, wait for me."

"Don Antonio, this is a surprise. Please come in."

"I wish that I could, but I can't. I have to get back to church for catechism for the little ones." He stopped to catch his breath. "Giorgio told me that your sisters, as well as your mother and *Nonna,* need new identity booklets. I already spoke with your mother. If your sisters are happy about it, we could go tomorrow morning to the Commune."

Marina clasped her hands. "That would be wonderful. Maybe on the way back, we can stop in the valley to shop for clothes, too. They have just the clothes on their backs, and I need to buy something a little bigger." She gently patted her belly.

"You women will have to figure that out." He laughed.

Marina offered a prayer of thanks to God later that night.

*   *   *

The October air had a chill to it. Happy with their purchases and grateful for their temporary identity papers, Marina drew her shawl around her head later that afternoon, and decided to visit Lisa.

Lisa greeted her warmly when she stepped into the house. "Come in. How are you?"

Marina sat down in front of a cheery fire next to her.

"I'm fine, just dazed. What about you?"

"With all that's happened, it's enough that we're up and about."

"Something strange happened two days ago." Marina recounted her encounter with the officer. "There's something about him that makes him stand out from the others."

"You mean he's *good*?" Lisa looked skeptical. "This *is* news."

"It's hard to believe, but I think so."

"For everyone's sake, I hope that you're right."

Suddenly, Marina felt the urge to leave.

Lisa noticed her restlessness. "Marina, what's wrong?"

"All of a sudden I feel that I have to go to the vineyard. Why, I don't know. I can only stay on the mule path. It's as if… as if Gianni is calling me there."

"You have to trust your instincts. Do you want me to go with you?"

"No, I'll be fine. Giorgio is at the house again… *oh Signore,…* I'll have to pass in front of it." Marina raised her eyes to heaven.

"I'm coming with you."

"No," Marina shook her head. "It's going to be bad enough for me to see it."

"Please be careful," Lisa pleaded.

When she arrived at the house, Marina cried out upon seeing the blackened stones of her home. She peeked into what had been the door of the kitchen and saw a mess of sodden ash, and charred and burned pieces of beams.

Giorgio was sifting through the muck. He looked at her, startled. "Why are you here?" he asked and got up, holding a tarnished, now blackened pot that had once prepared many a meal of *polenta*.

"I wanted to take a walk." Marina didn't want to reveal the sense of urgency that she felt.

"Well, here's a pot and here," Giorgio stepped to what was the sink, "are the pictures of Gianni and your father."

Marina gasped and reached for them. He had wiped the filmy glass as best as he could. She pressed them to her chest. "Mama will be so happy." She threw her arms around him and kissed him soundly.

Giorgio smiled. "Let's hope I find something else. Don't be out too long, alright?"

"I won't."

Reaching the path, she saw Carla walking in her direction, wiping her hands and muttering to herself. "Carla," she managed a smile. "How are you?"

Instead of a decent reply, all she got was a hard, sullen look. "I'm fine. Now I'm fine." Carla spat out.

"No," Marina said gently. "You're not. What's wrong?"

Carla fixed her gaze on her. "Everything's fine. The best is yet to come."

Marina stared quizzically at Carla, who rushed past her without saying another word.

She reached the path that led down to the vineyard. The thick blackberry bushes were almost bare of leaves as well as the once lush vines. A bird flitted about in its branches of the peach tree in search of perhaps a withered fruit.

She fixed her gaze on the path and frowned. A man's legs, and a pair of boots, such as soldiers wear made her cry out. She gingerly walked down a few steps, grabbing hold of a branch of a young oak tree. At a groan, her body tensed. She carefully managed to step over the man's legs and stared aghast, her hand on her chest. Lying on the ground, bleeding from a wound on the back of his head, was the German officer. Marina hesitated, not knowing what to do. Then she remembered the words they had exchanged in the street. *"Mia figlia e' giovane come tu,"* he had told her.

CHAPTER TWENTY-TWO

arina knelt down and tentatively placed her hand on the pulse at his neck.

The pulse of life beat against Marina's fingers. To her relief, the officer groaned and stirred. He had been struck on the back of his head, but Marina couldn't see anything lying near him that was stained with blood. What was he doing here? Who had struck him?

Again, the officer groaned, lifted his hand to his head and slowly turned on his side.

"Sono Marina." Marina gently reassured him of her presence. She looked around. The stable was too far down to get to the metal bucket always left outside for rainwater. She spied a little puddle of water on a large indentation on a rock a few feet away from her. It was better than nothing. She took off her bandana and dipped it into the puddle. "This will help you." She folded the bandana into a pad, and gently pressed it to the back of his head.

He winced and held the pad to his head on his own as Marina helped him to sit up. He looked up a her and managed a smile. *"Grazie."*

Hesitantly, she asked him how he found himself here

and if he remembered what had happened.

"Un Partigiano… e qui… qualcosa… mi… ha colpito."
Marina froze. He was here because of a Partisan. *Gianni!* Something had struck him. Raindrops began to dampen her. Her conscience told her that she couldn't leave him like this. Somehow, she would have to help him into the hayloft down below and pray at the same time that Gianni wouldn't be hiding there.

"Piove." Marina gestured as the drops thickened to a fine drizzle. *"Andiamo giu' alla stalla."* She gestured down towards the stable, and drew her shawl tightly about her, and helped him to his feet.

The officer rapidly scanned her body. *No, no. Tu… tu aspetti un bambino. Non puoi andare laggiu."*

Marina smiled at his consideration of her pregnancy. *"Ma lei…"* Her heart slammed into her ribs at the unmistakable voices of two German soldiers who were running towards them. She turned quickly to the officer whose face blanched.

He placed himself front of her as the soldiers advanced, their weapons drawn.

"No, no!" she cried out.

Grimacing, the officer shouted an order to them. The soldiers looked at each other, baffled, and lowered their weapons.

The officer turned to Marina and smiled reassuringly. *"Non avere paura,"* he said gently.

Marina swallowed hard, but she had nothing to fear.

The officer spoke in a firm voice to his men, apparently explaining what had happened.

"Marina, vai a casa. Io vado con loro."

Marina nodded, relieved to be able to go home, but she expressed concern that he was strong enough to return to the camp.

"Tutto bene." He smiled warmly. He extended his hand and helped her onto the mule path.

Marina felt a strange warmth deep inside as she gave him his hand. It was strong, yet gentle and reassuring. It had stopped drizzling, but the air was colder. She turned to the officer.

"Grazie, Marina. Grazie," he said in a grateful tone of voice and extended his hand again.

She gave him hers, which he held in both of his.

He turned and continued on with his men.

"Marina!"

She quickly turned to Giorgio who ran towards her, disheveled and desperate.

*　　　*　　　*

"I… I still can't believe this." Giorgio sat in front of the cheery blaze of the fireplace, along with Albina and Daniela, who were still in shock at what had happened.

"I can't either." Marina placed a hand on her still fast beating heart. Her encounter with weapons drawn and pointed at her was something that she would never forget. "The officer was so considerate of me. Who would have thought that a few words exchanged in the street with him would bring me to this?" She shook her head.

"Someone must have found out about Gianni and told him. But who?" Daniela asked.

Marina looked intently at her and then at Giorgio. "I'm beginning to think that we have someone to fear other than the Germans. One of our own is desperate to hurt us."

"I think you're right." Giorgio's jaw tensed. "Too many things have been happening, and I wish to God I knew who's behind it all."

"I do, too. Or maybe I don't. Oh, I don't know." Marina rolled her eyes. "I wish that I knew the officer's name. I feel as if he sees his daughter in me." She placed her hands on her temples. "If Mama finds out about this, it will kill her and it won't do Lisa any good either."

"We won't say anything," Albina shook her head. "Let's just hope that no one else will, though."

Later in bed, the tears that flowed freely as she lay in Giorgio's arms helped Marina to finally fall asleep.

*   *   *

After Daniela left for school the next morning and Giorgio was in the workshop, Marina and Albina brought the large kneading board to the table in the kitchen. Today they would bake bread. They had barely put out the flour before the front door opened. Alda and Lisa rushed inside, frantic.

"Oh mio Dio!" Alda cupped Marina's face, her eyes taking in every inch of her body. "Are you alright?"

"I'm fine, Mama," Marina reassured her and turned to Lisa. "I'm fine. Sit down." She pulled out a chair from the table and explained what had happened. "The officer immediately took command. He was so grateful that I helped him. Who told you?"

"It was all over the village. People are always on that path and someone was bound to see something," Lisa said.

Marina didn't argue. But something didn't feel right.

When they left with Albina to go to the shop, Marina lingered with Giorgio on their little piece of property. It was a small beginning, but Marina felt rich. Now that the weeds and the briars had been cleared, everything took on a new look, including the roses that already showed the results of tender loving care.

The ground was hard with years of neglect, but with a good dose of muscle, Giorgio had just dug up a corner of the garden for the planting of a few late winter vegetables. He paused to catch his breath and looked around, satisfied. "I think that it's all falling into place. Now I can really work on that shed."

"You should bring Pallino up, so that he can see his new home," Marina said gaily.

"I might do that."

"Being here in the sunshine does me good."

"I hope that I do, too." Giorgio looked at her keenly.

She stepped up to him and kissed him lightly on the lips. "That goes without saying."

"Marina! Giorgio!"

They both turned to Carla, who stood at the gate holding a water jug.

"Carla!" Marina exclaimed in surprise. "Come and see our property." Marina waved at her to join them.

"I was going to the fountain and saw the gate open." Carla stepped inside and looked around in amazement. "How lovely!"

Giorgio smiled, but without enthusiasm. "There's still plenty of work to do."

"Let's take a little break, Giorgio." Marina wiped her hands on her apron. "Come up, Carla." The least that she could do, in courtesy, was to invite her to visit.

"I don't want to keep you from your work."

"Don't worry," Giorgio said. "It will still be there tomorrow."

Marina didn't miss Giorgio's lack of enthusiasm as they climbed the garden steps. Courtesy wasn't her only reason for inviting Carla up. Maybe she could find out something.

Marina placed a few slices of bread and her last jar of peach jam on the table. She scooped up embers from the fireplace and placed them in the burners to heat water for the *orzo*.

"How are you feeling?" Carla looked a Marina with concern. "I still can't get over your experience. To have seen the soldiers run to you with their weapons drawn…" Carla caught herself.

Marina exchanged a quick glance with Giorgio, whose face had turned dark. Every fiber in her body had gone on the alert, but she kept herself in check. "I was terrorized, but thank God the officer explained everything. Who attacked the officer and on our property, I don't know, and maybe never will."

"Not only, "who," but why?" Giorgio asked grimly, his gaze boring into Carla.

Marina sensed his suspicion. She poured the *orzo* into glasses and placed them on the table. "I met you on the way to the vineyard. Did you notice anything unusual?"

"No, no. I… I know I sounded rude, but I'm just relieved that the Americans have arrived. We can finally be rid of these Germans." Carla sighed with apparent relief. She drank her *orzo* and rose abruptly. "Well, I'd better go. Thank you for the *orzo*, Marina. I'm glad that you're alright."

"Not half as glad as I am," Giorgio said through clenched teeth, his hard gaze resting on Carla.

After Carla left, Marina turned to Giorgio.

"What?" he asked.

"It's probably nothing… but now I remember that she was wiping her hands when I met her."

"She may be the answer to everything."

"What are you saying?"

"She could be the one who struck him," Giorgio said grimly.

"*What?*" Marina's eyes went wide. "I didn't see any rock or… anything bloodstained lying around. You… you don't think… that she could have done that… and…"

"And put the blame on you, or Gianni. I wouldn't be surprised. Too many things have happened and I'm getting suspicious," Giorgio said matter-of-factly.

"She… she couldn't detest me that much." Marina felt a little sick at the thought.

"Detest you? How about *hate* you? I have a feeling that we're going to find out more about our friend."

Marina sank down onto a chair, unnerved.

*   *   *

November arrived, bringing the first snow to the Alps. The day of the commemoration of the dead was a beautiful day, but this year it arrived with a biting cold wind.

Marina decided to forgo the predawn service at the cemetery, but visited a little later with Giorgio. She stood quietly at her baby's gravesite. A small stone angel now watched over it, and at its feet, a little narrow vase held a rosebud picked from the garden.

Giorgio adjusted the ferns that framed the oval mound and pushed a small, white lighted candle into the earth. He rose and put his arm around her shoulders. Marina leaned her head against his. "It's one year," she said softly.

"I know. I like to picture him in heaven playing with other children."

"Gianpaolo," Marina said softly, after they prayed together, "we love you." They were about to leave when Lisa and Marco entered.

Lisa joined her and smiled tenderly at the angel. "Gianni would be proud to know that a little bit of him is in his nephew. Can you wait a moment longer while I pay a quick visit?"

"Of course."

Marina wrapped her heavy shawl more tightly around her body. Thankfully, Lisa and Marco didn't linger any longer than necessary. At the wrought iron gate, Marina turned, gave one final glance, and closed the gate behind her.

She walked in silence, arm in arm with Lisa, immersed in her thoughts. From behind her, she could hear Giorgio and Marco. Although they were talking in low tones, there was no mistaking that their conversation was about the incident with the officer and about Carla.

They reached the crossroad. Marina and Giorgio took leave of Lisa and Marco and continued on in silence. They were soon in the *piazza*.

One of the few persons standing around there was Carla. Marina felt Giorgio's hand squeeze hers, hard. "Let's hurry home," she said quickly. "The wind is getting stronger, and we need to bring up wood for the fireplace."

"Yes, let's go."

They hurried up the street. When they entered the kitchen, Marina sighed with relief, and not just because she was in the warmth of her home. Chicco, who was curled up on the edge of the hearth, got up, arched his back, and stretched. Marina bent over a little to stroke his back, remembering how Giada had loved to sit on the hearth.

Giorgio entered with an armful of wood. "It's freezing out there." He placed the logs in the wicker basket.

"We're home and warm now, praise God. I had covered the embers. If we add some little twigs and a pinecone, we should have the beginnings of a fire."

Giorgio lost no time in warming the kitchen. A tiny spark became a little flame. With a little more kindling wood, he soon had a nice fire going. "Ah." He rubbed his hands together. "That's better. Sit down and warm yourself."

"I hope that the officer has fully recovered. It wasn't serious, but his head must have hurt for a while." Marina smiled.

Giorgio looked at her thoughtfully. "I never thought you'd take an interest in the enemy."

"If he was unconscious, I probably would have been taken as a hostage. Worse yet, if he had died, I could have been shot."

Giorgio winced. "Don't even talk about that. I keep cudgeling my brains to find an answer as to how he knew about Gianni. If Carla is behind all that has happened, I swear that fire and brimstone will be nothing compared to my anger."

Marina cast a sideways glance at him. His jaw was set, his eyes dark. If his suspicions proved true, fire and brimstone *would* be nothing. She felt the pieces of the puzzle were slowly fitting together, and she didn't like what she saw.

CHAPTER TWENTY-THREE

Marina took advantage of the late morning sunshine a few days later. The air was cold but she dressed warmly, reasoning that it couldn't be any worse than being in the house all day because of the rain. She crossed the *piazza* and met Carla, who had been to the store. For no reason, felt a shiver run along her spine. Nevertheless, she greeted her. "How are you?"

"I'm fine. How are you?"

"I'm taking advantage of a little sunshine, although my back is aching. I'm going to see Lisa and maybe go for a walk to the vineyards."

Carla's smiled. "The walk will do you good. Just be careful. There's a lot of movement going on today. You never know what might happen. Take good care of yourself."

Marina stared after her. Carla's smile and manner seemed almost diabolical to Marina. Suddenly, she feared for Gianni. Rather than visit Lisa, she decided to go to the vineyards instead. She inhaled deeply when she approached the blackened walls of her home. Giorgio, with the help of the village bricklayers, had reconstructed part of the façade of the house. After this, they would work on a part of the roof that had been damaged. Urgency took hold of her as she reached the mule path. She barely noticed that above and below her, the vines were bereft of their leaves, or that down in a field, a few sheep were nibbling amongst the dead grasses. From somewhere, a lone sparrow chirped. None of that mattered now.

Where the path curved, she stopped to look down at her family's vineyard and frowned at the sight of two figures coming up the path. An anguished sob escaped her and she hastened her pace just as Gianni stumbled onto the mule path. Behind him was the officer, pointing his weapon at him.

"No, no!" Marina cried out.

The officer whirled around while Gianni pleaded with her. "Marina… go… go home, please."

Defiant, Marina locked her eyes with the officer's. "What has Gianni done to you?"

The officer frowned at her. *"Tu conosci questo Partigiano?"*

She answered that she did know him although she didn't say how. She had to play on the uncertainty in his face. *"Tu hai salvato la mia vita. Lascia Gianni andare. Non ha fatto male a nessuno."*

She reminded him that he had saved her life, and to let Gianni go because he hadn't done anything wrong.

Again, Gianni pleaded. "Marina, go home. Think of the baby!"

Marina held her ground. After what seemed forever, the officer lowered his weapon. He closed his eyes and inhaled deeply. *"Quest'uomo e' tuo marito."* He turned to Gianni. *"Vai con la tua moglie. Vai!"*

Stunned, Marina looked at Gianni whose eyes went wide. The officer had mistaken him for her husband!

"Grazie," Marina said softly. She raised her face to Gianni.

He placed his arm around her shoulders. In a choked voice, he whispered, *"grazie."*

The officer inhaled deeply and inclined his head. When he turned to go on his way, Marina dared to place her hand on his arm. *"Il suo nome?"* She wanted to know who this man was.

"Tobias."

"Grazie, ancora, Tobias." Marina couldn't stop thanking him.

Tobias looked at them a moment, smiled and went on his way.

Marina turned to Gianni and wrapped her arms around his neck, her cheek against his. "Let's go home."

While they walked back to the village, arm in arm, Marina told Gianni about what had happened to their home and that *Nonna* and Alda were living at Amelia's and the girls with her.

Gianni couldn't hold back his emotion when they reached the charred walls of their home. He burst into tears. "Oh, no, no!" With his hand, he caressed a blackened stone. "Oh, Marina, our home…"

Marina took a deep breath. "Giorgio is working along with Bruno, Marco's father, and the village bricklayers to rebuild the damaged walls. It will be finished and… and it will be as good as new," she said gaily. "Come, let's go to Amelia's to see Mama and *Nonna*."

Each villager they met, at first stared, stunned, and then burst into expressions of joy that were followed by hugs.

Marina reached Amelia's and quickly opened the door. "Amelia, Mama, *Nonna*!"

Alda was the first to see Gianni. With a cry of happiness, she flew into his open arms. *"Bimbo!"*

Gianni held his mother tightly against him. He raised his head in time to see Nelsa and Amelia enter the kitchen, staring wide-eyed at him.

He let go of his mother and opened his arms to them.

Amelia quickly dried her tears. "We have to celebrate." She hurried out the door to go downstairs to the *cantina* for a bottle of Aleatico.

Alda couldn't stop caressing Gianni's face. "Marina was right. You do look nice with a beard."

"Enjoy it now, Mama, because I'm getting rid of it," Gianni warned her with a smile.

"If I have to die now, I'll be happy."

Gianni dried his tears and cleared his throat. "You'd better not. I want to enjoy your cooking again." He ran his finger along her cheek. "Poor Mama. You've been through so much. With Papa gone…" His voice trailed off.

Alda smiled. "I've been blessed with your sisters, especially Marina."

"We all did our best, Mama. Ooh." Marina gently patted her belly. "This is the second time the baby has kicked. I think it wants to know what's happening. I should go home now. We have to let everyone else know."

"I'll go." Amelia rushed to the door, then turned to Gianni. "We can all have dinner here. I'll tell everyone. Alda, have Gianni freshen up. There are towels upstairs."

"Oh, that sounds good," Gianni said gratefully.

Alda poured hot water from a pot into the pitcher that was always kept handy. "Come upstairs, and I'll put out towels for you. While you're freshening up, Marina and I will help to prepare dinner."

Marina rose, thrilled. Her heart burst with happiness at her mother's transformation. Her son had come home.

*   *   *

Giorgio sat back in the chair at the table and put his arm around Gianni's shoulders. "I still can't believe that you're home. It's... it's a dream."

Albina stared, enraptured, at her brother. "It *is* a dream."

Gianni grinned. "It's going to be a nightmare once we play *briscola.*" His face sobered. "I never thought this day would come. When I threw myself on the ground the day my unit was attacked and played dead..."

"Don't talk about it, Gianni." Lisa reached across the table for his hand.

Marina's throat felt tight. "He has to talk. It's the best way for him to begin to enjoy life again."

"I've seen it all, but now I hope to pick up where I left off. I'm looking forward to becoming an uncle, thanks to my sisters."

Marco lifted his glass. "I'll toast to that."

"Your return will make the rounds of the village, if it hasn't already," Giorgio said.

"I wonder how Carla will react when she finds out?" Marina smirked.

Giorgio looked at Marina in exasperation. "There's our dinner spoiled!"

Marina giggled. Her amusement faded when Gianni muttered something under his breath, his expression hardening.

*   *   *

Marina yawned and turned over in bed the next morning. She and Giorgio had slept little. They had talked late into the night and fallen asleep a few hours before dawn. He had insisted that she stay in bed and try to sleep while he went downstairs to light the fire. To her surprise, she did fall asleep and woke up after a couple of hours. She got up, dressed quickly, and went downstairs.

"This feels so good." Marina stretched her arms at the

warmth in the kitchen and sat down at the table. Chicco stretched and walked over to her chair, his little face turned up to her, his green eyes wide with anticipation.

"Did you sleep a little?" Giorgio kissed her on the top of the head.

"Yes." She reached up and touched his face. He had placed bread, some cheese, and a little bit of Amelia's flan from the evening before on the table. "Are you going to meet with the lady in Lucca for the measurements?"

"Yes, but before I do, I'm bringing up some wood and going for water. The weather is drizzly and promises snow. Don't you dare put your nose at the door, alright?" Giorgio gently admonished her.

Marina laughed. "Don't worry, I won't. I can't get over yesterday. It seems so unreal." Marina sipped her hot *orzo* and milk.

"It's going to take a while to absorb this dream come true." Giorgio nodded. "You know, I was thinking of the officer, Tobias. He may not be from Germany. I found out that some of the soldiers are born in northern Italy or come from other countries besides Germany. Could that be his story, too? You say that he speaks our language very well."

"Wherever he comes from, he's a good person. There's something about him that's different. I have a feeling that we'll find out his story."

*   *   *

Giorgio left after breakfast. It was just as well that Marina couldn't go outside. She had planned to visit Lisa where Gianni was staying, but he had to rest. There would be a lifetime to catch up with each other up as well as to make up for lost birthdays and holidays.

"Well, Chicco, let's see what we can do today," she said as she rose from the table. Chicco watched her for a moment, arched his back, and curled up in his box.

Marina tidied up in the kitchen and then went upstairs to make the bed. From the bedroom window, she looked across to her neighbor's garden, where the cycle of life and death repeated itself year after year.

The breeze gently ruffled the tendrils of the jasmine that trailed up the front of the house to her bedroom window. Marina hugged herself. The cycle of life had begun again in the baby she bore.

*   *   *

Marina kept busy with little tasks all morning. It was nearing noon, and with Giorgio away and not sure if he would be home to eat, she prepared something for herself. She was about to sit down when she heard a knock on the door and the key turned.

"*Ehi,* Marina?"

Marina quickly rose as Gianni entered the kitchen, his beard gone. "It's so good to see you." She hugged him as tightly as her body allowed. "I thought you were still fast asleep in bed."

"Lisa insisted that I have a good bath in front of the fire. Then I went to bed and slept like a rock." Gianni spread his arms wide. "It's so good to be home!" He looked around the kitchen with approval. "You're good here. This is really nice."

"We can thank Giorgio's father." Marina pulled a chair away from the table. "Sit down and eat with me. It's not much, but what I have is yours, too."

"It's good to see you like this. Remember when I told you to make me an uncle?"

Marina let out a deep sigh. "I remember. I was so depressed after I lost the baby. If it wasn't for Don Antonio, I don't know what poor Giorgio would have done." She placed a dish with some cheese and left-over *polenta* on the table.

"I'll never forget the day when you brought *polenta* to me. I was scared that you would be discovered."

"Instead, here we are."

He stared reflectively at his food. "The more I think about the officer, Tobias, the more I believe that he ended up in this war against his will. While we were coming up the path, he wasn't menacing. He doesn't have any of the characteristics that I've seen in other German soldiers, and we know who the SS are."

"Giorgio believes that he may not be from Germany but was perhaps recruited from up north or from somewhere else. Did Mama tell you about my experience with him?"

"No, but she doesn't have to." Gianni smiled.

"What is it?" Marina sensed that smile hid something known only to him.

"Sometimes, things are best left unsaid for the moment." He shivered. "What the SS have done to the people is beyond description. The massacre of Sant'Anna…"

"Who was to blame for that slaughter? Were the Partisans responsible?"

"No one knows for sure." Shadows darkened his eyes. "But I believe that, in part, they were. I'm only too happy that I wasn't present. Even the group I was with was getting out of hand. Some of them wanted to raid homes for food. I couldn't handle that. I still wanted to help the Allies, but harming our own people wasn't my way. One night, I left them and began my trek home."

"You did it in spite of the curfew? How?" Marina asked, shocked.

He laughed shortly. "I'd travel during daylight and then, before dark, share a stable with a pig or a cow, or sleep in a hayloft. It wasn't pleasant, but at least I had shelter."

"What is it with Carla, Gianni? Yesterday, you were joking at the table, and then when I mentioned her name, it bothered you. Is there something that you want to talk about?"

He chuckled and shook his head. "Nothing escapes you." He looked intently at her. "Be wary of her. She's deceiving."

Marina felt chilly in spite of the warmth of the fireplace. That was the same warning that Anna had given her a long time ago.

*   *   *

It was late afternoon when Giorgio returned home in the midst of snow flurries. The moment he entered the kitchen, Marina knew that something good had happened. With a big smile, he waved an envelope in his hand.

"She already gave me a deposit." Giorgio drew Marina to him and kissed her. "Now we can buy a little more food, so that you can stay nourished."

Marina raised her eyes heavenward. "Maybe this is the beginning of good times like you said. Gianni came to see me and stayed to eat."

"Good. I saw Anna as I was coming up. She told me that she saw him."

"I'm glad that she did. Who knows?" Marina murmured.

Giorgio raised an eyebrow. "Knows what?"

"Nothing." Marina answered quickly. She turned to the window hoping that the sudden flush that she felt on her face would be mistaken for the fire's warmth.

Giorgio looked keenly at her. "I know you, *carissima*. You're up to something."

Marina feigned indignation. "I am not. I'm just hoping that he can find the happiness that he deserves now that he's home."

"Perhaps with a certain someone that we both care about?"

She smiled as their eyes met.

*   *   *

A thin blanket of snow covered the garden the next day. The world outside was grey and freezing. Marina heard Giorgio's voice down below at the shed with Gianni. Giorgio had learned to read her like a book. She had no intention of playing matchmaker, and would let destiny take its course. But, if what she hoped for came to be, Anna would be well taken care of.

Down below on the valley road, a few jeeps moved in the direction of the American encampment. The war had intensified locally between the Germans and the Allies. Her heart went out to the people of a mountaintop town, Barga, to the northwest. Mussolini had once declared it a city, but between the artillery and bombs, it had been reduced to ruins.

Below the window, she watched Gianni carry out some debris. He and Giorgio had torn down a partially rotted wood partition to open up enough space to accommodate Pallino.

Gianni raised his head and waved to her.

Marina opened the window to the biting air. "Come up and have something hot to drink."

"Right away." Gianni disappeared inside to call Giorgio.

She had no sooner closed the window, than the door opened and she heard their voices.

Marina prepared the usual *orzo*. Now that they had a little more money, maybe she could buy cinnamon sticks and other spices and make *brule'*. She remembered how her father used to enjoy the mulled wine on winter days.

Gianni blew on his cold hands. "This is good of you." He hugged Marina.

"You're my brother. It's good of you to help Giorgio." She nodded toward the *soggiorno*. "Someone's at the door."

Giorgio rose as Amelia, barely visible in the heavy shawl wrapped around her head and body, entered the kitchen.

"Mama, what are you doing out?" Giorgio protested.

"You know I'm not one to stay cooped up inside the house all day."

"You're going to get sick. Come and warm yourself." Giorgio brought a chair to the fireplace for her. "You worry me when you do things like this."

"Coming here isn't like going to the next town, so *sta zitto.*"

Gianni exchanged a glance with Marina, who suppressed a chuckle. Amelia thought nothing of telling her son to button his lips.

Giorgio rolled his eyes in exasperation

"Have some *orzo*, Amelia." Marina handed her a steamy glass full.

Amelia turned to Gianni with a warm smile and squeezed his hand. "It's good to have you home."

"It's good to be home. You haven't changed, Amelia."

"I've had my setbacks and my moments of joy. The biggest joy for all of us now are the babies on the way and you being home, out of harm's way."

Giorgio smacked Gianni's knee. "We'd better get going. It's getting too comfortable here. Today, I'm bringing Pallino up."

"Thank goodness." Marina sighed happily.

Amelia contemplated Gianni as he rose and followed Giorgio out the kitchen. "I hope that Gianni keeps out of that witch, Carla's, way."

"Do you realize what you just called her?"

"You know that I don't mince words."

Marina frowned and leaned back in the chair while a feeling of uneasiness filled her. She recalled what Gianni had said that some things were best left unsaid.

*   *   *

Before evening, Marina heard a familiar braying and looked out the kitchen window. Giorgio had brought Pallino up.

Marina quickly went to the balcony just in time to see Giorgio close the stable door behind him. "Is everything alright?" She called out to him.

"It's fine. I'm coming up now."

"Wait a moment. I want to see him." Marina wrapped herself in a heavy shawl. The donkey, nibbling at the fodder, raised his head, alert. Marina caressed his neck while he rubbed his head against her arm. "You have a proper home now." She turned to Giorgio. "I'm so proud of you and Gianni for all of your hard work."

"Frankly, so am I." Giorgio smiled broadly and patted Pallino. "You have food to eat and you're nice and snug here."

Marina lifted her head to the sound of a window closing. Bianca, her neighbor, waved to her. Marina smiled and waved back but even from where she stood, she couldn't help noticing Bianca's taut face. Her heart ached at what was going on behind her neighbor's closed door. She turned and stepped inside the *soggiorno,* pensive.

Giorgio stomped his feet before entering. "It's going to be easier with Pallino here." His expression was one of relief and satisfaction.

"Yes."

"Is something wrong?" Giorgio didn't miss the almost absentminded answer.

"I saw Bianca up at the window. We're so close and yet so far away. I wish that I could reach out to her."

Giorgio warmed himself in front of the fire. "How long has it been now since her little boy died?"

"Ten years. I pray that she doesn't lose her daughter, too."

"I saw Michela a few days ago. She doesn't know what to do anymore to help her mother come out of the shell that she's in. Her father's leaving them didn't exactly help, either, although I can understand his feelings, too. Bianca has shut herself off from the world since her little boy died. To complicate things, Michela has a future mother-in-law who acts cold towards her, no matter what she tries to do to get into her good graces."

Marina remembered the circumstances. Bianca had never stopped grieving the sudden death of her little boy, who was about a year and a half old. She and her husband, Roberto, had a good marriage, but the years following their little boy's death had taken their toll. Roberto, feeling helpless and exasperated at the same time, left Bianca a year ago although he had never stopped loving her. Their daughter, Michela, who was engaged to a young man in the village, was left feeling resentful over their separation and dealing with her own problems. Not even Don Antonio's frequent visits, comforting as they were, seemed to have helped. It was a sad story. Marina's heart went out to all of them and she felt a small shiver at how close she had come to falling into the same despair.

*   *   *

December began wet. Marina frowned at the clothes draped on the chairs in the *soggiorno* and counted on her fingers the sunny days in November. If things didn't change, December wouldn't be any better and winter was just around the corner.

The light drizzle of the morning was now hard rain.

Because of the bad weather, the only major news lately was that the Allied Command, located in a town in the Serchio River Valley, had been transferred to Bagni di Lucca.

"We have to do the laundry," Albina moaned, "but where are we going to put everything?"

"Let's hope that tomorrow will be a little sunny. I can hang some things out on the balcony. Giorgio cleaned the stable yesterday. After he freshened up, I had him wear his good cardigan, while his everyday ones are drying out. I hope that it lets up before Daniela gets home." Marina straightened up, wincing.

"Your back hurts."

"I'm only six months along. I still have three to go."

The door slowly opened and Marina heard a now familiar voice. "Marina?"

"Come in, Gianni."

Gianni looked around. He scratched his head at the *soggiorno,* now turned into a makeshift drying room. "It seems that everyone I visit has the same problem."

"At least we have clothes. There are people who don't have any at all." Marina said brightly. "Let's go warm ourselves. Giorgio has gone to the house. Thankfully, the roof is done and now he's trying to put in new windows."

"Mama, *Nonna,* and Amelia are talking about Christmas, which is still three weeks away. I think they're trying to figure out how we can all be together." Gianni waited for Marina and Albina to sit down before he joined them.

Marina smiled that he had retained his gentlemanly manner.

"Your returning home has done wonders for Mama," Albina said softly. "Now that we're scattered about, I think she finds it comforting to have you as a pillar to lean against."

Gianni's face clouded. "I'd like to know who was behind the torching."

"Mama always says that the truth will come out in time." Marina decided to leave it at that, although she and Giorgio had their suspicions. "I wonder how Anna is doing? I haven't been to visit her for a while."

"I called on her before coming here. She was busy preparing a *torta di patate.*"

Marina clasped her hands. Gianni had just given her an idea for *pranzo* and knowing that he had visited Anna made her doubly happy.

Gianni visited a little while and made two trips for wood for the fireplace. After he left, Albina turned to Marina with a knowing smile. "You're up to something."

"What do you mean?"

"I saw your reaction when Gianni said that he had visited Anna."

"I have no idea what you're talking about." Marina smiled sweetly.

"You do, and you know what? I'd like to see them together, too."

Marina felt warmth rise to her cheeks. "Promise me that this is our secret. If it's meant to be, it has to come about on its own."

"Wouldn't it be nice? I think that Gianni never really forgot about her."

They both smiled at each other at the prospect of a happy outcome.

*   *   *

The war dragged on. Marina decided to have Christmas at her home. When Christmas Eve morning arrived, so did a biting cold. The Apennines were blanketed with snow down to the lower elevations.

"I'm so excited this Christmas." Marina clasped her hands joyfully. "We have Gianni home and we're going to have a baby. We'll have all the family, although with this cold, I worry about Lisa coming here."

"It will all work out, *amore mio*."

She and Giorgio had just set up a little juniper in the corner of the *soggiorno* where they would have the Christmas meal. Marina proceeded to decorate it with their few cherished, homemade decorations. This year there was an added touch. Albina wanted two booties hung so that the little ones to be born could already have a part in Christmas.

"What are we going to have for the meal? With the rations, it's hard to prepare something really good." Albina pursed her lips.

"We could make something special like *ravioli*," Marina said. She liked being able to cook and eat again without the nausea.

Giorgio rubbed his hands together. "Now that's a feast!"

"What are we going to substitute for the filling as well as making the *sugo*? Where are we going to get meat? Are we going to kill a chicken?" Albina asked matter-of-factly.

"I got ahead of myself," Marina said. "For the sauce, we could reconstitute some of the dried tomatoes as well as a few *porcini*. It would be plain, but we could add some dried basil. The filling… I don't know."

Giorgio opened to a knock on the door. It was Alda who carried a sack.

Marina studied the sack. Judging by how her mother held it, she dared to hope that it was a chicken. Before she could ask anything, she got her answer.

"The weasel tried to feast on the chickens. It killed two and ran away when Amelia heard the commotion in the chicken coop. I brought one to you."

Marina exchanged a glance with Albina and Giorgio before they burst out laughing.

Bewildered, Alda looked from one to the other.

Marina managed to compose herself. "It's alright Mama. The weasel solved our dilemma. Now we can make some nice sauce for the *ravioli* and have the filling too."

Before evening, Marina looked at the rows of freshly made *ravioli* on the table, made with Giorgio, Albina, and Daniela's helping hands. The *sugo* bubbled gently on the burner. Nevertheless, she was disappointed because her mother as well as Giorgio had counseled her not to attend the Christmas morning Mass because it was too cold. Lisa also would remain home, but she had invited Bruno and Valentina to have Christmas with her and Marco.

Later, when Giorgio entered with an armful of wood, Marina looked wistfully at him. "I suppose it's for the best," she told him.

He kissed her on the forehead. "It is. I didn't want to say anything earlier, but you need to pray extra hard. A German attack is going to take place in the valley on the 27th. The Americans are on alert."

Marina's eyes filled. It was Christmas. Where was the peace announced by the angels?

CHAPTER TWENTY-FOUR

Marina closed her prayer book, her mind lingering on a favorite prayer. Except for the crackling of the fire, silence surrounded her, Giorgio, and the girls in the kitchen. Albina and Daniela were intent on their handiwork. Giorgio sat thoughtfully, gazing into the crackling fire.

As she contemplated the cheery flames and sparks that shot up the chimney, her mind drifted back to the Christmases of years past when her father was alive. Her parents had engrained all of their children with a deep respect for the sacred. It seemed only fitting, now that she was expecting a baby, that on this holiest of all nights, she raise a heartfelt prayer that mothers and the babies they carried be protected.

After a little while, they let the fire die down. Giorgio scooped up embers and placed them in the *scaldino*. Upstairs, he hung it in the igloo shaped frame and placed it under the bedcovers. Daniela and Albina smiled, happy at the idea of finding a nice, warm bed. Giorgio repeated the procedure for their bed. While it warmed, Marina stood at the bedroom window and raised her eyes to the starry heavens. After a few minutes, she undressed quickly and slipped into the cozy bed, not daring to dwell on what the coming days would bring.

*   *   *

"This is special to have the Christmas *pranzo* as a family again. Marina, thank you for having us all together here." Alda's eyes were damp with tears as she looked from one face to another around the table in the *soggiorno*. "Lisa is having her Christmas at home with Bruno and Valentina and *Nonna* is there, too, so it's alright."

"It is special." Albina turned to Marina. "I wish I'd had the *scaldino* with me this morning. It was freezing in church!"

Marina smiled at Albina's expression, but then sobered. "Let's enjoy this moment while we can. I wonder what Tobias is doing?"

"I don't know, but I doubt that his Christmas is as good as ours," Gianni said.

"It's hard to believe that on both sides, Christmas is being celebrated in one way or another. I heard that in the German encampment, they've put up a Christmas tree. Why is it that what unites us today can't keep us together tomorrow?" Giorgio smacked the table. "Instead, no, all hell will break loose."

"This has to be the ugliest war ever fought." Amelia shook her head in dismay.

"Let's make the best of these moments." Marina rose from the table to take the plates away. "Daniela, why don't you bring out the *torta di riso* that you baked?"

Smiles broke on everyone's face as Daniela emerged from the kitchen with the rice torte.

"Here's the *Aleatico* to enjoy with it." Giorgio brought out a flasket of the dessert wine. After he poured it into glasses, he raised his glass. "Here's to our Christmas!"

*   *   *

The next morning, Marina felt edgy, because Gianni had said that he wanted to go down to the valley to see what the situation was like. "It worries me to know that he's down there," she told Giorgio.

"He's learned how to stay out of harm's way," Giorgio reassured her. "He'll be fine."

Marina finished washing the breakfast cups as the winter sun's rays played on the water in the dishpan. She raised her eyes to thee icicles that hung from the eaves. "Ooh, it's going to be another freezing day."

"It may be freezing outside, but we have warmth here." Giorgio hugged her. "This is getting harder to do."

Marina laughed. "It won't be for much longer. Before we know it, it will be March, and our baby will be here."

"A springtime baby. What a perfect time."

The front door opened and a pale Gianni entered the kitchen and slumped into a chair.

"What is it? What's happened?" Alarmed, Marina warmed up some leftover *orzo*. "Drink this."

Gianni reached for the hot drink with shaking hands. "I can't believe what's happening down there. I ran into a Partisan who said that the Buffalo Soldiers as well as soldiers from India are facing an uphill fight."

"Do… do you think that the Allies will win?" Marina asked tremulously. She knew how much Giorgio and Gianni counted on the Allied victory for the total liberation of the valley and of Italy.

"They have to! There's no other way to free us from the Nazi Fascists." Gianni got up and paced restlessly to and fro. "In a way, I wish that I was out there fighting with them."

It was self-centered of her perhaps, but Marina breathed a prayer of thanks that he was home instead.

*   *   *

The hours that followed were a nightmare. Death and destruction rained down. Cannon fire pounded the towns and blew holes in homes.

In late afternoon, Marina tried to concentrate on the tiny baby sweater that she was trying to finish. Although the kitchen was warm, she felt cold. Every blast of a cannon meant one more home destroyed or worse, one more death.

Giorgio trudged into the kitchen, his face taut. He stood at the fireplace, his arm on the mantelpiece.

Marina got up and placed her hand on his chest. "You're troubled."

Giorgio cleared his throat. "It's hell in the valley. People are fleeing the barrage of machine gun fire and the cannons with little more than the clothes on their backs." He stepped away and walked to the window. "It doesn't' look good for the Americans. Who knows what the coming hours will bring."

Marina put her arm around his waist and rested her head against his shoulder.

Giorgio turned and rested his forehead against hers. "I'm almost ashamed that we have a roof over our heads."

That night in bed, Marina offered a prayer of thanks that she and Giorgio were together and, as they said, that they still had a roof over their heads. She placed a hand on her belly and once again reassured their baby that everything was fine, but she was far from feeling confident. It was a long time before she finally fell asleep.

*   *   *

The next day, the twenty-seventh, intent on kneading dough, Marina jumped when Giorgio and Gianni rushed into the kitchen, both out of breath.

Marina looked from one to the other, her sticky hands suspended in air. "Something's happened."

Giorgio's words tumbled out before Gianni could say anything. "The… the Americans have begun a counteroffensive by air. We… we walked to the cemetery to look at the other end of the valley. It's… it's nothing but one bomber after another diving down on the Germans. I… I can't believe the airpower!"

Gianni grinned from ear to ear. "For a while it looked like the Germans had the better of them, but… but now it's a whole different story."

Marina didn't feel enthusiastic. "It's good, but it will mean more deaths and more destruction."

Gianni placed his hands on her shoulders. "It's the only way that we will be free," he said grimly.

"I know, I know, but when I think of the many more lives that will be lost…"

"Lives lost? *Ehi, amore mio,* if anyone should be thinking of lives lost, not only now, but ever since this wretched, ugly war began, it should be someone in the Republic of Salo'. Him and his glory for Italy," Giorgio flared.

The bombings continued until evening and were then followed by intense cannon fire that lasted all through the night.

*   *   *

"I'm so sleepy. What a night." Giorgio yawned and pushed back the covers on his side.

Marina tried to stretch a little and placed a hand on her belly. "Good morning, little one. Ooh!" She winced. "I think the baby isn't happy that I didn't sleep. This kick was strong."

Giorgio kissed her on the forehead. "It's a sign that he or she is well. If it's sunny, I'm going to tidy up around the stable."

"Well, let's begin the day." Marina slowly rolled over.

"Let me go light the fire before you get up." Giorgio rose and opened the shutters. "It's nice and sunny outside. Good."

"May the good Lord have it be a good day." Marina snuggled under the covers for a moment longer. When the baby kicked again, she began to laugh. It seemed that her baby was telling her to get up. She threw back the covers and got up to the biting cold. She dressed quickly and went down to the kitchen, letting Chicco out a moment.

The reverberations of the bombings echoed through the valley and made the walls of the homes shiver.

Daniela entered the kitchen and stood with a dejected expression on her face. "Again? When will it all end?" she moaned out loud.

"I'm going." Giorgio pushed his cup and plate aside and rose from the table.

"You hardly ate." Marina looked with dismay at his plate.

"You know that when I'm tense, I can't eat." Giorgio said glumly.

"Please be careful," Marina pleaded.

"I'll be fine. We don't have bombs falling or cannons

firing here, by the grace of God. You stay inside, alright?"

"If I'm dressed warmly, I could go and see your mother." She was more than a little tired of being confined in the house all the time.

"No." He shook his head vigorously. "You could get sick."

Marina rolled her eyes.

"He's right, Marina," Daniela said gently. "You've come this far. You don't want to risk anything."

"There you go." Giorgio grinned and left.

"Traitor!" Marina feigned indignation at Daniela.

"I hope that the children can bring some wood to heat up the classroom." Daniela sat down to have some breakfast, her expression pensive. "Was Gianni going back down to the valley? It seems that the Partisan is still in him."

"I suppose that he saw so much when he was out there. He probably has a better sense of what's happening than we do. Do you know the farmhouse on the other side of *Nonna's* home, where the new family lives? The young woman was tending her sheep when she heard a drone and saw a bomber swoop low. Frightened, she ran and hid inside the trunk of a large, dead chestnut tree while the sheep scattered. The bomber swooped down. She heard a roar, and, in a matter of seconds, a bomb exploded in the area where she had been tending them a few minutes earlier. The Americans definitely missed their target."

Daniela shuddered. "I hope this all ends soon."

Albina came down from upstairs, rubbing her eyes. "Why didn't someone wake me up?"

Marina smiled at her. "Come and have something to eat. None of us slept very well."

"I'm going. Albina, be sure that Marina doesn't go outside." Daniela put on her heavy jacket.

As the hours passed by, the news was staggering. In one town, a church had been reduced to dust, and there were more deaths and more wounded to add to those of the preceding days. In another town, a miracle had happened, instead. A bomb had exploded in a house leaving only the walls. The owner, a woman, had been left unharmed.

Marina and Albina busied themselves with handiwork or tasks in the house.

"Marina, do you think there are other worlds out there besides ours?" Albina laid down her embroidery.

"I would think so. Why?"

"If there are, I wonder if they are as war torn as this one?"

"Only God has the answer to that."

Later, just before dark, Marina and Giorgio were coming up from the stable when they heard someone running up the street, gasping. They turned to see Gianni, who stumbled in front of the gate, nearly losing his balance. "It's... it's happened," he gasped. "The... the Germans are... are retreating!"

*   *   *

The next day the soldiers from India once again re-gained control of four towns. German soldiers were deserting, and some officers were giving up their command.

Giorgio chuckled as he leaned against the mantelpiece. "Can you believe that in one town, four Buffalo soldiers spent four days in an attic while the Germans were on the lower floor? But the Fascists just won't give up. They're still saying that the Germans are gaining, in spite of the Americans taking over."

"How can they be so blind?" Albina asked as she neatly folded the towels that had finally dried.

"When people are so pumped up with pride, they don't give in easily to defeat." Marina held up the tiny sweater that she had sewn buttons on. "What do you think?" she asked Giorgio.

"I'm proud of you. I can hardly wait…"

The door burst open and Gianni stumbled into the kitchen gasping, his face ashen.

Giorgio jumped to his feet. "What's happened?" He held him by the shoulders.

Gianni sucked in his breath. "It's… it's Tobias."

Marina dropped the sweater as her heart slammed into her ribs. "What happened to him?" She held on to the back of a chair.

"I… I was coming from the vineyard… I… I found him on the mule path on his knees, sobbing." Gianni swallowed hard. "His… his rifle was pointed at his throat. I… I was close enough to launch myself at him and grab it, but it fired and… and it grazed the side of his head." Gianni sank into a chair.

"No! Why?" Marina cried out.

Daniela and Albina gasped.

Gianni inhaled deeply. "He kept saying, *"Mia moglie, mia figlia… morte!"*

Marina covered her face. His wife and daughter, dead! "Poor Tobias… How terrible!"

"How… how did… did they die?" Daniela asked softly.

"I… I don't know." Gianni rolled his eyes exasperated. "He's wounded and in no condition to talk."

"Where is he now?"

"At Marco's office. Someone came along, and I told him to go to Marco for the stretcher and to tell him what had happened. In the meantime, I made a pad with my handkerchief and held it against the wound. Fortunately, Marco was in and we managed to get him to his office. He treated him and… and gave him a sedative. He's asleep now."

"I have to see him." Marina grabbed her heavy shawl.

"Marina…"

"Giorgio, I'm going. I have to see him… please!" Marina looked fixedly at him and then at Gianni, determined to have her way this time.

"Alright, alright." Giorgio nodded reluctantly.

Marina couldn't walk fast enough to reach Marco's

office. When she did, she let out a cry as she entered what used to be Marco's bedroom. Tobias was fast asleep with his head bandaged. Gut-wrenching grief showed plain as day on his face. "I'm staying with him."

"Marina, I don't think…"

"I said that I'm staying." Marina spoke through clenched teeth, interrupting Giorgio. "You'll be here, won't you?" She turned to Marco.

"Of course I will. There's no way that he can be left alone."

"A soldier serves his country and ends up losing those he loves. It's been like that since time immemorial. When will man ever learn?" Giorgio muttered.

"Gianni, go tell Lisa what has happened," Marina said.

Gianni nodded, spent. "This… this has worn me out. I've… I've been in the war, seen death, but seeing someone trying to kill himself…" He swallowed hard. "God, I'm… I'm so grateful that I… I managed to save his life."

Marina looked at Tobias and back at Gianni. She shuddered. In the attempt to save Tobias's life, it could have cost him his own.

CHAPTER TWENTY-FIVE

Waking up from a restless night, Marina squinted in the faint light of dawn that peeked through the shutters. The stretcher that Marco always kept handy for emergencies had proved useful, not only for Tobias, but for Marina to sleep on. Marco had fallen asleep at the table with his head resting on his arms. She heard a soft moan from the bedroom and lowly rolled over. She lifted herself on an elbow and gently woke Marco. "I think Tobias is waking up."

Marco rubbed his eyes, rose quickly, and helped Marina to her feet. They entered the bedroom where Marco bent down and placed his fingers at Tobias's pulse. "It's a little fast but steady."

Marina sat down on the chair next to the bed and reached for Tobias's hand.

Tobias looked at her, confused for a moment. When he recognized her, tears welled in his eyes. "Marina. *La mia moglie, la mia figlia... morte!*"

Marina squeezed his hand. She wanted so much to comfort him but struggled to ask the difficult question. "What... what happened, Tobias?"

Marco moved over to Marina's side and sat down at the foot of the bed.

Between his sobs, Marina managed to discover something about this man. He was from northern Italy, born to Polish Catholics. Marina couldn't help smiling when he said that his father was a cabinetmaker and that he had taken up his trade. He had fallen in love and married a young woman from the same village, who was also a Polish Catholic. They had been blessed with a daughter.

They had lived a quiet life until Poland was invaded and the war broke out. He was called to serve, but he rebelled at the idea of serving under Hitler, especially after the invasion of Poland and the atrocities that had been committed by the Nazis. But, he feared that if he refused to serve, his family would be harmed. Reluctantly, he left, and with time became an officer. When the commander here had been forced to leave because of illness, he had been sent to replace him.

"Now I know why I had never seen you before." Marina smiled.

Tobias had received letters from his wife, but he hadn't heard from her in a long time. Worried, he had written to her family. Yesterday he had received a letter, three months old, telling him that his wife and daughter had been shot and killed when they were discovered sheltering a Polish Jewish family.

Marina took a deep breath. "Tobias, *noi... noi ti vogliamo bene.*" He had to know that there were people who cared about him, she thought. He wasn't alone.

"Grazie," Tobias murmured.

Tentatively, Marina asked what his daughter's name was.

"Nora." Tobias smiled wistfully as tears rolled down his face.

*   *   *

Later, at home, Marina told Giorgio and the girls Tobias's story. Giorgio smacked his hand on the table with such force that a plate jumped.

"I… I never thought that people could be so heartless as to kill people who are trying to help others," Albina flared.

"Poor man." Daniela shook her head sadly. "What does he have to look forward to now?"

"He said that all he wants to do is to go back home." Marina got up and walked to the window.

"I can understand that," Giorgio agreed. "But if he can wait until we are totally free, it will be safer for him to return home. It's only a question of time."

"Where can he stay in the meantime?" Marina's mind was a whirlwind as she tried to find a solution.

Giorgio ran his fingers through his hair. "We don't have any room."

"We just can't leave him on his own, not with everything he's going through," Daniela protested.

"I have an idea. It's not the most inviting place in the

world, but what about the hayloft over Pallino? We can make it comfortable for him to sleep there and... and he can have his meals with us and... and perhaps help with some outside tasks." Marina, like Daniela, was not about to leave him to himself.

Giorgio's face lit up. "Mama has an old cot stored in the *cantina*. I'll bring it up and he can sleep on that. Your idea might work. You do remind him of his daughter. It may be just what he needs in this moment. We'll tell him tomorrow."

*   *   *

Marina accompanied Giorgio to Marco's office the next morning, carrying a basket with a small jar of broth and boiled beef, a small bowl and spoon, and some bread.

Tobias sat on the edge of the bed. Marina felt relieved to see that his face, although sad, was much clearer. "I brought you something to eat."

Tobias gratefully accepted the gift of food.

As he was eating, Marina told him about the plan. *"Tu stai con noi."*

Tobias looked up, his eyes widening with surprise. *"No... no... e' troppo disturbo."* He shook his head.

"It's no bother," Giorgio said quickly. "We're happy to have you with us."

After much convincing, Tobias gave in. He stopped eating and looked keenly at Marina and Giorgio. *"Questo e' tuo marito?"* he gently asked Marina, pointing to Giorgio.

Marina smiled sheepishly and admitted that Giorgio was her husband and not Gianni, whom he had spared. Gianni was her brother.

Tobias smiled and shook his head. He extended a hand to both of them. *"Grazie, Giorgio. Grazie, Marina."*

*   *   *

Cannon fire and bombings in the towns around them continued as the year drew to a close. On the morning of New Year's Eve, Saint Sylvester, the feast of the village church's namesake, Marina and Giorgio woke up to a surprise snow fall.

"Well, we're going to have our own feast for sure here at home. The snow is ankle deep and it's still snowing!" Giorgio exclaimed.

Marina fell back on the pillows in dismay. "I was *so* looking forward to going to Bruno and Valentina's. It wasn't all that cold these past two days."

Giorgio went downstairs to light the fire. Marina lay in bed a moment longer, reflecting on Tobias. More than ever, she was convinced that they had done the right thing in giving him shelter. Giorgio had been able to find a long hop pole to hang across the inside of the door of the hayloft. Marina, with Albina and Daniela's help had found an old blanket and hemmed it so the pole could slide through. When Tobias retired for the night, he could hang the makeshift curtain to keep out the cold air and sleep on the cot, covered with a comforter. He deeply appreciated the care he was given, but he couldn't hide his grief. They had seen him more than once quickly wipe away tears when he was busy with a task. To kill people just because they were helping others was beyond her understanding. She pushed back the covers and got up.

Down in the kitchen, Giorgio, Daniela, and Albina were preparing a frugal breakfast.

"I suppose that we're going to have to make our own feast today," Albina said glumly, looking outside at the falling snow.

"What matters is that we are here together and that we are well." Giorgio knelt down to add another piece of wood to the fire that crackled merrily.

"The church bells are ringing." Marina opened the kitchen window just enough to hear the festive sound. "I can't go to church, but the three of you can."

"Where's Tobias? I've told him not to hesitate to come up when he wants to." Marina feared for him. When someone had experienced what he had... she shook herself from the terrible thought.

"Let me go and see." Giorgio quickly rose.

"Poor man." Daniela shook her head sadly. "He probably needs a moment."

To Marina's relief, Giorgio returned with Tobias, who handed her a tiny packet. *"Questo e' per te,"* he said smiling.

Marina carefully opened it and lifted up a silver chain with a medal of the Virgin Mary. "Tobias…" She couldn't continue. Her throat tightened with emotion.

"La mia moglie me l'aveva data. Ora e 'tua."

Marina pressed the medal to her heart. His wife had probably given it to him when he had left for the war. Now it was hers.

Giorgio fastened the chain around Marina's neck and she touched it gently. It was a precious gift, not only because of the Virgin Mary, but because it had held so much meaning for Tobias.

Marina had Tobias sit down with them for some breakfast. When they finished, Tobias shyly asked if he could go with Giorgio and the girls to church.

"Of course you can." Giorgio smiled warmly.

Gianni was about the same height as Tobias and he had given him an extra pair of trousers and a cardigan.

After breakfast, Marina watched him leave with Giorgio and the girls. She offered a prayer of thanks. If Tobias felt the need to go to church, it was a good sign.

A little later, Marina heard their voices in the *soggiorno*.

Tobias entered with a little smile on his face. *"Questo mi ha fatto bene."*

"It did you good. You also met other villagers," Giorgio said.

"Was Mama there?" Marina asked.

"Yes," Giorgio nodded. "Tobias met her, *Nonna,* and

my mother. They send their love and Marco told me that Lisa is staying home, too, so she decided to host the main meal instead of Valentina. Your mother and *Nonna* will be with her."

Marina sat down dejectedly. "I wish that we could all be together, but it is for the best. Giorgio, go tell your mother that we want her here. We'll have our feast for *pranzo*." She smiled at Tobias who sat quietly. "Tobias, you know that we want you to join us, right?"

Tobias nodded, smiling.

"Tobias, come and see how my work is progressing." Giorgio got up and they both left.

Daniela had prepared an almond torte the day before. "Well, we have this, but that's about it."

"What shall we do, Marina?" Albina pursed her lips. "It's a special day."

Marina scratched her head as she tried to come up with an idea. "We managed to have a little feast last year. Now that we are close to liberation, there's more reason to celebrate, but what can I put together? We're still under rationing."

"We had rations last year, too." Daniela countered. "But I suppose that we also had more zest for them because we weren't scattered all over."

"That's no help," Marina groaned even if she agreed.

"I know," Albina said brightly. "We still have some *porcini,* don't we?"

"Yes. What are you thinking?" Marina was ready for

any idea to save the day.

"Why don't we make *polenta di neccio,* and have a nice sauce on the side? *Nonna* has given us cheese and we still have olives from Giorgio's vineyard."

Marina exhaled, relieved. It would be a simple meal of *polenta* made with the chestnut flour. There were still some dried tomatoes to make the sauce and the *porcini* and the olives would enrich it. "We'd better get to work! Daniela, go and remind Giorgio to tell Amelia to come here. We should also visit Lisa."

"I can see both of them." Daniela put on a heavy shawl and shoes and was out the door.

A little before *pranzo,* Marina fidgeted, wondering what was keeping Daniela. She heard the front door open and Daniela entered with Marco behind her, holding a basket. Their hair and clothes were flecked with snow and their cheeks were red from the biting air. Daniela sailed into the kitchen, her face radiating sunbeams.

"Marco! Sit down and warm yourself." Marina pulled a chair away from the kitchen table while staring perplexedly at Daniela.

"I can't sit down. I have strict orders to do the rounds of the family." He placed the basket on the table and lifted out the contents.

Marina gasped with delight at the pieces of roast chicken, roasted potatoes, and several slices of *torta di riso.*"

"How… where…?" Albina stared wide-eyed.

"Isn't this wonderful?" Daniela clasped her hands. "Valentina and Bruno had just brought the meal to share with Lisa. Valentina insisted on sharing some with us."

"Mama got up so early this morning and cooked up a feast. Here you go." Marco said.

After Marco left, Marina stared incredulously at the bounty. God was good.

*   *   *

The New Year had arrived with the hope of liberation and peace.

Marina stood at the kitchen window in early afternoon with Anna, who had come to visit a few days later. They were watching Tobias bring water for Pallino. "He is so grateful to be here. When one task is finished, he'll find another to do before we even think of it," Marina said, smiling.

"You and Giorgio have gone above and beyond what anyone else would have done," Anna said emphatically.

"Gianni started it by saving his life." Marina placed her hands at the small of her back and rubbed it gently.

"Your time for the baby is getting close."

"My back is a good reminder that I'm in my seventh month." Marina turned from the window. "I hardly see anyone anymore. What is our friend Carla up to?"

Anna arched her eyebrows. "I haven't been out that much either, so I don't know, but knowing her, be prepared for plenty of gossip over Tobias.”

Marina waved it off with her hand. “I know, I know, but Giorgio and I could care less.” She turned again to the window. A brisk wind had begun to blow, sending wisps of snow up in the air from the stable roof. “I have to call Tobias to come and having something warm to drink.”

“I’d better go for water and get back home.” Anna reached for her shawl. “If you need anything, you know where I am.”

Marina walked Anna to the door. She opened it just as Tobias approached. He stepped aside for Anna, who greeted him with a smile that he returned.

“Ahi, sono sporchi.” Tobias looked disdainfully at his dirty boots and bent to unlace them on the doorstep.

“No, no.” Marina quickly drew him inside although she appreciated his consideration.

Tobias didn’t sit down but gratefully drank the hot *orzo* that Marina poured for him. *“Tutto bene?”* he asked.

Marina assured him that she was fine. Giorgio had gone to the valley to buy a little meat. Tobias had assured him that he would keep an eye on her.

Tobias gratefully drank the *orzo* and left to bring up a couple of armfuls of wood.

Marina contemplated his tall frame as he went out the door. She prayed that he would be able to find peace.

*   *   *

Marina knew immediately that something was amiss when Giorgio returned home in late afternoon. He was downcast and a little pale. "The situation down there must be terrible," she said.

Giorgio sat down. "All I can say is that we're blessed up here."

Marina looked at him questioningly. There was something that he wasn't telling her. "Giorgio, has something happened?"

He raised his head. "No. Everything's fine."

Marina smacked the dish towel on the table. "No, it's not. Out with it!"

Giorgio hesitated a moment. "When… when I was on the path coming up from town, I… I stopped a moment to catch my breath and heard a deafening blast." He closed his eyes. "A piece of shrapnel whizzed by in front of me. If I hadn't stopped…"

Her knees buckling, Marina sank down on a chair. "When will this fear end? When will life return to normal?" Marina pressed her hands to her temples. "I… I can't handle this anymore, Giorgio!"

"I'm alive, I'm alright." Giorgio drew his chair close to her. *"Ehi,* calm down." Giorgio took her hands in his. "You're tired. Go upstairs to rest."

"I'm not tired physically, just emotionally." Marina buried her face in the dishtowel. "My family is without a home. Daniela could have lost her life when she was taken hostage, Tobias almost killed himself, and Gianni could have died saving his life."

Giorgio inhaled deeply. "Yes, your family is here and there, but they have shelter. Daniela could have lost her life, but she didn't. Tobias is alive, and so is Gianni." Giorgio squeezed her hands.

Marina lifted her face and looked at him. "You should have been a doctor for people who get depressed."

Giorgio kissed her lightly on the lips. "And you're my first patient."

Chicco jumped up into Marina's lap and stared up at her, his eyes wide.

"Little one, all is well in your world." Marina stroked him and his purring proved that she was right.

*   *   *

Daniela and Albina returned home just before dusk, having visited Alda and Lisa. "This is a *giostra*!" Albina exclaimed sitting down on the edge of the hearth.

Marina couldn't have agreed more. It *was* like a merry-go-round to keep up with everyone.

Daniela pulled a chair away from the table. "Who knows when we'll be able to go back home? To think that I fell for that soldier. Thank God that you made me see how wrong I was. I would rather have died than to live knowing that we lost our home because of me."

"We ended up losing it anyway." Albina unsuccessfully stifled a giggled and then sobered. "I still say that someone was behind that."

"What matters is that you were freed." Marina kissed the top of Daniela's head. "Everything else we can handle. Loving the soldier was nothing if it was just a question of giving it time, but I was afraid that you weren't willing to wait. But the good news is that one charred bedroom wall has been rebuilt and Giorgio is testing a new window there now. Little by little, they'll all be done."

Daniela's face brightened. "Hopefully, they won't rattle as much when the *cavallone* blows."

"Or break as easily when certain people swat a spider with the first thing in their hands." Albina turned her gaze to Daniela, who blushed.

Marina laughed outright. "Mama wasn't happy about that."

"Neither was the spider being swatted with a shoe," Albina added.

"Oh, stop it!" Daniela laughed.

Marina placed a hand on her belly and winced.

"A kick?" Albina asked.

"I don't know." Marina bit her lip and grabbed hold of a chair.

Daniela sprang to her feet. "What is it? Are you alright?"

A moment went by before Marina spoke. "Yes, I think so."

"Should… should we call Marco? Tobias?" Daniela asked.

"No," Marina shook her head. "It's not necessary. I'm

alright, really." She straightened up and walked to the window but deep down, she was concerned and wished that she had her mother with her. That stab of pain had been strong.

Albina quietly dried a few dishes, exchanging a glance with Daniela, who raised her shoulders as if not knowing what to do.

Marina breathed a sigh of relief that nothing more had happened as she closed the shutters. *"Oh, mio Dio!"* Suddenly, she placed her hands on her belly and bent over, squeezed by another sharp pain.

Albina flew out the door to call Tobias.

Daniela tried to hold Marina as she slowly sank to the floor. "Marina!"

"I'm losing the baby!" Marina cried out, terrified, as something warm oozed from her body. "Please… please…" She clutched the medal at her throat.

Daniela eased her to the floor, leaned over, and hiked up Marina's skirt.

Albina rushed into the kitchen with Tobias who launched himself onto the floor next to Marina.

"Marina, *sono qui.*" Tobias calmly gave orders to a frightened Albina and Daniela as to what was needed and how to help him. He took her hand and squeezed it reassuringly.

Marina took a deep breath between the stabs of pain, grateful that he was there. She gritted her teeth, holding fast to the medal. "Please, Mary!"

CHAPTER TWENTY-SIX

Perspiration trickled down Marina's face. She cried out with the final push and squeezed Albina's hand hard.

"Eccola!" Tobias exclaimed as he lifted a tiny creature in his arms.

"It's… it's a girl! Oh, Marina, you have a baby girl," Daniela cried out.

Marina burst into tears as the cry that she had longed to hear so badly now filled her ears.

Tobias gently cleansed the little body with warm water, while Albina warmed a towel to wrap the baby in.

"La tua bambina," Tobias said softly as he handed the baby girl to Marina.

Laughing and crying at the same time, Marina reached out for her baby. "She's… she's so small. *Oh Signore!* Please let her live, please!"

"E' tutto bene, Marina." Tobias reassured her. Everything had gone well.

"Here's a pillow and two blankets." Daniela placed a pillow under Marina's head while Tobias wrapped her in the blankets.

Marina gazed lovingly at the little rosy face and then at her sisters and Tobias. "What would I have done without all of you?"

Tobias turned to Albina. *"Chiama Marco e la tua mamma."*

Marina laughed. "Be sure to find Giorgio, too."

"I'll get them all." Albina raced to the door.

Marina reached for Tobias's strong hand. *"Grazie! Grazie!"*

"Pensa ad un nome per la bambina," Tobias said softly.

Marina and Giorgio had decided already what to name their baby if it was a girl. *"La chiamo Nora."*

Tears welled in Tobias's eyes. *"Nora,"* he whispered. *"Grazie."*

*   *   *

Before she knew it, Marina heard the front door open and the quiet kitchen came to life. Giorgio rushed in followed by Alda and Marco. Albina staggered in behind them, out of breath.

"We have a girl," Marina announced.

Giorgio knelt down and kissed Marina on the forehead, then gazed in wonder at his little girl.

"We have to get you upstairs and tend to you," Alda said quietly. "Tobias, can you carry Marina?"

"Giorgio, will you carry Nora? Giorgio?" Marina

waved a hand in front of his eyes, giggling. "Are you still here?"

Giorgio shook himself and very cautiously took the wrapped bundle of his daughter in his arms, looking in rapture at her.

With Marco's help, Tobias carefully lifted Marina in his arms and carried her upstairs. When he laid her on the bed, he placed a hand on his chest.

"Tobias, are… are you alright?" Marina looked at him with concern.

"Si… si. Sono contento."

"That makes two of us who are happy, Tobias." Marina extended her hands to him.

"Rest and relax. You're doing fine, and so is Nora, even if she'll need extra attention since she came a little earlier than usual," Marco reassured Marina.

"She won't lack for that," Giorgio exclaimed.

"I'm going home now," Marco said.

"Please tell Lisa that everything is fine," Marina pleaded.

"We'll be downstairs, alright? You and Nora have something important to do." Giorgio whispered to Marina.

Down in the kitchen, Giorgio embraced Tobias impulsively. "Thank you."

"Mia figlia… vive nella tua." Tobias turned quickly towards the *soggiorno.*

"His daughter lives in my daughter." Giorgio exhaled deeply.

*　　　　*　　　　*

News of the baby quickly made the rounds of the village. Marina gazed lovingly at her three day old daughter. Except for her family and Amelia, Marina felt reluctant to have many visitors.

"She's coming along beautifully," she confided to Alda, "but I'm afraid that she may catch something."

"One can't be too cautious." Alda cast a loving glance towards the crib. "Is Giorgio at the vineyard?"

"Yes. He had to go and cut down an old pear tree that had died." Marina held up a pair of tiny booties that Albina had made as she sorted out the various baby items that had been lovingly prepared. "Honestly, Albina must have knitted a pair for every day, judging by how many there are. Who would have thought that when Giorgio made the crib last year that we would really have a baby sleeping in it so soon?" At her baby's cry, Marina stepped over to the crib. "I think my little one is hungry." She lifted Nora and sat down on a nearby chair. "Here you go, my love." Marina settled back into the chair and began to nurse her baby.

"I'd better go for some water. I'll lock the door downstairs, alright?"

"Be careful, Mama. The streets are slippery."

When Nora was satisfied, Marina placed her back in the crib. Her gaze fell on a tendril of jasmine that Giorgio had trained on a cord and which now had reached up to the bedroom window. She gasped and turned to the sound of shattering glass down in the *soggiorno,* followed by a thud. She cast a glance at the sleeping Nora and slowly descended the stairs. She cried out at the sight of the broken window. Among the shards lay a small rock with a note secured to it by a thin cord. Marina reached for it and, with shaking hands read the familiar, sloppy handwriting.

I hope that your daughter isn't a good for nothing like you.

The door burst open and Alda entered, frantic, almost dropping the bucket of water. She looked from Marina to the broken window. "Wh… are… are you alright?"

"I'm… I'm alright." Marina nodded and handed her the note. She heard Giorgio's familiar step and winced at his cry of dismay.

"No, oh no…" Giorgio stumbled through the door, shocked.

Marina exchanged a worried glance with Alda, who reluctantly handed him the note.

Giorgio read it, cursed under his breath, and slammed his fist into the wall. "This has got to stop. If… if I ever find out who's behind all these notes and everything else, I swear that there will be hell to pay." He crumpled the note and launched it across the room. "There's hate involved here. Tell *me* I'm good for nothing, but don't say that about my wife and newborn daughter!" He gritted his teeth and cradled his wrist.

"Now you've done it!" Marina brought her hand to her forehead, dismayed that in his burst of fury, he had injured his right wrist.

"Cosa e' successo?"

They turned to Tobias as he rushed inside and gasped audibly. He had been securing the post at the gate when he heard the commotion.

Giorgio picked up the crumpled note and handed it to Tobias, who immediately took in the situation. As he read the note, his face turned dark with anger. He walked to the balcony door, then turned around, muttering under his breath.

Marina didn't understand what he said, but it was clear that he was angered. *"No fa niente,"* she said to him. It didn't matter.

"A woman is behind all this." Alda began to sweep up the shards of glass. "I've felt it since… She pressed her lips together as if not wanting to say more.

"What are you saying, Mama?" Marina felt sure that her mother wanted to say something.

"Let's finish cleaning up." Alda walked to the kitchen.

Marina exchanged a glance with Giorgio and Tobias, whose expression was tense. "It's jealousy. It's always been about jealousy." She looked at Giorgio. "Maybe you're right. Someone does hate me. You'd better go and see Marco. You're hurt."

"It's not as bad as what I'm feeling inside." Giorgio clenched his teeth.

*   *   *

They weren't even a month into winter, and if it didn't snow, it rained. Once again, they celebrated the feast of the *Epiphany,* and once again, the children were blessed by the little old lady who came from the mountains.

"This time we have our very own special gift." Marina gently covered Nora with a blanket that her mother had knitted.

"What a gift," Giorgio whispered.

"Does it hurt very much?" Marina touched Giorgio's bandaged wrist.

"A little bit, but more than anything, I'm mad at myself for having lost my temper. What have I gained? It's my right wrist and I can't do much with my left hand."

"Thank heaven we have Tobias. He can help you. Remember that he helped his father as a cabinetmaker."

Giorgio's face brightened at the thought. "Somehow, things were meant to be. He was here to help you give birth, and he can help me in the workshop. I'd better go and stoke the fire. The weather can't get any more miserable than this."

Marina heard a familiar whistle. She rushed to the top of the stairs and greeted Gianni, who hadn't been to visit because he'd had a cold. "I'm so happy to see you." She wrapped her arms around him.

Gianni held her close, too moved to speak. He cleared

his throat. "Where's my little niece?"

Marina took his hand and led him to the crib. "Remember when you told me to make you an uncle? Here you are."

"Hello, little one," Gianni whispered.

Nora opened her eyes and turned her head towards him.

"She can hear me." Gianni's eyes went wide.

"Of course she can." Marina smiled, delighted at the expression on his face.

Nora moved her little arms and what seemed like a smile appeared on her face.

"Is she smiling?" Gianni asked.

"I think so." Marina nodded. "All is well in her world."

Gianni sat down on the edge of the bed. "This is too much for me. It's… it's a miracle.

*   *   *

January came and went, and February didn't seem to promise anything better with the weather. Marina had resumed her normal life even though she stayed mostly in the house or, at most, went for water. To her happiness, Nora continued to gain weight.

The kitchen was always toasty, and she didn't lack for food.

Anna visited one day. Marina welcomed her into the *soggiorno*. Giorgio had brought down the crib, so that Marina had Nora close by during the day.

Anna tiptoed over to the crib. Nora lay with her brown eyes wide open. "She's beautiful! What dark hair."

"We were so afraid because she was so small."

"Thank you for letting me see her." From her cloth bag, Anna lifted a little packet. "This is a little something that I knitted. I hope it will come in handy."

"You shouldn't have done that, but thank you!" Marina opened the packet and lifted a little white sweater with a matching bonnet from the wrapping. "This will be perfect for when we baptize her in a few weeks."

"Giorgio told me what happened here. I'm sorry that you can't have any peace, even with the baby." Anna frowned. "To make it worse, he hurt himself."

"More than his wrist, I'm worried about the hurt he has inside. I'm afraid, Anna." Marina swallowed the tears that wanted to surface. "Giorgio is seething."

Anna raised her arms to heaven. "Can you blame him? Too much has happened."

"Mama knows something. The trouble is, she won't tell me."

"When the time comes, we'll all know who this person is and when we do, it's not going to be pretty. You know how news gets around, and people are frustrated. They want to know, too."

Anna clenched her fists and pressed her lips together, which Marina found a little odd. After she left, Marina joined her hands in prayer. "Please, Lord, let the moment of truth come soon."

*　　　　　*　　　　　*

The war had turned desperate for the Nazi Fascists as the Allies continued the fight alongside the Partisans to free the entire valley. Together, they conducted night patrols in the hope of finding out as much as possible about the placement of enemy lines.

Marina looked longingly at the bright, sunny day outside the kitchen window.

"Why don't you go and get some fresh air?" Alda suggested. "It's not too cold. I'll watch Nora for you."

"I think I will. She should be alright for a little while. I'll visit Amelia and Lisa and then go to the house and see how Giorgio and Tobias are coming along with the windows."

"Dress warmly," Alda cautioned.

Marina put on her winter shoes but when she reached for her shawl, she hesitated. The one she always wore had been washed. This was the one that she had worn the morning she had fallen down the garden steps. *That was then,* she told herself as she resolutely wrapped herself in it, crossed the *soggiorno,* and walked out the door.

She continued down the street but didn't stop at Anna's Her neighbor's black dog trotted alongside her and stopped to eye a cat that arched its back in a "don't even think it" message. "I wouldn't try it if I were you." Marina laughed.

The dog seemed to think the better of it and went on its way.

Her first stop was at Amelia's, who welcomed her with open arms. "Here you are."

Nelsa emerged from the kitchen. *"Bimba!"*

"How is Nora?" they asked at the same time.

"She's doing well, but how are you?" Marina placed an arm around each of them as they went into the kitchen.

"I'm doing fine," Nelsa said. "But I don't know about Amelia, who has two more mouths to feed."

"I'm happy to have you here. Without Giorgio, it can get a bit lonely." Amelia sighed. "Is he at the house?"

"Yes. I'm stopping to see Lisa first, and then I'll go there. It feels strange to leave Nora, although she's under Mama's watchful eye."

Amelia turned to Nelsa. "We might just take a walk a little later. We've been cooped up like chickens."

Marina stayed for a little while and then left. She paid a quick visit to Lisa, who wanted to know everything about Nora, and then continued on to the house.

"Oh Signore!" Marina clasped her hands as she approached the blackened walls of her childhood home.

Giorgio was testing a new window in her mother's room. *"Ehi, carissima!"* he called down to her.

Tobias leaned out from the other window. *"Marina, buon giorno!"*

Marina felt a glimmer of hope at the new windows that Giorgio was installing little by little. It had hurt to see the simple, white curtains that had hung at the windows tattered and burned. She turned to Pallino who nodded his head up and down, his bells jingling. "I'm glad to see you, too." Marina smiled and stroked his neck.

Her gaze rested on the pot where once the pretty red geranium had bloomed. Now, just sticks jutted from the cold dirt. The once clean basement steps were strewn with dead leaves. Blackened rubble lay next to the house. She brushed away soot from the cross etched into a corner stone. The Cross. Death and victory at the same time. She tried to convince herself that everything would return to normal, but now all she could see spoke of anything but hope.

"Everything looks so desolate." She blinked hard and tore her gaze away to look up at the blue sky.

"That's where I come in." Gianni came up from the basement holding a broom and began to sweep vigorously at the cobwebs and the steps, working his way down.

Marina leaned against the post at the top of the stairs and watched him. She turned to Pallino who was shifting about restlessly and approached him. "What is it? Is something biting you?"

Pallino snorted. At Marina's gentle patting on his neck, he calmed down and shook his head, his bells jingling again.

Marina approached the steps again and smiled down at Gianni. Gone were the dead leaves and the cobwebs.

Pallino brayed loudly. Suddenly, a feeling of dread

filled her for no reason and a chill coursed through her body. She sensed someone at her shoulders. Before she could turn around, someone shoved her hard.

CHAPTER TWENTY-SEVEN

arina cried out and grabbed blindly for the post as she lost her balance. She fell down on both knees onto the rough stone step. It hurt. She bit her lower lip from the pain, raised her head and reached up for the post with the other arm. Her hands smarted from the slivers of the weathered wood, but she regained her footing. She screamed as two arms grabbed her. It was Gianni.

"It's alright, it's alright." Gianni put his arms around her, holding her tightly.

Frightened and relieved at the same time, she clung to him. "I… I was pushed."

Gianni swallowed hard and cupped her face with shaking hands. "I… I know. I… I saw who did it."

Marina stared at him, shocked, as he gently lifted her to her feet.

Gianni steadied her and she slowly stepped up onto the street in time to hear a furious outburst followed by a scream.

"You… you good for nothing whore… you witch! I… I saw you push her. This… this time you're not getting away with it." Daniela had grabbed Carla by the hair, wrestled her to the ground, and now slapped her hard across the face.

"I'm not the only one who saw her." Gianni smirked.

Marina gasped audibly as Carla struggled, but Daniela's fury proved stronger. She twisted Carla's hair in her hands. "You were behind everything… all the notes, Giada's death. You… you pushed Marina down the stairs and… and made her… lose… lose her baby!" Daniela slapped her again. "We lost our home because of you! Deny it if you can!" Tears of anger flowed down Daniela's face as she pummeled Carla, punching her and slapping her again and again.

"Daniela, stop! Please, stop," Marina cried out to her infuriated sister. She grabbed Gianni by the shoulders. "She'll kill her! Oh, Gianni, stop her!"

Tobias had rushed down ahead of Giorgio at the commotion and stopped short at Marina's side. He smiled broadly and folded his arms across his chest.

"As if that's a loss!" Gianni scowled. He ran to Daniela, but his sister's wrath was too much even for him. He finally managed to grab her by the waist and, not without effort, lifted her up off of Carla. He swung her away. "That's enough!"

Daniela elbowed him in the ribs. "Let me go! I'll tear her hair out! She's a witch!"

Gianni cursed as she elbowed him again. "I said that's enough!" He tightened his grip on her.

Spent, her face red and wet with tears, Daniela turned and looked up at him. "She… she… pushed…"

Gianni exhaled deeply. "I know. I saw her, too."

Daniela fought no more and let herself be led away from Carla who huddled on the ground, her hands shielding her face. He didn't let her go until she was at Marina's side.

Marina took her in her arms and then held her at arm's length. "I love you," she said softly.

In the meantime, Carla had scrambled to her feet and now broke into a run, but Tobias was faster and grabbed her by the arm. *"Ah no. Tu rimani qui!"*

The last thing Carla wanted was to stay there. She fought Tobias. "Let go of me, you filthy German!"

Marina winced. She couldn't imagine what Tobias must have felt like in that instant. His face had turned dark with anger, but he held himself in check. He almost dragged Carla over to stand in front of all of them.

Giorgio, trembling, took Marina's hands in his. One hand was stained by a trickle of blood. *"Amore mio,* you're hurt," he said in a shaky voice.

"I don't know what hurts more. My hands, my knees, or my heart." Marina shook her head in disbelief that her childhood friend had really reached this point. Up to now, she had only suspected. She straightened her shoulders, determined to find out the truth. The *why* of it all. "Let her go, Tobias. It's alright."

Tobias hesitated but at Marina's smile and nod, he let

her go. Carla roughly freed her arm from Tobias's grip and rubbed her cheeks, red from the slapping. She glared at Marina and walked towards the post, leaning against it.

Giorgio's face grew dark with anger and he clenched his good hand into a fist. "You're fortunate that I didn't see you push Marina, because Daniela would have been nothing compared to me."

"Let me handle this, Giorgio," Marina said calmly. "She can't hurt me now.'

She saw Carla move dangerously close to the edge of the basement steps. "Why, Carla? Why did you do this and… and everything else?"

"Why? Because it's always been about *you*!" With one hand, Carla brushed a lock of hair, damp with perspiration from her face.

"You…" she pointed to Giorgio, "you got him with your wiles. *I* wanted him. I could have given him something better than what you ever could, but no, he chose you instead."

Marina raised her eyes to heaven. "Carla, I didn't use any wiles! Yes, I loved him even before he realized that he loved me, but I let destiny take its course. Is all that you have done to me because… because of… of this? Were you so desperate?"

"I had more to give him than that skinny body of yours," Carla spat out. "You had to pay! He had to pay!"

"You killed my baby," Marina said softly.

For a moment, Carla's expression softened. "I felt sorry

for the baby, but I didn't feel sorry for you. In losing you, Giorgio would have found solace with me. I would have given him everything that he could want. He knew what I could give him." She smiled seductively at Giorgio.

"I told you then, and I'm telling you now that the only left-over I like is food." Giorgio measured every word, his tone icy.

Even without looking at him, Marina could see his anger. She turned to the sound of muted voices at the junction. Her *Nonna* Nelsa, Amelia, Albina and Don Antonio were hearing revelations that would answer all their questions. She turned again to Carla, whose look was defiant and, Marina felt, hateful. Her childhood friend had become insane with jealousy.

"You… spied on us, made… made us lose our home." Daniela glared at her and turned to Marina. "When you came that day to tell me not to have anything to do with Heinrich, he told me later that he saw her eavesdropping at the door."

Marina remembered that day. "You listened at the door, Carla. You listened while Daniela and I talked about him. When she said that the sentinel wanted to desert to the Americans, that was your chance. Before I left, I heard someone running. It was you. I remember the quizzical look on Heinrich's face, and I thought it was odd. He knew what he saw. You helped him to desert and then you reported Daniela to the commander in charge at that time. She was… was rounded up along with other villagers.

When the other sentinel returned, the hostages were released, but the commander had found Heinrich's uniform in the basement and ordered our home torched." There was one more thing Marina had to know. The one thing that had almost driven her and Giorgio apart. "Did you plant that comb in Giorgio's jacket?"

"When Stefano left for the war, Giorgio wanted to protect the poor, helpless wife that was left behind." Carla smirked at her. "She found out that she was pregnant. Of course, Giorgio took her to heart even more, maybe too much."

"No snake is as evil as you," Giorgio growled and took a step towards Carla.

Marina gently pushed him back. He was a thundercloud ready to burst. "She's not worth it." She smiled at him.

"She's also responsible for injuring Tobias," Gianni said.

Tobias shot him a startled look. *"Come sai questo?"*

Gianni smiled wryly. "I know because I saw you walking along the mule path with Carla sneaking behind you that day. I crouched low beneath the blackberry bushes at the slope of the path. You had barely started to walk down towards the vineyard when Carla struck you on the head with. a rock. You fell unconscious. I didn't know what to do, but fate had Marina come along to help you. I managed to get away."

Marina looked from Gianni to Carla. "You suspected that Gianni was a Partisan and told Tobias. You had planned for Gianni to be blamed to get back at me." Tears welled in her eyes. "I'm sorry that you have spent all this time hating me when we could… could have enjoyed our friendship."

"I'm only sorry that I didn't do a good job when I pushed you down the stairs the first time." Carla raised her arm to strike Marina.

Although she had remained calm, Marina had been on guard all the time. As Carla lifted her arm to strike her, Marina quickly lifted hers in the same instant to defend herself.

"I will kill you!" Carla lunged toward her, but she had stepped back—too close to the edge of the steps. Arms flailing, she lost her balance and fell backwards with a scream. She tumbled down the steps and struck her head hard midway down. At the bottom, she lay still, her body crumpled. Blood slowly pooled beneath her head.

Marina turned away. Giorgio took her in his arms and pressed her face against his chest. "I… I should have warned her to not get close to the steps. I… I didn't and… and now she's dead," Marina cried.

"No," Giorgio said gently. "Carla died a long time ago." He kissed her on the forehead. "Justice has been made to happen. Let's go home," he whispered.

Don Antonio ran toward them. He shook his head in disbelief at the crumpled figure and descended the steps along with Gianni.

Amelia, Nelsa, Daniela and Albina quietly followed Marina and Giorgio home.

*   *   *

"She tried to kill me twice." Marina still couldn't believe what had happened. Alda, the girls, Nelsa, Amelia, and Marco sat around the kitchen table, still in shock. Tobias was tending to Pallino. She cast a glance towards the *soggiorno* where little Nora lay fast asleep in the crib. The experience had left Marina badly shaken, but she had still been able to nurse her. Now she had to put all that had happened behind her.

There was a knock on the door. Alda opened it to Anna, who opened her arms to Marina and hugged her tightly.

"I… I have to talk." Anna inhaled deeply. "There… there are things that you need to know that I've kept to myself out of fear."

Giorgio brought an extra chair for Anna to sit on. "What is it, Anna?"

"I suspected that Carla was behind a lot of things from the beginning." Anna took a deep breath.

"You don't have to say anything now if it's too difficult for you," Giorgio said gently.

"No, it's best that I do it and be done with it. When Giorgio was assaulted, Carla seemed unlike herself. I got the impression that she was obsessed over what had happened to him."

Marina exchanged a glance with Giorgio, who nodded.

"Then came the incident with Giada. When you told me

that she was missing, I happened to bump into Carla. She was carrying a small, rectangular box. Afterwards, when… when I heard that… that Giada was found dead in such a box, it seemed like a strange coincidence. But, something didn't feel right." Anna paused and closed her eyes. "Then… then you became pregnant with Gianpaolo…"

"The dirty witch!" Daniela exclaimed.

"She's dead, Daniela. Let it go," Alda said softly.

"I remember how you recoiled from her when she came to visit me afterwards. It was she who… who stood behind me on the church steps last summer. Only Giorgio and Don Antonio coming out of the church saved me."

"You never told me about that." Giorgio frowned.

"I didn't know that she had pushed you that morning, believe me," Anna continued. "I would have spoken up if I had seen her myself, but the suspicion kept growing and growing. I pretended to be mad at you for something and played up to her. She was insanely jealous of you, Marina. You had lost Gianpaolo, but you had survived. Then, there was the incident with the comb. You had told me that you were helping Lisa in her new home that day. I happened to be coming down from the fountain when I saw Carla approach Giorgio's workshop, look around quickly and go inside. I stepped back, and I saw her come out of the workshop almost immediately and leave the garden. When I found out about the comb, I understood why she was at the workshop."

"That explains the overturned pot," Marina said quickly, "and why the workshop door was open. In her haste to leave, she forgot to close it."

"She was trying to drive a wedge between Marina and I… and she almost succeeded." Giorgio ran his fingers through his hair.

Anna burst into tears. "Please… please forgive me for… not telling you anything, but I… I was afraid for myself and my children." She wiped away her tears with the back of her hand and sniffled. "I… I should have told you… but… I couldn't. It's not easy when you're left alone with two babies." She wiped her tears and got up. "It's all over, Marina."

Marina hugged her tightly. "The bad is over. The good is beginning." With her arm around her shoulders, she walked Anna to the door.

Anna stopped a moment to contemplate Nora who had awakened and looked around with her big brown eyes. "Be happy, little one," she said softly.

Back in the kitchen, Marina's gaze fell on Gianni who had a faraway look in his eyes. "Gianni? You seem lost in your thoughts."

He got up and turned to look at his family. "You know how much Anna meant to me before I left for the war. Stefano had more courage than I did when he confessed his feelings to her."

Alda smiled at him. "Go slowly, Gianni. Remember that she is a widow. Give her time."

"I know." He smiled. "But that's no reason why I can't

begin to make her feel cared about."

Giorgio smacked his thigh, delighted. "This is better than a game of *briscola,* Gianni! I know you'll win!"

*   *   *

Marina recovered from the incident. She and Giorgio and all the family vowed to put all that had happened behind them. On April eighteenth, a joint operation, helped by bombers and machine gun fire in the towns above them, was underway. The liberation of the entire valley was getting closer. She prayed that as the dreary winter gave way to the beauty of springtime, it would be a time for renewal all around.

That afternoon, Marina watched, delighted, as Nora placed her little hand against Tobias's cheek as he held her up. "She loves you, Tobias."

"E io voglio bene a lei." He loved her, too, and gently lowered Nora to sit on his lap. He looked at Marina. *"Questa e' la mia famiglia ora."*

Marina's heart ached for him. He had received more sad news. His wife's family had also been killed by the Nazi-Fascist's. The bodies of his wife and daughter had been buried in a mass grave along with others who had been brutally shot. His desire to return home had waned. It was a bittersweet moment. He no longer had his family, but he had acquired a new one.

"Someone is at the door," Marina said. She opened it to

Don Antonio.

He greeted her warmly. "Is Tobias here?" he asked.

"He's in the kitchen with Nora. Come in." Marina led him into the kitchen.

Tobias stood up and greeted Don Antonio, who lost no time in taking Nora in his arms. "How is our little one today?"

"Thanks be to God, she's doing fine. I think that we're all spoiling her." Marina laughed as she pulled a chair away from the table for Don Antonio.

"Tobias, I came to ask a favor of you," Don Antonio said.

"Bene." Tobias smiled.

"You may not think it good when you hear it." He smiled. "But I am in sore need of help. Would you be sacristan in church?"

Tobias smiled broadly. *"Si! Oh, si!"*

Marina clasped her hands. "This will really help him to get to know the people more. He will be good, Don Antonio. I know he will. He's also good with wood. He... he can repair things, too."

"You have a job, Tobias, and I can sleep at night now." Don Antonio happily sat back in the chair, beaming at Nora, who held tightly to his finger.

Marina looked at Tobias, who looked a little dazed. Not only did he have a family, he had a job now, too.

CHAPTER TWENTY-EIGHT

Towards the end of April, the Partisans and the Allies broke through the second Green Line. All of the valley had finally been freed. Benito Mussolini and other Fascists with him were captured by the Italian Partisans and on April 28, they were all executed.

The longed for news of the total liberation of the valley and the death of *Il Duce* spread quickly throughout the village. The sad part was for those families who had lost loved ones as well as those families who had a husband or a son taken as a prisoner of war. Marina didn't know which was the worse of the two. On one hand, you grieved the loss of a life, such as Stefano, but on the other hand, your loved one was alive but a prisoner of war.

That evening after dinner, Gianni visited.

The days were longer and a little warmer. Giorgio, Marina, and Gianni sat outside on the little balcony discussing the recent events.

Gianni shook his head. "I don't know what to make of Mussolini's capture. That part I can see and maybe his execution, but I think the Partisans overdid it."

Marina shuddered. "Did they have to hang his body by

the heels? He was what he was, but…"

"Only God can judge him," Giorgio said softly. "Let's leave it at that."

That night as she prepared for bed, Marina glanced at Nora, who was fast asleep in her crib. She looked at Giorgio who was lying in bed with a look of happiness on his face.

He noticed her gaze on him. "What is it?"

Marina slipped into bed next to him. "Never take life and those you love for granted," she said softly. She turned towards him and nestled in his arms.

Giorgio held her close. "I wonder what news we will have tomorrow?"

"I don't know, but for now, I'm just happy for what we have today," she murmured.

*   *   *

The next day, Marina swept the street in front of the house while Giorgio and Tobias were repairing the gate down to the garden below. Pallino nibbled at the grass outside the stable.

"Eviva! L'Italia e' libera!" The shout rang down the street.

Marina stood with the broom in hand. "Italy is *free?*" she asked aloud.

Giorgio's eyes went wide.

Tobias rushed down the street to find out what had happened.

Marina walked down to Giorgio and they stared at each other, hoping yet not daring to believe the news.

Tobias ran back up and hugged both of them as he relayed the details. The Fascists Italian armed forces had all surrendered in Southern Italy.

Marina stood dazed while Giorgio laughed and cried at the same time.

Tobias's eyes twinkled. *"Celebriamo con un bicchiere di vino?"*

Giorgio nodded in assent. "You're right. We have to celebrate with a little wine. Marina, bring out the *ciambella* you baked yesterday. Tobias, let's go." Giorgio went into the *cantina* with him.

After toasting the liberation with a little wine and a slice of cake, Giorgio was the first to recover from the excitement of the moment. "I'd better go to the vineyard and see what has to be done there."

Marina contemplated him as he went into the *soggiorno* and tenderly kissed Nora. He sauntered out the door whistling a tune. This was the day that he had longed for.

"Io vado su alla chiesa," Tobias said.

Marina followed him to the door. His step was brisk; he was eager to assume his role of sacristan in church. With Don Antonio's help, he had found a little house that had stood abandoned for years. It needed a lot of work, but with Giorgio's help, he would make it a home. He spoke a few tender words to Nora, who smiled at him, and left.

Absorbed in peering at her fingers, Nora moved her

little hands about. Taking advantage of the moment, Marina took a water bucket, locked the door behind her, and rushed up the road to the fountain. While the water poured from the spout to fill her bucket, she glanced at the uppermost part of the village, where the crenelated bell tower of the church was clearly visible. The bells began to ring. There was no village feast, but freedom needed to be celebrated.

When the bucket was full, she carefully walked back down to the house.

"Marina! Marina!"

Marina lowered the bucket to the ground, alarmed as Daniela ran up the street.

"What… what's happened?" Marina rushed towards her.

"Lisa… is in labor," Daniela gasped, leaning against the house wall. "Mama… is at the house."

"I have to take Nora with me." Marina rushed into the *soggiorno* and gathered a few essentials for her. She lifted her. "Come, sweetheart. Your aunt needs me." Although anxious to be with Lisa, she didn't want to hurry down the street with Nora in her arms. This was the first time that she had taken her outside. Suddenly, she stopped short. Her younger sister who had been so sick and tired of *polenta*, who had stood faithfully by her side when she had become pregnant with Gianpaolo, was about to give birth.

"What?" Daniela's eyes widened.

"I can't believe how far Lisa has come. Has it been all that long?"

"We've all grown up," Daniela said softly.

At Lisa's, Daniela opened the door. Alda greeted them, anxious and happy at the same time. Albina, Gianni, Nelsa, Valentina and Bruno were gathered in the little dining room.

"Mama, I'll go upstairs and be with Lisa. You take Nora."

"The midwife is already here. Marco is in another world in this moment." Alda's eyes shone with delight as she took her little granddaughter in her arms.

"Just like his father when he was born." Valentina reached for Bruno's hand.

Albina and Gianni fidgeted about with excitement.

"We'll take turns with Nora," Gianni said.

Marina smiled as she dashed up the stairs. Her baby wouldn't lack for attention.

Lisa lay in bed, enjoying a moment of calm after a contraction. She inhaled deeply. When she saw Marina, she reached for her hand. "I'm so glad that you're here."

Marco sat on a chair, pale. "I'm a doctor, but I feel like a wet dishrag in this moment."

Lisa glanced at Marco, then at Marina and raised her eyes to heaven. "You're of no help."

Marina burst out laughing. "It's one thing to deliver someone else's baby, but when it's your baby, that changes everything."

Lisa cried out and grimaced. "I think that… that some-thing's happening!"

The midwife, who had sat quietly, smiling at the exchange between them, was immediately at Lisa's side. "I think the baby is ready."

Marina placed her hand on Lisa's shoulder, still holding tightly to her hand.

Marco knelt down, taking Lisa's other hand in both of his. "It's going to be fine."

Lisa cried out again and gritted her teeth. *"Signore Gesu', aiutami!"*

Marina well remembered that moment. How she had prayed for help.

"You're doing fine. One more push, Lisa," the midwife encouraged her.

Lisa cried out again with the effort and then breathed deeply.

"Good, good. You have a boy!" The midwife held up the baby boy for Lisa to see.

"Is… is he alright?" Lisa asked quickly.

As if in answer to her question, the baby let out a lusty cry.

"He's fine. Come, little one," the midwife said tenderly, "let me make you nice and clean."

When the baby was ready and wrapped in a warm towel, Lisa reached out for her little boy.

Marina choked back tears as she relived her own moment.

Lisa's eyes shone as she looked tenderly at Marco. "Here's your son."

Too overcome for words, Marco leaned over and kissed Lisa on the forehead. He took his son in his arms, beaming with happiness.

"I'm calling Mama!" Marina flew downstairs. "We have a boy! We have a boy," she announced.

Alda didn't waste any time and quickly disappeared upstairs.

Valentina cried out in happiness, cupped Bruno's face in her hands and kissed him soundly.

"I hope that there will be more babies," Bruno murmured, smiling at the enthusiastic kiss.

Giorgio had arrived. Nora sat on his lap, her brown eyes taking in everyone and everything. He looked at Marina. "Another baby. How…" He bit his lower lip not being able to continue.

"What's this?" Marina asked softly.

Giorgio swallowed hard. "I… I can't believe what we have all gone through these past few years. Now here we are, free, and… two babies have been born."

Albina whirled around, her arms wide." Can anything be lovelier than this? We have so much to look forward to."

"We have so much to be grateful for." Nelsa joined her hands together.

"We have a new family member in Tobias," Marina added quickly.

Nora squealed as if in approval.

"She recognizes his name." Giorgio lifted Nora above his head to her delight.

"We also have a romance in bud." Albina turned to Gianni.

Gianni smiled bashfully. "Yes. Anna is happy. Who would have known?" he asked in a low voice.

Marina understood. Gianni had let destiny take its course when Stefano had fallen in love with Anna. It was a bittersweet moment now. Life had been cruel to Anna with the loss of Stefano, but now Gianni was able to care for the woman he had never stopped caring about.

"Giorgio and I were wondering if you and Anna would be godparents to Nora?" Marina asked.

Gianni nodded. "I'll talk to Anna, but I feel that she'll be happy to do it."

"We can also go back into our home again." Daniela signed happily.

Marina hugged herself. She was living the most beautiful dream…

*   *   *

April ceded to May and the countryside was in the full splendor of spring. The fruit trees were in bud, and the wildflowers bloomed in a profusion of white, pink, and blue. The grasses rustled gently in the breeze. Marina and Giorgio, with Nora in his arms, decided to visit their loved ones' gravesites. Although they had Nora, they never forgot about the little one who had never gotten a chance at life.

Marina felt a moment of bitterness. "Every time we come here, we'll always be reminded of what she did. Because of her, he's dead."

Carla's gravesite, marked with a temporary wood cross, lay next to Gianpaolo's. It was the only one available where her father had lain for many years.

Giorgio shook his head. "Is he really dead, *amore mio?*"

In that moment, a meadowlark warbled somewhere in the trees. Marina smiled. Gianpaolo was only a thought away. She had gathered a bouquet of wildflowers and placed a few in the vase for Gianpaolo. She hesitated and then placed a stem of blooms on Carla's grave.

They prayed at the other gravesites and then closed the cemetery gate behind them. They took the mule path home. It was a longer walk, but the day was lovely, and they wanted Nora to enjoy the fresh air.

"This path holds so many memories." Marina stopped to look around her. Below her was her family's vineyard. "Down there, I saw Gianni. Here on the path, I came across Tobias when he was injured."

"You know," Giorgio said thoughtfully, "we were never really alone in reaching this moment. Hard as everything was, we lived through it."

The day before, on May 8th, the war had officially ended in Europe.

Marina slipped her arm through Giorgio's. He was right. They had never been alone. Through it all, God had been by their side. Now, they could all look ahead to a brighter future. They could look beyond the hardships and horrors of the war. They could look beyond today.

382

–END–

ACKNOWLEDGEMENTS

This book would have never have come to existence without the dedication, patience, and encouragement of my late editor, Mary Rosenblum.

I wish to thank Sylvia Frost for all of her help and suggestions for the cover design.

I wish to thank Dirk Wentling of Wentling's Studio for my photo.

My heartfelt thanks go to my brother, Mario, for being a bookworm. He leafed through many pages of his books on wartime Italy to help me find information that might come in handy.

Thanks to my publisher, Andrew Benzie of Andrew Benzie Books for calmly guiding me through a critical moment.

Last, but not least, I want to thank Giuliana, my cousin in the village where my story is situated, and Silvana, my neighbor, for going back in time. Giuliana was one of the youngsters playing in a field who saw first-hand the American fighter plane come down.

Information was also gathered from the Internet. I do recommend a book for reading called Trapped in Tuscany by Tullio Bruno Bertini. He was literally trapped in Tuscany with his parents in the town of Diecimo, in the Serchio River Valley, when the war broke out.

ABOUT THE AUTHOR

Mary Franceschini was born in Los Angeles, California, the daughter of Italian immigrants. After high school graduation, she, along with her brother and her parents visited the little village of her parents' birth in Italy. They returned home and two years later, although her parents were American citizens, they moved to Italy. Her brother remained in Los Angeles. In twenty-seven years of living in the mountain village, she learned how the village was affected by World War II and the German occupation. After both her parents died, she returned to the United States to live with her brother. She calls it fate that she received a letter from Longridge Writers' Group where she tested her writing potential. She entered their program *Breaking into Print.* In this time, she and her brother moved from Los Angeles to Concord, California, and her first short story was published in *The Storyteller* magazine. She wasn't paid but the satisfaction of being published meant more. Her late *Breaking into Print* instructor, Mary Rosenblum, helped her to write this first novel. It will be published by Andrew Benzie of Andrew Benzie Books.

For pictures of the region where *Look Beyond Today* takes place and to find recipes for some of the classical local dishes mentioned in the book, visit her website at: www.maryfranceschini.com.

www.ingramcontent.com/pod-product-compliance
Lightning Source LLC
Chambersburg PA
CBHW070349170726
48291CB00001B/240